AND THE CREEK DON'T RISE

R.M. GILMORE

and the creek don't rise

a *Southern fantasy* novel by

R·M· GILMORE

MAC
GILLE
MHUR
PUB

Creative Design: RMGraphX

Executive Editor: Becky Johnson

Page 354 Illustration: T. Ottemoeller

mac gille mhur

Publisher's Cataloging-in-Publication data

Names: Gilmore, R.M., author.
Title: And the creek don't rise / by R.M. Gilmore.
Description: Dallas, OR: Mac Gille Mhur Publishing, 2020. | Summary: Small town girl, Lynnie Russell, unwittingly unearths a deadly familial secret—she's death incarnate.
Identifiers: LCCN: 2020921564 | ISBN: 978-1-7358635-1-1 (Hardcover) | 978-1-7358635-0-4 (pbk.)
Subjects: LCSH Death (Personification)--Fiction. | Fairies--Fiction. | Folklore--Southern States--Fiction. | Folklore--Ireland--Fiction. | Fantasy fiction. | BISAC FICTION / Fantasy / Paranormal | FICTION / Fairy Tales, Folk Tales, Legends & Mythology | FICTION / Fantasy / Contemporary
Classification: LCC PS3607.I452148 A53 2020 | DDC 813.6--dc23

Thanks to my southern heritage for the
advanced degree in colloquialisms.

For AJ

The power of the universe
lies in every stroke

Ivy
wild, parasite

gort

ciert

apple
rebirth, life cycle

alder

bridge between worlds

Fearn

dair

oak

strenghth, protection

elder

ruis

endings, death

and the creek don't rise

HOW'DO?

My name is Sharlene Carolynn Diamond Russell. It's a mouthful, I know.

To most of the world, I was a redneck. Hillbilly. Poor white trash. Just a little ol' Southern brat who'd never amount to anything. But in Havana, Arkansas, I was just an American girl. Raised on promises.

Actually, I'm pretty sure that's a Tom Petty song.

They were wrong. So was I.

I can't tell you what I *really* am without telling you how it came to be. Most stories start just before the action begins, when the juicy bits are ripe. I think mine is better told from the beginning. Or close enough to it.

It's what kicked it all off. The day I turned twenty.

HELL—BENT

"*What* are you doing here, Lynn?" Sam asked from behind a rack of chips. "You're off today."

A grin pushed my sun-kissed cheeks into mounds. "Just came to get my—"

Sam—the best boss a girl could have—pulled my paycheck from the pocket of his apron, gripping it tight between two thick fingertips. "Don't you go spending it all down at Maldoon's, ya hear?"

I looked up at him from under my lashes. "You know I ain't old enough to be down there at that old bar, Sam. Just a quiet evening at home with Garret and Hattie." And lied through my teeth.

I reached out to snatch the handwritten check and he pulled me into a hug. "Happy birthday, sweet pea," he rumbled against my ear.

I nuzzled his broad chest. Sam always smelled like diesel fuel and even though he was about a hundred pounds heavier, it reminded me of my dad. The biological one.

Daddy drove long-haul. He was never home, and when he was, it wasn't long enough to get to know him. Didn't doubt he loved me—brought me gifts and things; he just didn't give up his time too often.

"Thanks, old man."

"You be good out there tonight, girl." He ran a heavy hand over the thick cushion of tight black curls at his neck, clearly a few months since his last trip to the barber shop.

"You know I will." I winked over my shoulder and shoved the check into the back pocket of my cutoff shorts.

"Carolynn Russell, I don't want to hear about you wrapping that old truck around a tree down there in Logan county." He wagged a calloused finger at me.

We're taking Hattie's truck. I smirked. "I'll be fine. Don't you worry about me. It's Havana, Sam. What in the world could I get up to?"

"You tell your mom and them I said hi," he shouted after me.

"Will do." I pushed out the door, ringing the bell that hung from the corner. "Whenever I see her," I grumbled on my way out.

My mama, God love her, never could stay in one place too long without a man to keep her there—Daddy was gone too often, too long to keep her put. She loved us kids with all her soul, but if it weren't for me and my brother, she'd have left Havana a long time ago and never looked back.

I had a mind to do the same, but I'd never get out of this damn town working part-time at Sam's pump station.

I always figured I'd be out on my own by twenty. Maybe I'd be living in a college dorm miles away from my parents and this hick town. Poor life choices and lack of funds kept me trapped in Havana, Arkansas. Or what I like to call, bum fuck.

My old beater bounced along the pocked road up to our property. Dead of summer, the weeds were lighter than my blonde hair and tall as my knees. You'd think with humidity thick enough to bathe in, the foliage would get a little drink every now and then.

Stifled by my overbearing—yet equally aloof—mama and ignored by my absentee daddy, I didn't have too many opportunities to spread my wings, as they say. Moving in with my brother had been my best option.

Garret bought himself a few acres and a double-wide just out of my town. Havana only had a few streets to its name, so just outside of town wasn't saying much. But it was far enough away from home that I didn't have to see Mama out there mowing her lawn in a pair of short-shorts every Saturday morning.

I knew eventually I'd break free of my backwoods, redneck prison. When and how were the only things I hadn't yet worked out.

Clouds of dust settled behind me as I pulled up in front of the house. It wasn't much, but I was happy to call it home. Even if it was shared with someone who liked to fart in my gravy.

It was twelve on the dot when Garret walked through the front door. "Whatchu got on the stove, girl? Damn," he hollered from the front mat. The clonk of his dirty work boots echoed when they tumbled to the hollow foundation.

If I learned anything being stuck at home with my mama, it was to always have something on the table. "I got beans in the pot and the bread's just 'bout done," I said, grinning at him from over my shoulder, and he smiled back.

We looked a lot alike, my brother and me. Our smiles were almost the same. Bright and shiny and showing a lot of teeth.

"Did you talk to Mama today?" he asked while he picked at the beans in the pot on the stove.

"She called at eight. Woke me up on my day off to say happy birthday. You know the speech. It's the same every year. 'Twenty years ago today you were born. It was eleven fifty-four at night, your birthday could have been tomorrow, but out you popped, cryin' and hollerin' all the way.'" I copied Mama and Garret laughed. I looked too much like her to keep it up for long without making myself shudder so I changed the subject. "You coming to Maldoon's with us tonight?"

Thanks to my brother and my one and only real friend, Hattie, it was Maldoon's for my birthday celebration. I wasn't really into honky-tonks, but Carolynn Russell never turned down a good time and living in Havana opportunities for that were slim.

I was one of the lucky twenty-thousand county residents who couldn't drink, legally, regardless of age. Yell County, Arkansas was a dry county—dry as in no booze. Ever.

Maldoon's was just over the county line, technically in Logan County, just up the highway from Blue Mountain Lake. The old place was nothing big, basically a glorified barn with a full bar and a bandstand. It was regularly chock full of cowboys in tight jeans and muddy boots, but it was the closest place to Havana that served alcohol.

Old Leroy would get anyone drunk for a price, or a smile and wink. Leroy Maldoon was pushing eighty, feisty as all get-out, and had been the sheriff of Yell County in the sixties. He always said, when you're the law, you can do what you want. Kids had been running off to Maldoon's to drink since before I was born. In fact, I had it on good authority that yours truly was conceived in that very parking lot.

"You bet." He gulped a glass of milk. "I'll be bringin' Rusty." I scowled. Garret grinned around a spoonful of beans.

Rusty Kemp was a scoundrel. Ornery. No good. A goathead in my heel since I'd hit puberty. He'd also been my brother's best friend since grade two.

My fork clanged against the plate. "Jesus H., Garret, why you bringin' that idiot?" From day one Rusty made my blood burn under my skin. He'd ask to play but always ended up being mean or embarrassing. I usually just kicked dirt at him. My mama used to say it was 'cause I liked him. I never could figure out why my mama would ever think I liked a boy I kicked dirt at.

"You know he can't be left alone too long. He might chew things up," Garret said with that stupid grin.

"It is *my* birthday, you know? Maybe I can have a say in *somethin'*? Y'all wanna blow my candles out too?" I sat back in my chair and folded my arms across my chest. "Can't you leave him in the kennel?"

Garret watched the corners of my mouth tuck into a frown. He shoveled one last heap of beans into his mouth, never breaking his smile. The squeak of his spoon dropping into his bowl ruffled every one of my feathers. My rotten brother's ocean eyes locked onto mine, a sniggering call to arms. One blink. Two. He wiped his mouth and tossed his napkin over top of the spoon. One of my eyes twitched as I scowled. Long legs pushed his chair back away from the table.

"Com'on now, Lynn. Every girl wants a puppy for her birthday." He kissed the top of my head. "He just ain't housebroke yet." Garret laughed over the sound of the running sink.

It was useless to argue, one never left the house without the other, and if I wanted my brother there for my birthday,

I had to take the shit with the dog.

I was alone in the house, which typically was how I liked it. I used the time to clean up lunch and straighten the house. I swore my brother only let me move in so he'd have a live-in maid. He was too scared of marriage to get a wife, so his sister was the next best thing.

I realized that comment could be taken wrong by certain folks seeing as though we're from Arkansas. But it was not that way. I loved him and he loved me. In a "take a bullet for each other" kinda way, not the marrying kind. He was all I had to lean on coming up in that fake-smile, Daddy's-gone-again home of ours. Garret was the only man I ever trusted. We got close.

I cleaned for well into two hours, but the old shag carpet and dull wood-paneling still looked unkempt. You can't polish a turd, as they say. And a crusty old double-wide full of yard sale furniture sure was turd-like. I finally gave up and decided to leave it be.

I headed off to my bedroom to figure out what I'd wear. It wasn't like I was overly excited about the plans my people had made for me. I didn't like Maldoon's all that much and I couldn't stand Rusty Kemp, but I was determined to have fun if it killed me.

Normally, I'd be working till five, but it was tradition at Sam's to get your birthday off, so I had the entire day to relax—if you call cleaning the house relaxing—and wash the stink off me. On any other night, I'd've just pulled on a pair of shorts and a tank top, but it was my birthday so I figured I'd gussy up a bit.

I put a dress on for the first time in six years. Sticky Arkansas heat didn't account for heavy fabrics, so I chose a short cotton summer dress with tiny pink flowers printed on it. It showed my chest off. My mama would've never let me leave the house in something that revealing, but I was a grown woman free to do as I pleased. Hell, by twenty, she was nursing Garret. I figured I had myself on the right track in life, all things considered.

The front screen squeaked open and slammed shut, boots tumbled to the floor. Four of them. I let out a sigh heard by even Satan himself. "Lord, so help me," I grumbled, swiping a coat of mascara on my lashes.

"Whoo-wee! Look at you." My brother's voice came from the doorway of the bathroom a few moments later.

A smile spread before I could stop it. "Oh, shut your mouth."

"Well, I'll be damned, Lynn." Rusty squeezed in the doorway beside Garret.

"You shut your mouth too, Rusty." I snarled.

Behind me in the mirror, Rusty grinned and mussed his hair. If there'd been a pile of dirt nearby, I'd've kicked it at him.

I ignored him and gave my big blonde hair one last coat of hairspray. I'd set it in hot-curlers and the result was big curly hair. The last of the hairspray promised it would stay that way for at least an hour in that damn humidity. The higher the hair, the closer to God, my nana used to say—she may have stolen that from Dolly Parton. I was pretty damned close.

I plopped down on our hand-me-down couch and started pulling on my boots. Rusty sat in the Barcalounger by the front door. Dark gray smudges around his blue eyes made the color pop. My lip curled instinctively and I looked away. Him and Garret worked together over in Russellville laying asphalt and they both regularly came home looking like something the cat dragged through a damn chimney. I knew under all that dirt was a handsome face. But under that handsome face was an ornery, no good, rotten pig's ass. Curly tail and all.

Garret came through the room and brought us both a beer that they snuck over the county line in their lunch pails. Garret tilted his at me to toast. "One year closer to legal."

"You ready to get goin', birthday girl?" Rusty said with a wink.

"Go wash your face, Rusty. You got shit all over it," I said to him and guzzled down my beer.

The doorbell rang as the last drop hit my tongue signaling the end of the round. I grinned at the timing and leapt from the couch to answer the door. Hattie stood on the porch, one hand on her hip, a monstrous box of chocolates in the other.

Been friends since kindergarten, Hattie and me. She'd spent every birthday with me since I turned five. And every year I got the same thing. Chocolate. Henrietta Ruby Savanna Willits knew the way to my heart. We also shared long, obnoxious names. Her daddy's named Henry, she's Henrietta. How you get Hattie from that I don't know, but that's who she was. Just Hattie. The only sister I'd ever known.

"Your hair is so big, Lynn. Mine don't get that big," Hattie said with a pout, fluffing her hair.

I just smiled at her. There was a part of Hattie that could be a bit uppity. She was Arkie as shit, but she sure as hell didn't think so.

"All right, y'all meet us there?" I asked Garret over my shoulder.

He grinned at Hattie. "Yeah, we'll be along. Go on now, scoot," he said, pushing me out the door.

I poked my head back in. "Wash your damn face," I said to Rusty with a sneer.

Me and Hattie piled into her daddy's pickup truck. The oversized tires kicked up rooster tails when she stomped on the gas and peeled away from the house. I hooted, shouting out the window, "Hurry on up, boys." Hattie smiled from ear to ear, bouncing in the old truck seat as we bounded over potholes.

The sun was about set and the two-lane highway that connected Havana and Logan county was getting dark. The only lights were the high beams on the old Ford. I wasn't scared though. I knew that highway like the back of my hand. Hell, everyone old enough to reach the pedals could get to that lake blindfolded. And drunk. Maybe not at the same time, but you get the idea.

YOU REALLY ASKIN'?

Maldoon's was crowded for a Thursday night. The dirt parking lot was filled with old beat-up trucks, classic muscle cars, and a few shiny new ones too. Everyone from Logan and Yell counties came out to Maldoon's—probably more. It was a pain in the ass to find if you'd never been there before, but once someone showed you the way, you never forgot how to get there.

The big, red wooden barn stood in the center of a wooded area. Christmas lights hung from the eaves of the roof and a huge canvas banner stretched over the double barn doors. The banner read Maldoon's, painted in giant black letters. As far as I knew, the place had never changed as long as it'd been there. A fresh coat of red paint or new hay bales in the dancehall maybe, but other than that, it was the same as when my mama and daddy were honky-tonkin' before Garret came along.

I kicked up dirt with the toes of my boots as Hattie and I walked through the open doors. An old woman on the fiddle stomped a bare foot with the beat of an old country song. Couples swung around the dance floor. The whole place smelled like cheap cologne, hay, and beer, reminding me of home.

"Get this girl a beer. And make it on the house, Leroy; it's her birthday!" Hattie yelled over the makeshift bar at the old man behind it. She slapped imaginary drums against the wood while we waited.

Damn near eighty years old and the man was still pouring drinks. Those folks who say drinking and smoking causes an early death obviously ain't met Leroy Maldoon.

"You got it. You turnin' twenty-one again, Miss Lynnie?" Leroy winked a wrinkly blue eye at me. Wrinkles he'd earned outright on a ruddy face, topped with dove white hair, made for a comical character.

I nodded and beamed. He handed me a bottle of beer without charging me for it. If he could, I'd bet Leroy wouldn't charge anyone for anything, ever. But I guess you just can't run a business that way.

Me and Hattie clutched our cold beer bottles and moved on from the bar to the dance floor. The band plucked along to some country tune when I caught Garret and Rusty making their grand entrance. Nearly everyone in the place knew my brother and the idiot he'd walked in with. In a town of four hundred people, everyone knew everyone. But Maldoon's was a midway where all the folks from three different counties—Yell, Logan, and Pope, probably more if someone took a census—came out to have a good time. Garret might as well have been hung on the wall as a decoration. I don't think the women would mind.

I waved at my brother and snarled at Rusty when he puckered his lips and kissed the air in my direction. Garret was good-looking. Like our daddy. Thank the Lord he didn't act like him. Wouldn't know what I'd do if I only got to see Garret on Christmas and random weekends. They shared the same rough and handsome face, dark blue eyes, and a thick, manly jawline. It was because of this ladies flocked to him in droves. But I knew my brother. He wasn't any closer to getting hitched than I was of winning the Nobel Prize. It took a few minutes, but Garret finally broke free from the horde of drunken women pawing at him and worked his way over to me.

"Hey, birthday girl. Leroy got you started?" Garret said, nodding at my half-empty beer.

I smiled and chugged the rest down my gullet to finish it off. I shook my empty bottle and swallowed the mouthful of beer I had stored in my cheeks.

A stupid grin spread across Rusty's face and he headed off to the bar, yelling over his shoulder, "Ya' need another'n." Hattie followed behind him swinging her girthy hips.

"That damn redneck boy's gonna be the death o' me," I said to myself, watching him walk away.

"He loves you, ya' know," Garret said.

"Yeah, 'bout as much as he loves his truck and his dog." I was starting to sound like a poor-me country song.

"Eh, Lynnie, he ain't just yankin' your chain. You got his heart." Garret made it sound like a joke, but I knew by his voice he wasn't kidding.

"Come on now." I looked at him with eyes that said I'd punch him good if he was lying.

He poked me in the chest. "And you know in there somewhere you love him just as much. Ain't nobody hate someone so much that didn't love 'em first." It wasn't often Garret got to be a deep-thinker, even if he did use the word "ain't."

For one second, Garret had me believing that Rusty Kemp was actually in love with me. He'd been pestering me for years, but I'd always figured he was just being a fool. Everything he did made me want to pull my hair out. He was always breaking my toys, eating my lunch, pulling my hair, even before I got smart and started kicking dirt at him. If anyone knew Rusty, it was my brother, so he'd be the first to know if Rusty was in love. Garret had never said anything before about it. Maybe Rusty finally confessed, or Garret finally told me, or he was full of shit. Oh, hell. Either way it was Rusty Kemp—there was no way I'd ever bed that man. Ever. I caught a mental image of Rusty and I together and my body winced with disgust.

"Here you are, my lady," Rusty said, trying to mask his accent with a British one, as he handed me a shot glass filled to the rim with brown liquid. Whiskey, from the smell of it. Rusty had a few more tucked in his big hands, but Hattie handed a shot to Garret.

The four of us raised our miniature glasses in the air. "Happy Birthday, Lynnie," they said together and flipped the glasses bottom-up.

I did the same and the spicy fluid hit my tongue. A hot poker on my throat, I was right—it was whiskey. I shuddered and smacked my lips. Before I knew it, Rusty was handing me another glass filled with the same spicy brown nectar of stupidity.

"This one's to you from me. Happy birthday, Lynn." Rusty grinned at me. He'd cleaned his face, washed his hair too from the look of it, and knocked the stink of fresh tar off him. For the first time in something like fifteen years, I didn't want to spit in his eye. A twinkling blue, like clear water at sunrise.

I wished then that Garret had kept his damn mouth shut. I didn't wanna think about Rusty's eyes. I didn't want to wonder if he loved me, if Garret had been telling the truth. And I damn sure didn't want to get drunk enough to sleep with him.

The smell of expensive whiskey filled my nose as Rusty held the glass closer to my lips. I rolled my eyes and snatched it, spilling a few drops. Normally I'd have licked it off, but I let it sit out of spite. The three of them clapped and cheered when I parted my lips and let the liquid fire fill my mouth.

"A'ight, that's enough for now," I yelled over the bluesy bass guitar plucking on stage.

I had to shake my head over and over till the three of them stopped egging me on for more alcohol. I knew my limit, knew I needed to slow it down even if it was just for a minute.

The band started a new song. I didn't recognize the singer, or the band, as anyone I'd seen play at Maldoon's before. Leroy was good about bringing in folks who were just starting out. The singer's voice, a deep rumble, matched the heavy bass and slow beat of the song. I wasn't much of a dancer, especially to slow songs, but Hattie dragged me to the dance floor. I looked back to the spot we'd been standing to find Rusty and Garret had disappeared into the crowd. I'd never cared much where Rusty went or what he did. Until Garret opened his big fat mouth.

Hattie and I danced together as best as two girls can without turning too many heads. The man on stage sang his heart out. His grumbly voice was a perfect fit for the song. The lyrics I could understand were mostly about being lost, losing God maybe. And being stuck in the night. Wasn't exactly what you normally hear in a bar in the middle of nowhere, but I liked it. After being stuck in a place that hadn't changed much in twenty years, anything new was welcome.

Rusty was suddenly at my right, a silly grin plastered on his face, and two fresh shots tucked into one of his hands. I tried to fight it, shook my head to tell him no, but Hattie pushed and Rusty handed it to me anyway. He clinked his glass against mine and flung his shot back. I sighed. It didn't burn quite as much that time.

"My twenty-first birthday ain't gonna be half as fun if I drink this much before I'm even legal," I said with a loud drunken giggle.

Rusty only grinned and produced another shot he'd been hiding in his other hand. I grumbled and whined, but me and him repeated the same clanking and drinking routine. My cheeks tingled and my eyes were getting heavy.

The music picked up to a banjo-picking tune. Even though I actually liked that particular brand of old country, I let Hattie pull me away from the dance floor and Rusty, back to the bar to see Leroy. Rusty followed behind like a puppy dog—or was he the *shit*? I looked around for Garret. *He's probably off wooing some poor girl*, I thought to myself. My big brother wasn't looking for a wife, but he was still a man and he damn sure wasn't dead.

Hattie and Rusty sat on either side of me at the bar. I was four shots in and though it wasn't my first rodeo, I wasn't exactly a seasoned drinker. I asked Leroy for a glass of water. He laughed, shook his head, but got it anyway. I drank it up in a few hefty guzzles.

Rusty ordered another round for the three of us and a basket of chips to help soak it up. "Don't want you gettin' sick on yourself now, kid," he said with a wink.

"I can hold my own," I slurred. He was right to get some food in me. After four shots and a beer, I'd started to not care so much about all those years I'd wanted to toss Rusty Kemp off a bridge.

"Hm," he scoffed, lips turned up at the corners. "Drink your drink."

Hattie leaned against me, the two of us sang along to an old Cash song playing on the jukebox while the band took a break. Rusty watched us, holding back a grin that looked painful.

"Hey, Leroy, can you get us some beers and a few more whiskeys?" Rusty shouted over the music.

"Well, Mr. Kemp, if I didn't know any better, I'd say you were trying to get me drunk."

A smile crooked the side of his mouth. "Well, Miss Russell, I'd say it's your birthday so might as well get drunk on me."

Before I could stop myself, I tucked my blonde hair behind my ear and bit my lip. *Damn it, Lynnie, knock that shit off.* Hiding my embarrassment, I looked at anything but Rusty Kemp, who was staring a hole into the side of my head. Why did Garret have to go and tell me about Rusty? I could have gone my whole life without knowing. I'd done well to come up with that boy and not have killed him twice over by now. Let alone fall in love. In a town like Havana, the dating pool was small, very small, and Rusty Kemp was a good catch. I won't lie about that. He was handsome and honest and responsible and had a good job, and despite what Mama said, I was not, absolutely *not* in love with Rusty Kemp.

"What are y'all up to?" Garret slid in between Rusty and me, saving me from making eye contact with the one man I swore on my life I would never see naked.

"Flirtin' with your sister," Rusty joked and took a swig of beer.

Garret held up two fingers to Leroy. "Good to see nothin' changes 'round here." He looked over my head and winked at Hattie.

"Shut your mouth, Garret Llewellyn. Ain't nothing of the sort," I grumbled.

"Why you smiling like a dead pig in sunshine?"

I glared at him. I knew well enough what I was doing. And why I was smiling. And I couldn't stop it no matter how hard I tried. Garret winked at me, crinkling the corner of his eye. If he were Robert Redford—which was a close comparison—Rusty was Paul Newman. More than just the classic duo, Rusty shared the same broad chin, which was usually covered in sandy scruff. An angled nose he'd grown into eventually, shiny now under the lights and sticky sweat.

Leroy slid two fresh beers across the bar to Garret. "Thanks, old man," he said with a nod. "Come on, girl, you're looking like you're ready for a dance." Garret handed Hattie a beer behind my back and slid his arm around her shoulder. "You be good, Lynn." He kissed me on the top of my head. "Take care of our girl, son." And flicked the back of Rusty's hat with a single finger, sending it flopping over his forehead. That stupid brother of mine hustled Hattie off to the dance floor before I could argue with him.

Damn it.

My heart leapt. Forty horses galloped through my stomach. *Why, Garret?* Leroy finally set my potato chips down in front of me alongside my millionth shot of whiskey and an icy beer. Nervous sweat dripped down my back. I needed something to cool me off. I swallowed hard—a foamy lump of beer shoved through to my gut.

"Thank ya, old man," I repeated my brother, and Leroy

winked at me—less charming than Garret's.

Rusty raised his glass. "To Lynnie on her twentieth birthday." Our eyes locked and I blushed red. "What're you blushing for?" he asked like he didn't already know. Like Garret hadn't let him know he'd spilled the beans.

"Just hot is all," I said, my nose growing five inches. I clinked my glass with his and let the liquid set fire to my gullet.

Mama's voice wouldn't leave my head. She'd never said those exact words before, but it was her voice telling me to give it up and admit I'd been lying to myself all these years. Maybe she'd been right, that old, rode-hard woman who couldn't find love herself—that didn't drive off on eighteen wheels.

Rusty Kemp, all dressed up in his least-faded Levi's and off-white Stetson, could've had his pick of girls. Garret had a line of them to choose from. But there he sat, staring a hole in the side of *my* head as if he hadn't ever seen me boot and rally—not a pretty sight—in this very establishment. Or eat a pan of cornbread to myself, or shovel chicken shit in my daddy's hand-me-down jeans, or any other disgusting thing we got into coming up together.

Whiskey flushed my cheeks. Sweat dripped down the back of my knees. Rusty Kemp, I couldn't hardly think his name without bringing up memories of some stupid, annoying, rat-faced thing he'd done. Rusty was an ornery little shit if I ever saw one, but damned if I wasn't starting to not mind that so much sitting there letting him look at me.

I ain't nothin' if I ain't a sucker for a good-lookin' cowboy, my nana used to say. Nana wasn't wrong, not about much anyway. I'd always thought he was a two-tailed pig, but as it was turning out, he was just a dumbass boy in a big ol' man-body.

I'd never been nervous around that man in my life, but there I was shaking in my boots, blushing red at the thought of what could be. Courage finally convinced me to look at him. His eyes shifted toward the dance floor and he swigged his beer as if he hadn't just got caught staring.

Sweat shined on his forehead, a workingman's sweat. Hair-pulling, lunch-stealing, shithead extraordinaire aside, there were worse choices than Rusty Kemp out there. One day I'd get out of Havana where the dating pool was bigger, filled with people I hadn't seen crap their pants on a baseball field. But until I made that happen, Rusty wasn't going away.

I had a choice to make. Ignore Rusty's mostly typical bullshit, act like Garret hadn't said what he did, and continue to pretend I didn't like Rusty, or actually consider the possibility of him and me in a romantic-type situation.

I knew two things in that moment. I could never go back to pretending I didn't—in some backassward, slap-me-in-the-morning way—*like* Rusty, and I was piss-ass drunk. Whether it was lucky for me or not, so was Rusty. Maybe he needed it for courage. Maybe I did too. Two drunks full of bad decisions.

"You hot?" I said without thinking. Sweat dripped from under the rim of his hat.

He looked at me with glassy blue eyes and swiped a hand down his stubbled jaw. "Got the whiskey sweats." A lazy grin tugged one side of his mouth.

I looked away from him, took a drink of my beer. "Wanna go outside and cool off?" And said something really stupid, regretting the invite the instant it left my bumbling lips.

He took a second to answer. Long enough I thought maybe Garret had lied. "You bet," he croaked, half choking on his beer, and jumped off the stool.

By the hand, he dragged me out the front doors. I thought about fighting him, changing my mind and running back to Garret—who I thought deserved a kick in the shin—but I didn't. My hand in his, I followed Rusty out the old barn doors and to his truck parked out in the lot.

Dirt kicked up off our boot heels, shuffling awkwardly to his old Chevy. The damn thing had about four different shades of primer on it from him and my brother running into stuff all tanked up, but she ran like a champ.

Rusty leaned against the tailgate, looking up at the stars. "Better," he said, drawing up a deep breath and letting it out slow. He smelled like whiskey. A smell that would soon enough come through his sweat. Redneck cologne I couldn't get enough of.

A country girl till the bitter end, I couldn't wait to get out of this godforsaken town. Get out and see the world and all it had to offer. There was still nothing better than the smell of an old truck, a fresh dip, and whiskey on a man. Like my mama that way, I guess.

We stood out in the night, leaning against his truck, staring at our own feet, for a whole five minutes before either one of us said anything again.

"Nice night, eh?" I rolled my eyes at my own damn self. It was bad enough I was outside looking at the stars with the likes of Rusty Kemp. I didn't have to be an awkward mess on top.

"Yup. Beautiful," Rusty said, staring at the tips of his boots.

"You all right, boy?" I asked, just as I would have before Garret told me what he had.

He sucked his teeth, the Rusty sign of deep thinking. "Why you out here with me?" he asked, still staring at his feet.

I shrugged, shaking off the truth. "It's a nice night." I knew that was a lie, but there was nothing else I wanted to say out loud.

"Com'on now, Lynnie. I know you better'n'at. You don't go anywhere with the likes of me. Shit, you ain't looked at me twice unless you was trying to take aim." He lifted his hat and ruffled a hand through sweat-damp hair.

I stood up straight and looked him in the eye. "Maybe 'at's 'cause you're a pig, Rusty Kemp. Treat me like the lady I am and maybe it'd be different." I poked his chest.

He blew air through his lips. "You ain't a lady. I watched you drink whiskey like a man and more than just tonight. I seen you change an alternator in your prom dress. You are a lady 'bout as much as you're a cat, Lynnie Russell." He laughed his stupid little boy laugh that I'd hated for years.

"Do you love me?" If I hadn't been drunk, I'd've never said it.

He stopped laughing and swallowed hard. "You really

askin'?" His eyes went back down to his boots.

I didn't know if I wanted to know the God's honest truth. Or, even if Rusty would actually tell me the truth. Instead of making up my drunk mind right then, I changed the subject.

"You wanna go out to the lake?" I ducked under his head to look him in the eye.

Rusty looked up at me from under the brim of his hat with big eyes. "You really askin'?" he repeated.

A sly grin pushed my lips together. "You bet." I was really asking; that was for certain. Was I sure heading out to the lake, drunk, in the middle of the night was a good idea? Nope. Not one little bit.

Rusty didn't say a word before he had my door open, me in, and the old truck roaring. Like he knew if given long enough to think about it I'd have changed my mind. We were sliding out of the dirt parking lot before I could decide not to tear off into the night with my brother's best friend. A boy I'd known since I was old enough to start knowing people.

At damn near midnight, drunker than Cooter Brown, and coming from Maldoon's, there was only one thing folks did out at the lake. Well, two, really. I was only planning on doing one of those. As long as Rusty didn't pump me up with whiskey until I forgot I'd hated him that morning, I'd be all right.

"Here's a beer." He pulled a cold beer can out of an old red cooler on the floorboard. "You sure you wanna go out to the lake? It's hot enough for swimmin' tonight. That's for damn sure."

He talked fast, nervous. I was thankful he didn't mention the *other* thing folks did at the lake after dark. I did my best to tell myself I wasn't there to do that. Just swim. Just take off some clothes and swim. That's it. Two old, drunk, mostly naked friends cooling off in a secluded lake under the cover of darkness. I was worried that I wasn't worried at all.

I'd never been in love before. I didn't know what it felt like. I knew I'd never thought of Rusty as anything but a rotten, no-good turd until the night I ended up sitting shotgun in his truck on our way to swim naked in Blue Mountain Lake.

KISSIN' & SACRIFICES

I didn't have time to finish my road-beer before Rusty was slowing the truck down just off the muddy bank. Silver ripples of moonlight danced on the lake under a full moon hanging big and bright in the black sky like someone was backstage with a ball on a stick.

Rusty left his headlights on long enough to find a stick to whack the water and scare away snakes. It sounds ridiculous to swim with snakes, but we all just mostly try to forget they're out there until we see one. But drunk and all hyped up on hormones? What snakes?

He kept the radio on, low enough to hardly hear over the sound of the katydids singing their long-awaited summer song.

Rusty leaned against the grill of his truck and pulled boots off one by one, watching me from the corner of his eye, nearly glowing in the reflection of the moon. I pretended not to watch him tug his T-shirt from his jeans. Feet sunk into sandy soil, prickly grass poking between my toes. I almost didn't pull my dress off, exposing my underthings, letting Rusty see them. He hadn't seen my undies since I was seven and Granddaddy built us a mud pit to roll in like the pigs— maybe that's why I saw Rusty as a short-snout swine. The flash of the two dimples above his butt ripped that hesitation right out from underneath me.

He cleared his throat once and folded his jeans to lay on the hood and did everything he could to not look at my boobs.

Heart doing somersaults in my chest, I ran into the water. The chill brought goosepimples up my arms. "Come on, shithead." I splashed in his general direction.

Rusty hollered when his nether region hit the water. I kicked water at him. He lost his footing and slipped neck deep into the lake. I cackled like an old drunk witch. Other than the sexual tension, it was a typical summer night on the lake.

Me and Rusty splashed and laughed and sang along with Willie and drank beer under the big moon for what must've been an hour. Sticky heat, surely hotter than hell itself, melted away in the cool water.

We'd made our way from the bank near the truck to a small cove just up the way. The area was small and only about chest high with rocks large enough to sit on. Perfect for two drunkards who had no business trying to swim in the dark.

I perched on a rock, my top-half out of the water. Blonde hair, long enough to cover my boobs like a mermaid, did nothing of the sort, and clung together in twisted chunks on my back. Rusty squeezed on the rock beside me. It wasn't a two-person rock.

His arm pressed against mine, our legs floating together. I waited for him to pull my hair or shove me off the rock into the lake or pop my bra strap or some other stupid man-boy thing he was notorious for doing.

"You doing okay?" I was pretty certain he hadn't ever said those words to me.

I nodded. "Fine."

"We can go back… if you want." He was giving me an out I should have taken.

"Do *you*?"

He breathed. "No."

"Okay."

"Okay."

Rusty breathed beside me, quiet and smelling like whiskey. "Lynn."

"Yeah?"

"Would you marry me?"

I laughed, one great bark. "Rusty Kemp, what in the… *what*?"

He huffed. "Shut up, Lynnie. I mean, like, am I someone *someone* would marry."

Hurt peppered his voice and it stung me inside. "Oh." Yes, actually, he was. Definitely. Would *I* marry him? "You're a good man, Rusty. I'll give you that one."

"Hmm."

"You know what I mean." He'd never asked me what I'd thought of him before. Probably because I'd always made it clear I mostly hated him. But I didn't. Not really. Not inside where it counted. A wise man once said, can't truly hate someone you didn't love first. "You're a hard worker. I think you'd be a good provider." I grinned at the time he put on Mama's girdle and strutted around the house like a hooker in a whorehouse. "You're funny."

"Yeah?"

"Yeah."

I listened to him breathe for a solid few minutes. I knew Rusty well enough to know when he sat still, just breathing slow and soft, he was thinking. Sometimes he was just thinking about what was for dinner, but that night sitting on that rock with me, he was thinking about his future. It rolled off him, steam from hot skin on a cold night.

"Rusty?"

"Yeah?"

I waited long enough to finish my thought that he turned to look at the side of my head and watched me say, "I wish you weren't so mean to me."

"I was a kid, Lynn," he said, his voice desperate.

"You're a man now, Rusty."

"Yeah." He turned on the rock to face me, taking up too

much space on the one-person seat. Clenched cheeks clung to the rough surface for dear life. "I ain't mean to you like that anymore. I'm just teasing. And you're mean to me. I tried to say something nice about your hair tonight and you told me to shut up."

I looked up at the moon. "What else was I supposed to say?"

"Thank you. Just say thank you."

Our voices had grown louder and echoed back at us. "Well… I don't know how to be with you any other way," I said hushed.

"I ain't expecting you to."

"What are you expecting?" I turned to look him in the eye. His face just inches from mine.

"Nothing. Sure as hell not this." He waved his hand through the dark. Moonlight gleamed off his blue eyes.

I looked away before truth spilled out of my mouth. "Garret told me…."

He got quiet, still. "Yeah?"

"Yup."

"Is that why you're out here with me?"

"Mostly."

He sighed. "Fuck." Water splashed between us when he kicked his foot. "Damn it, Garret," he mumbled.

"It's fine."

"No."

"Yes. Someone had to have the balls to say it."

"I have balls," he shouted, and his echo said it three

more times.

"Not enough to tell me you love me." I swallowed the word, but it bobbed in the back of my throat, threatening to spill out.

I turned to look at him. His mouth hung open. No words escaped. Tan skin was muted in the moonlight, but his eyes sparkled. Bright white and ocean blue.

One breath. Two. "I gotta take a leak." He waded out of the lake and ran over to a tall tree that stood just in front of a set of head-high bushes. He turned his back to me.

"Just piss in the lake like the fish do, Rusty." My voice echoed through the tight inlet. Our echoes made me nervous, like someone was gonna come out of the woods and catch me naked in the lake watching Rusty let loose a six-pack onto a tree.

I could hear his pee hit the ground and tried not to laugh when he said, "I ain't pissing in there while you're in there."

"Since when?" Whether the emergency piss break was necessary or not, he'd successfully avoided the subject. I slid off the rock and let cool water cover my chest.

From the corner of my eye, I watched the top of his butt cheeks peek out from the waistband of his skivvies, two divots overtop. I wondered how I'd feel about him when morning came, when I wasn't drunk.

I tried hard not to judge my feelings by the fact that Rusty had, until that day, made me want to kick him in the knee. I also tried to pretend Rusty hadn't known me since I was in kindergarten. And, if I'm being honest, I tried to pretend I wasn't admiring the way the moon landed on the muscles of his broad back.

His loud splashing and hollering snapped me out of my thoughts. He opened the lid of the cooler that bobbed beside us on its tether, and tossed me another beer.

"I can't drink anymore more, Rusty," I said while I popped the top open and chugged it down.

"Yeah, bet you can't." He chuckled and rustled a hand over wet hair, sending drops of water to my pink cheeks. That nervous gesture of his used to drive me insane, to the point I couldn't even look at him. Under that moon, I couldn't get enough.

"Catch, bitch." I tossed my empty can at him. He caught it and shoved it into the cooler.

I swayed with the movement of the lake. Rusty was quiet, leaning against a rock, mostly underwater, watching the moon dance on the surface. I laid back, letting the water lift my body flush with the surface. The moon, so damn big in the black sky, called to me as I floated weightless on top of Blue Mountain Lake.

To Lynnie on her 20th birthday. Rusty's words played over in my head. If Garret hadn't said anything, would Rusty have gotten the guts to? Would I have eventually figured it out on my own? If it weren't for Garret, would I have thought twice about Rusty? Five million questions and the only answer was the simplest. My life was about to turn ass up.

Rusty's arms slid under me and he picked me up like a bride over the threshold. I screamed. "You put me down." I kicked my legs, laughing too hard to break free.

His arms, strong from manual labor, only held me tighter. "You gotta kiss me first," he said, so quiet I damn near didn't even hear him.

Rusty had always played stupid childish games like that when we were growing up. I never paid him mind. I never actually thought for a minute he meant any of it. He'd pretend to be a gentleman, even charming sometimes, but he'd always follow it up by pulling my hair or puttin' a frog in my bed. Then, drunk in the middle of the lake in my undies, I finally figured it out. The simplest answer. Strange what happens to a girl's sensibility when a good lookin' southern boy falls in love with her.

"You'll put me down?" I asked.

He breathed, watching my face for any sign of bullshit. "You really askin'?" he asked just before I kissed him.

It wasn't a long, deep movie-style kiss. Just a small innocent type, but it made butterflies burst to life in my stomach. His mouth was soft and beer-flavored. Underneath the beer and lake water, the whiskey was still there. Water dripped from his hair onto my cheek. It fell across my face like an escaped tear. I had no reason to be crying. I was fairly certain I was in love with Rusty Kemp, and the promise of what could be filled my heart.

He pulled his head back and smiled so big I thought his cheeks were gonna fall right off. "I can't believe you did it," he said, all lit up like a boy at Christmas. "I been waitin' a long time for that, Lynnie Russell." That first kiss would be with me until the day I died. "You asked; I'm tellin'. I love you. I do. Ain't never been a day I didn't," he said, breathless.

I stared at him. I couldn't believe he'd actually said it out loud. Three words that would change my world.

I was twenty years old officially. I was drunk and half-naked in a lake under a perfectly round moon, sprawled across the arms of someone I had thought was a jackass, still did. But I'd be damned if I didn't want to ever stop kissing Rusty Kemp. Maybe mama was right. Maybe I had really just loved him all along.

His chest pressed against me with each breath. Water droplets reflected a dozen moons across his shoulders. I wrapped my hand around the back of his neck. He pulled me closer, beyond the sweet stench of alcohol, into the deep woodsy scent of him. I knew that smell. My living room smelled like it most days. It was familiar, and safe, and unexpected.

Rusty's scruffy cheek pressed against mine. If I'd been sober, it would have been weird. Too awkward to get around. I thanked the whiskey gods for letting my stupid head shut up long enough my heart had a moment to speak.

"Why'd you make it so hard to love you, shithead?" I slapped his shoulder.

He shrugged. "Probably because I'm the biggest fool you've ever met." His grin curved crystalline eyes into half-moons.

I should've been highly uncomfortable cradled in Rusty's arms, watching moonlight glimmer in his eyes. I should've been closing down Maldoon's with Garret and Hattie, puking out the window of her daddy's truck down highway 10. I should've been a lot of things. Had it been fate? Was it that big ol' moon? The whiskey and beer and piney sweat?

I took a deep breath. "Is this even gonna work? Like… *us*?" Chewing on my cheek, I almost bit a hole right through it. What if it didn't and our lives were never the same? What if it *did* and they were better than I'd ever imagined?

He watched my mouth for a solid few seconds before answering. "Divine Providence and the creek don't rise." His voice rumbled deep in his chest.

I pinched my lips together to keep my smile from getting out of control. Knowing it was bad luck—Granddaddy Higgins had carved that saying into the hawthorn tree out in front of their house the year they built it. We'd spent every summer out there taking naps under it, snickering at Nana's stories about wood spirits. It was the cleverest thing Rusty Kemp had ever said in his whole life.

All the things I wanted to say were stuck on the tip of my tongue. Once said could never be unheard. I swallowed, licked my lips. He watched, a sly grin tugged the corner of his mouth. The sweet stink of whiskey filled the narrow space between us.

Brows pulled tight at the center, he lifted his head. His eyes shifted, focused on a thick, dark section of woods. "What the hell is that?" He stared into the shadows on the other side of a ring of tall bushes just off the bank.

We'd floated far enough that I couldn't see the truck

anymore, just dark dense woods.

"What?"

"Are those…" he leaned closer to the sound "…*ladies* talkin' over there?" His voice was low, but his slur was undeniable. He always sounded more redneck the drunker he got.

I cranked my neck to look and wiggled until he got the hint and carefully put me down, holding my waist until my feet touched solid ground. His focus was on the woods, but his hand never left my back. We stood still and quiet for long enough to hear more than just our breath and the sound of water slapping wet skin.

It wasn't exactly abnormal for that time of year. Blue Mountain Lake was a popular party spot. But to hear a bunch of women out there in the wee hours of the morning, all talking at once, was too much to resist for two drunks desperately trying not to sleep together.

After a few more minutes of looking and listening, curiosity won out. We hauled our drunk asses out of the cold water and sloshed through the dirt. Prickly grass stuck to wet feet. The voices grew louder the closer I got, but they were still garbled turkeys from where we stood.

"I think they're singin' a song."

"Probably soused and lettin' loose," I whispered.

"Nah, that ain't no drunkard's tune I ever heard before."

"That's not surprising, Rusty. You haven't heard of a lot of things." He ignored my jab and moved closer.

My mouth gaped. "Damn it, Rusty," I grumbled and

followed him. "I'm kind of in my skivvies here," I hissed.

We crouched behind a row of bushes on the far side of the cove. Yellow flames tickled the trees surrounding a clearing a dozen yards away. Four elongated shadows danced across the trunks. Rusty poked his head up above mine for a better look and ducked down quickly.

Eyes wide, he whispered, "They're wearing some kinda black gowns."

"*Gowns?*"

I didn't trust Rusty as far as I could throw him, and peeked over the top of the bushes to see for myself. They weren't gowns. Not any kind of gown I'd ever seen, anyhow. Black, yes, but these had hoods and long pointed sleeves. They weren't gowns, they were robes. Not what someone would be wearing out there in that sticky summer heat. Or any time in a place like Havana. Maybe Halloween.

"They're like robes, or cloaks, or somethin'," I whispered as quiet as I could without looking away.

Crouched behind a spiny bush, water-blurred eyes a butt hair above the top, I hid. If they'd have looked, they probably would've seen me no matter how stealthy I thought I was at the time.

One of the robed women pulled a hefty chicken from a makeshift coop sitting by the fire. A taller woman slid a shiny blade from its sheath. The chicken squawked once, but it was over before it started. The red-haired woman ran her knife around the chicken's neck, nearly chopping the damn thing clean off. My eyes went wide. I slammed a hand over my mouth to stop myself from squealing like a girl.

Something cold and wet touched my back. I jumped almost out of my panties.

"What're they up to?" Rusty whispered, so quiet I almost didn't hear him, his hand pressed against my back.

I shook my head. "I don't know," I said hushed. "Killin' a chicken."

"A *chicken*?"

Rusty and I peeked cautiously over the top of the hedge. The chicken's head was gone, blood poured from the stump, hanging by its feet. The chicken woman held a bowl—or some odd thing—in her other hand catching every drop. The other women kept on with their singing. At first, I thought maybe they were speaking English, just really fast. Closer, I could tell it wasn't any language I had ever heard before.

Hot breath puffed through my nose, speeding up to match my heart, dragging in the stinging stink of the fire.

The women chanted the same words over and over again, "*Cu sidhe an laoch díoltas.*"

Electricity charged the air, drawing the hairs on my arms up, covering them in goose pimples. Fear mingled with a cool breeze and a chill ran down my spine. I looked at Rusty, who's eyes were saucers, mouth a gaping fly trap. "What the hell is happening?" I mouthed, hardly a breath.

He shook his head. "I feel like I might be dreamin'." His eyes shot in my direction, looked down then back up again. "I definitely have this dream a lot."

I blushed and turned back to the glowing fire in time to

see the red-haired lady toss the headless chicken into it. A blast of flame billowed out to the sides, and then shot up like a rocket engine through the center of the circle of trees. All four women raised their hands to the sky. Hoods fell away to show each wore a skull headdress, circled in twigs and flowers.

The whispered voices of so many mouths at once, the hiss of a thousand snakes. "Gort, ciert, fearn, dair, ruis," they chanted.

Sparks popped and flashed in the billowing fire, gunpowder in open flame. Yellow first, then little bursts of green. They sang on and the fire crackled into a curling swirl of green. The color of first spring grass.

Eight hands clapped in unison. I flinched, breath gone for good. My heart galloped in an all-out sprint. I gulped back the thick lump trapped in my throat. With the slap of their hands, the fire flashed to yellow again, crackling gone.

A pair of glowing purple eyes locked onto mine. Tingling crackled over the baby-fine hairs on my neck. The blonde woman dropped her raised hands and pointed one eerily straight finger directly at *me*.

"Oh, hell!" Rusty yelled as he jumped up from behind his bush, drying undies hardly hanging on to his narrow hips. "Com'on," he shouted.

I clamped my eyes shut and tucked my head to my knees. I was too drunk to handle stressful situations. No fight. No flight. All freeze.

Rusty's bare feet slapped sandy soil as he ran away from

me, kicking up leaves and cracking twigs all the way. A rough fist clenched hold of my hair. I screamed and kicked, and struggled to wriggle away. The harder I kicked, the more determined her steps. Screaming in the woods under a full moon only let me know how loud I could scream from the echo that came back to me. There'd be no one coming to help. No one could hear me. No one but Rusty.

Tiny cuts on the backs of my legs nipped like bee stings as twigs tore up my backside. I screamed for Rusty. I knew he didn't leave me. He wouldn't. There was no way. *I should've ran with him. Lord, help me, I should have ran.*

I skidded to a stop next to the fire pit. "What—"

She held tight to my hair, forcing me to my knees. Hush voices hissed foreign words.

I gulped, terrified vomit—sweet and spicy like whiskey—stung the back of my throat.

My daddy hunted my whole life, and I lived with my brother, who thought guns and knives were the best things since titties. I knew a knife when I heard one. A sharp blade sliding quickly from its sheath had a particular sound. Deadly steal gliding over well-aged leather. Nearly indescribable. It took knowledge and a good amount of fear to understand that sound.

Unfamiliar screams ripped through my throat. I tried to scramble to my feet, but one of them shoved me to the dirt. Blood splattered from my head onto a large pale rock surrounding the fire.

Lungs stiff with fear, I rolled to my back. Through hazy

eyes, the red-haired woman towered over me. Her chicken-killing blade glinted in her clutch. I kicked at her, but she grabbed my hair again, taking near about my whole scalp with it.

Wriggling and kicking, I jerked away from her, almost yanked my hair from its roots when I did. Off in the distance, lit only by moonlight, Rusty snuck through the brush. He'd put his pants on. I opened my mouth to warn him, beg him to run away, but only a strangled squeaking came out.

If a knife is sharp enough, you don't even feel the cut. Air gurgled through the thick gash across my gullet. Blood poured from the gaping line like someone had opened a flood gate. She held the wooden bowl under my chin and let the blood fill it up.

"Gort, ciert, fearn, dair, ruis." They circled the fire pit, cottony robes tickling my toes as they moved around me. Each swiped a finger through my blood in the bowl, drawing angled lines across their faces. Blondie sat a headdress on her head—a five-point buck, crowned in dried bits of nature. Red-spattered soil clenched in my fists, I begged the heavens to take me quick or give me the strength to kill them all. "Cu sidhe iompróir a bháis bheidh mé a bheith," they cried.

Red left the circle, dragging me by my hair to my feet—tips of my toes hardly touching the ground—and held me over the flame. Blood poured, fueling the fire. In a searing flash, lime green flames plumed, engulfing my face, licking the trees above. The stench, my own burning flesh, the last true scent of my young life.

Death isn't something you plan for, even though we all know one day it's coming to round us up. I should've been somewhere else. Anywhere else. Fate brought me there. It must've been that creek Granddaddy was talking about.

Happy fucking birthday. I choked a rattling breath. Blackness filled my vision.

The force of a pissed off bull slammed into us. The woman dropped me and I fell to the dirt. She tumbled away. Shallow breaths hardly registered. I peeled open one heavy lid. Shadowy blobs rolled and scuffled. A slow, forced blink cleared my vision. *Rusty.*

Emerald fireworks burst from the now raging fire. Ragged breaths puffed dirt at my lips. Heart only a whisper, I silently begged the Lord to keep him safe. My ornery boy. Lime green flames shot up through the center of the trees. I clenched cool soil in my fingers, one desperate grasp of earth before I took my last breath.

Blackness, a void never ending, swallowed me whole. Nothingness. An eternity in an instant.

As if God himself commanded it, I popped back to life, eyes wide, stomach curdled with agony. Sorrow, a sound so vile, screeched from my lungs. Blood and bitter bile spewed from my lips. I coughed and sputtered and spit the last of it to the dirt.

"Lynn?" Rusty cried.

I pushed myself to my knees, freshly resurrected and too weak to stand. "Rusty," I gurgled, a soggy hole gaped in my throat.

I should've been dead. Flat out on my back *croaked*. I blinked at the madness unfolding, head swimming with a thousand thoughts—and the equally void blackness that called me back home. On shaky legs, I climbed to my feet. My boy wrestled with all four of them—each caked in my blood—winning for just long enough to scramble closer. I reached for him, desperate for his touch, lost in the chaos of the last few minutes.

The fire puffed out into a mushroom, curling around each of us, sending them to the ground. Pain shot through my limbs. They gave out and I fell back to the dirt, sandy soil stinging my palms. My back arched, spine popping, each vertebra shifting into an unnatural curve. Cartilage and bone cracked and echoed in my head.

I dug into the dirt, clinging to something familiar. Soil-covered fingers clicked at each joint, bending, lengthening. My thumb retracted into my arm, deforming into something animalistic. Long, sharp claws pushed from my nailbeds.

A garbled, messy almost strangled version of Rusty called for me. I couldn't talk, couldn't move. Whatever was happening to me had taken my voice, trapping me in silent horror.

Tendons stretched and snapped. Skin reformed, a slopping gooey mess that dripped on my hands. I cried out, hollered and begged Jesus himself to save me. No words came out. Eyes and teeth shifted in soggy, slurping sockets.

Squelching and crackling echoed up my limbs and drowned out muffled sounds around me. Pain blinked my vision in and out, a slow camera shutter. Chills raced down my crackling spine with each pop. The sound sickening. A tooth pulled with nothing but whiskey and brute strength. Tangy puke clawed its way up my throat.

Stinging tingles spread over my skin. Murky green fur erupted from each pore, covering my arms in a thick, shaggy coat—which shook, flinging gooey remnants and letting loose a woody musk.

Unspeakable awareness of the monster I'd become dragged terror from my lungs in a long, piercing scream. Not a scream. A howl. Screeching into the darkness.

FOUND GIRL LOST

I opened my eyes to a white sky. That unsettling shade that comes just before sunrise. The early morning chill sent shivers down my arms, aching every inch of my skin. The beds of my nails, my eyes, even my damn scalp hurt. For a second, I thought I'd laid out all night, drunk as a skunk. And somehow naked.

I sat up slowly, trying not to set free a pint of beer from my rumbling belly. White coals smoldered, little puffs of smoke twisted out. Blood. Dirt. Rocks and limbs, striped and speckled with red. I'd have given anything to go back to that blissfully ignorant second.

I scrambled to my feet and fell instantly—knees in the dirt, hands tangled in soft black cotton. My throat caught and vomit popped out where a scream should have been. Red hair stuck to a mangled face in sticky clumps.

I scrambled backward on my hands and feet, as far away from the body as I could. Twigs and debris carved tiny cuts on my backside, stinging like little bits of fire on my skin. Something squished against my palm. I swallowed hard and looked cautiously over my shoulder.

For the first time in fifteen years, I realized that I loved Rusty Kemp with my entire soul. Anguish—a word I'd never known before that moment—poured from my lungs, strangling me on the way out. I gulped air but nothing broke through. Choking gasps held tight to my throat.

For a moment, I truly believed I died all over again.

Hot tears fell on Rusty's face, washing long lines of flesh through the red mask that dried on his skin. My cries echoed through the trees, rousing a flock of birds that rustled late-summer leaves from the limbs. I wrapped a trembling hand around his chin and moved his head to look at me, silently begging the whole of the universe to make it not so. When I squeezed, thick, long lines of flesh pushed open, bone peeking through from under all that blood and meat.

I jerked away, wiping the tingles of terror on my hand into the dirt. My chin quivered. We should've been elsewhere. Shaking hands hovered over his body, searching for a clean place to touch, to lay my spinning head.

Thick rusty lines striped his chest. Jeans, left unbuttoned in haste, were stained red to the ankle. Not an inch of him hadn't been marred by blood. I stared at red speckled feet, dragging in air, snot and tears and drool falling in a gooey mess to my hands.

One long *whoosh* stole the last of my breath. Like an old movie, single frames of time clicked through on fast-forward.

A blade. My throat. The fire. Dying. Changing.

Powerful legs pounced. Catlike swipes sliced open the brunette. The others fought, trying to tame the beast I'd become. I bucked, a bull from a chute, flinging one through the air and onto the fire. She wailed as the flames overtook her. The other flipped through the dirt in front of me. With one mighty paw, I drew four wide, gory stripes across her middle.

Rusty let out a gurgled scream. I turned my big furry body and bounded on four muscled legs to the jumbled mess of purple and green.

Glowing neon purple, the last robed woman straddled Rusty—green as a spring afternoon—hands around his throat. I leapt. Claws so fierce and deadly, landed wildly, Rusty in the way. I slashed at him without hesitation—a simple casualty. Electric violet spurted from the woman's wounds. She collapsed onto her side, and rolled away. Rusty's glowing eyes stared at me, blood glugged from his gullet, lime green milk from a tipped jug.

The film jolted to a stop.

Searing hot air filled my lungs, freezing me to the bone. I curled my legs to my chest and fell to my side. A fierce shiver took over my body, shaking me from head to toe. There I lay, not a peep, eyes wide, staring at the bloody mess I'd left behind.

Summer sun peeked over the mountains turning the white sky blue, shining glittering light on Rusty's sweet face. I plucked a leaf from his sticky skin; nuzzled against his cold stiff body. He smelled like a jar of pennies, but if I pressed my nose against a spot of blood-free skin, I could catch the hint of his cologne. He'd been wearing the same damn cologne since high school. I'd always hated it. Laying there next to his dead body, all I wanted was to breathe in the scent of that stupid cologne.

The rumble of a heavy truck crunched along the bank of the lake. It sounded far off, but it slowly moved closer. Help had come. They had to've been there for me. To save me. The monster.

Heavy boots clomped through the underbrush nearby, coming closer to me and the bloody heap beside me. Fear hit, a hard lump of ice in my gut. My claws, my strength had torn into those women, into Rusty. The people of Havana would tie me to a post and burn me alive. How in all the heavens in the sky would I explain to the law—and the torch-holding townsfolk—that some witches—that's what they had to've been, no doubt in my mind—had turned me into some beastly thing? A ravenous creature that just might kill again. I gulped down stinging bile.

He'd call the State Police. He'd call my mama. He'd call Garret. My icy stomach dropped when I thought about my brother.

I'd killed his best friend. My boy.

Tears rolled down my cheeks and plopped into the dirt. "I'm sorry," I breathed.

Silent, still, I laid there and waited for those heavy boots to find me. A beast. *Lord, don't let them burn me.*

Strong arms scooped me up from the chilled earth.

Garbled words, like talking underwater, I watched his mouth move but didn't understand a word of it.

He squeezed me tight to his chest, his panting breaths echoed in my head. We moved quickly through the brush, me draped naked over his arms. I listened to his heart pick up speed. Shoving through the rim of bushes where Rusty and I had hid, golden rays of sun hit my cheeks. I winced away from the light.

"You okay?" he rumbled. "We're almost there." His breaths came too quick, heart almost not able to keep up. He should've put me down. Dragged me out by my feet. "What in the hell happened here?" he whispered.

That question would haunt me the rest of my living days. What was this nightmare? When would I wake up?

He stumbled the last few steps to his truck, where he laid me in the bed. "Stay right there, honey. Don't move." I laid on my side and let the morning sun warm my skin. "What in the world…." the man said confused.

His badge glinted in the light. Deputy Morely. He covered me with a heavy wool blanket. Too much for the hot summer morning regardless of my nakedness. The deputy's radio crackled. "I got her. I got her," he shouted with short breaths.

It seemed like only seconds passed before the sirens were coming. *They* were coming. The state police, the sheriff, my mama, and my brother. I cried hard and loud.

Deputy Morely jumped, laid his hands on my hip and shoulder. "Talk to me, honey. You okay?" he said.

"No," I howled. My body shook with every breath I

dragged into my lungs.

"It's gon' be a'ight. They're comin', honey. You're a lucky girl. Lucky your brother knows you good enough to know you'd be all the way out here." He ran his hand over my head. I winced from the pain that shot down my spine.

Sirens screeched close by, clawing through my splitting head, before they cut short and the sounds of a dozen car doors popped my ears. More heavy boots and a chorus of crackling radios. They all shouted to each other. A sound so penetrating my head vibrated with it, split with it. I curled into a ball, peeking out from over my knees.

The police cars were parked at least a hundred feet away and all the men in uniform and big brimmed hats stood around the edge of the lake. No one was crowding me or yapping their mouths right over my head. But I could hear them like they were having a party on the tailgate.

I let out a long breath, failed to stop my trembling, and sat up. Off a ways up the bank, parked right where we had left it was Rusty's old truck, one of the officers wound yellow tape around trees to block it off. His white shirt glowed in under the intense sun. A shining reminder of what was.

Death hung in the air. Dense. Pungent. I couldn't see the bodies from where I sat, the ridge of brush hid the circle of trees and the fire pit that sat center. Their stench—a smell I'd never quite get rid of—clung to the hairs inside my nostrils. Deputy Morely must've smelled them too. Had to've.

A Logan County deputy wrapped me in a heavy coat without saying a word and helped me off the end of the tailgate. We walked together—my legs threatening to give way—to the ambulance that waited away from where the action was. The young deputy smiled and held my hand while the paramedics looked me over. The victim. The lone survivor.

No one knew I was the monster.

One of the paramedics said I had a high fever. Said I was probably in shock but wouldn't rule out internal injuries—as if she could see my broken heart right through my chest. They strapped me to the gurney, covering me in a thin cotton blanket. She poked me with a needle and hooked me up to a bag of clear liquid. I watched them work in silence.

Time ran forward and back in my mind. Wild, frantic thoughts. Flashes of memories, fear and sorrow, flowed into my head in waves. Agony, sheer and total, ripped through me. I thought it'd kill me right there.

"Where is she?" My chest seized. "Where's she at?" Garret's voice was at full volume when he came flying into the back of the ambulance.

Garret's blue eyes stared down at me. How could I ever look at those eyes again? I'd killed his best friend. Our best friend. His almost brother.

Snuffing out the life of someone you love, truly love, feels like God himself is ripping your heart out straight through your chest. My soul was dying, rotting from the inside out. I prayed to Jesus that wasn't true, begged him to save my soul.

A DAMN MIRACLE

Other than the soul-crushing, heart-ripping destruction left behind after ruthlessly murdering someone I loved and four strangers, I felt fine. Doc said I had a fever, sent me for X-rays, sucked my blood. Which I was happy hadn't turned to toxic sludge.

I'd cried for hours, soul pouring right through my eyes, leaving nothing but an empty hole. I wasn't rotting from the inside out anymore. Or maybe I was; I just couldn't feel it. Couldn't feel anything.

Blistering afternoon sun glared into the windows. Wincing away from the light, a low groan rumbled in my chest. I wanted to get up and close the blinds, but machines and tubes plugged into my skin kept me put. Whatever they'd been pumping me up with for pain had stopped my tremors and the hellacious ache in my head.

Garret's voice carried from the hallway. "How could this be?" and "How did *she* make it?" I knew the answer. And if someone thought hard enough, they'd know the answer too.

I was no survivor.

I was the beast.

Even now that the shock of what happened—what I'd done—had lessened, and I could actually consider the possibilities, I couldn't figure out for the life of me what and how I became what I had. Whatever that was. A beast no matter how you looked at it. The only thing I could figure it was magic. Honest to goodness magic.

"Hey, darlin', how you feelin'?" Garret came into the room with a look on his face that I had only seen him have once before, which was when his old dog died.

"Can I go home?" I asked. My voice, scratchy and deep, didn't sound like mine.

"Not yet." He ran a hand over my head. "Doc says you're a miracle, a damn miracle." I gulped back the gaping hole I imagined on my throat. "Logan County Sheriff can't figure how you didn't get yourself in that mess right along with Rusty and the rest. They don't know who the ladies are still. Trying to get to the bottom of that," he mumbled, his face drooped into a frown.

I knew he was thinking about Rusty. I hadn't stopped thinking about him. The picture of his bloody face popped into my head.

"I'm sorry. I'm just so sorry," I sobbed, head in my hands.

Emotions flooded in and that soul-shredding feeling settled into my gut.

"What're you sorry for? You can't go up against a bear, Lynn." They'd assumed and I hadn't corrected them. "It's a good thing you didn't." He sniffed back tears.

I fought hard against the urge to tell Garret what really happened. It was a battle I wasn't willing to lose. If I wasn't careful, I'd get myself thrown in prison. Or a damn nuthouse. Knowing Havana folk, I'd just as quickly be burnt at the stake. No, I had to keep my mouth shut to save my life.

Tears came where words couldn't. Loud and long, I sat in that hospital bed and cried till my face burned from salty tears. Garret stared at me with watery eyes. My sweet brother, nearly as lost as I was.

Red streaks flashed in my memory, I buried my face into the pillow. Snot and spit and tears and sweat soaked into the stiff cotton.

"Lynn, it'll be all right. It will be. You're alive. We can thank God for that. He was watching out for you last night." Garret kissed the top of my head and rubbed his hand through my ratty hair over and over again.

God was nowhere to be found when that woman slashed into my throat. While my bones popped and cracked. When I killed Rusty. Where was God? Not with me, I'll tell you that much.

"I'm fine. I'm fine," I said, muffled against the pillow, pushing my loving brother away from my bedside.

"Okay. Okay, I'll go find the doc, see when I can take

you on home." I watched Garret walk away with one half-covered eye. He walked out the door without looking back.

I was hoping it was Garret come to take me home when I heard hard-soled boots clicking outside the door. It felt like hours since Garret left me crying. Since I'd seen another human face. The constant drip of high-quality painkillers made the wait tolerable. I turned over in the bed to see Hattie in the doorway.

"Hey, girl," she said in a whisper.

A tight grin tugged one side of my mouth and I tried not to cry, again. I knew there would come a point that I would have to atone for what I did. What'd happened to me. Deal with God. Before then, all I could do was cry. I felt weak. Weak for crying and blubbering. I didn't much like that feeling. But it was better than my soul rotting top down.

"Hey." I couldn't look her in the eye. She'd surely see my sins reflected back at her.

"Garret asked me come down and pick you up." I squinted raw eyes. He couldn't come get me himself? Maybe he'd seen the beast in me. "Said he had to get the house ready for you."

"Damn it, Hattie, I ain't dyin'!" Weakness didn't last long before anger took over. "Get those nurses in here to unplug all this mess and I'll walk outta here myself. What's Garret thinkin'? Sendin' you all the way down here to fetch me?" I shoved the weakness down deep, sat up in the bed and pushed the nurse button till I thought my thumb would fall off.

"You're 'bout to walk home, Carolynn Russell." Hattie stood with her hands on her hips like my mama.

I thought then about my mama. Where was she in all this?

"Where's Mama?"

"She ain't here. Get up so I can get you home. You look like a dog pissed on ya all night." Always honest Hattie.

"Well I spent most of it half dead in the woods," I argued. By the last word guilty vomit burned my tonsils. "How'd the deputy know where to find me, anyhow?" She swallowed and looked away, fussing over the trash on the bedside tray. "Garret called the sheriff when Rusty didn't show at work this mornin'." *Sniffle.* "You didn't come home last night." Her boots clicked the floor while she paced, garbage bin in hand. "We just knew you'd finally run off with Rusty Kemp, and we didn't wanna get in the middle of two kids in love." Sadness glittered her eyes. "*Ahem,* we knew you'd probably headed on up to Blue Mountain when you tore off from Maldoon's, but nobody'd heard from you. Then when Rusty wasn't at work, Garret just knew ya'll must've gotten yourselves into trouble."

Panting breaths sped my heart. I had to tell Hattie. Had to. There was no way in all the heavens I'd be able to keep a secret like that from her. Knowing her like I did, she'd never believe it. They say two can't keep a secret, and she'd surely tell Garret—*the mouth of the south*—and he'd lose his ever loving mind.

"He called the sheriff from work, and then he headed out there to look for himself. I thought he was being a little dramatic calling the law in so soon, but he was right. You're lucky your brother loves you so." She nodded up and down like I might not believe her. Like for a second, I might forget how insanely protective Garret Russell could be.

The nurse finally shuffled in, fake smile plastered on her face. "Looks like you're goin' on home. Lemme get those."

She smelled like burnt toast and pickles. I was in no mood for niceties and manners. I didn't need smiles, I needed to be mad. Because if I wasn't, I'd be sad and that just wouldn't do. She jerked the tubes out of my skin like a sloppy drunk. When I winced, she snorted at me like I was being dramatic.

"There. All set," the chubby little nurse said with another plastic grin.

I didn't have a smile for the woman. Not too sure why. I just didn't like the burnt toast lady. She took one look at my face and hightailed it out of the room.

Hattie handed me a pair of old rundown shorts and a big T-shirt. I didn't know where she'd come up with those clothes, but they sure as hell weren't mine. I pulled on the shorts that were a bit too big. I figured they must've been Hattie's; she was a little plumper in the end section.

The door opened two milliseconds after a gentle knock. "Miss Russell, how are we feeling?" He flashed a bright, white smile. If he'd have been in a toothpaste ad, they'd've sparkled. "Doing any better with some fluids?" Doc was surely no local boy. California or something sounded like. Why a California doctor would come all the way out to Yell County to work at a Podunk hospital like the one in Denville, I didn't have the slightest.

"Just wanna go home is all." I looked around the room for the rest of my stuff and realized I didn't have anything. "I am free to go, right?" I was starting to lose the gusto I had built up.

"Of course. I would prefer it if you'd stay the night, just to keep an eye on you. But if you'd like to leave, I see no reason why you can't go home and rest in your own bed." He smiled again. I liked his smile, it was real. And he didn't smell like pickles or toast. I liked that too. "I do have to tell you, you still have a slight fever, just under one hundred degrees. It's not life threatening, but you should keep an eye on it. We gave you some antibiotics for your abrasions and I'd like you to fill this prescription for more as soon as you leave. You'll need to take them twice a day for the next week, until they're gone."

"That about it?" I knew I was behaving like a snot, but it felt better than crying and making a fuss.

"Yes, I suppose it is." He put a hand on my shoulder. "Miss Russell, I don't know how you did it and I don't know what kind of believer you are, but I feel *God* was with you last night. Other than your scratches there on your, um—" He cleared his throat and carried on, "—and a slight redness in your throat, likely from a long bout of crying and screaming, you are in perfect health." His voice was near angelic, but I wanted to kick him straight in the shin for bringing God into this. "After you fill the prescription, perhaps you should send some thanks to whatever you believe in for keeping you safe when others weren't so lucky." Dark eyes watched my face. Like he was gauging my reaction. Like maybe he didn't believe I'd just gotten lucky.

That last bit pulled bile up into my mouth. I didn't know whether I'd cry or slap that handsome doctor. I just stood there and stared at him until he handed me a small piece of paper with some chicken scratch on it and left the room. Still smiling.

"Well, now that you've done run that good-lookin' doctor off, you ready to go home?" Hattie scolded, brown eyebrows tucked tight at the center.

I didn't talk to her after that. Couldn't. I knew I would only say something, it'd come out. I was being too ugly for it not to. Anger had kept the gut-churning sadness under wraps, but it was making me wild. Unruly. Volatile.

Hattie and me drove from Danville back to Havana in her rumbly old truck. I spent most of the ride staring out the window watching the sun move across the sky. I didn't think I'd been in the hospital that long, but it was damn near dusk. The sun was coming up when the deputy found me in the woods crying over Rusty. All damn day in the hospital for a doctor to tell me I had a sore throat and some scratches on my ass. Hell, I could've told everyone that for free if I had the right mind to speak up. Not talking was better I figured.

If I ain't talking, I ain't accidentally telling anybody I'm some kind of monster.

Less talking meant more thinking. And I didn't want to think about anything. Thinking led to crying and I damn sure didn't like crying.

ARGUING WITH GHOSTS

Hattie walked me to the door and made sure Garret was there ready for me before leaving in a hurry. She'd wanted more from me than I could give. I'd tell her sorry on a day I wasn't recovering from second-degree murder. Or would it be manslaughter? I'd slaughtered a man and I didn't mean to do it. Maybe I could claim insanity. I didn't know anything about the law but what I watched on *Law & Order*, and not one of those episodes covered accidental creatures killing under a bright blue moon.

"I made your bed up, Lynn. I got some pot roast in the cooker on the counter if you're hungry." He tried—hard as it was for him to be nurturing. I wasn't even angry with him anymore for leaving me in the hospital. He was hurting more than he could handle. It rolled off him like heat on the pavement. There wasn't anything I could do for him. I was hurting enough for the both of us.

"I'm fine. I just wanna sleep. I need to lay down a bit." I walked past him, head down, to my bedroom at the end of the hallway and shut the door.

The second I was alone, my cheeks flushed and my bottom lip shook, but I downright refused to cry again. I swore to myself then that I would not cry over any of it until morning. I would sleep, eat, and then figure out what in the hell I was gonna do with myself.

I laid back, pulled the covers up over my head, and tried not to think anymore. Garret rustled around in the kitchen. I knew there'd be a mess for me to clean in the morning. He didn't cook much, which was fine with me because I tended to have more work when he did the cooking than when I did.

I listened to my brother fumbling around in cabinets and drawers and tried to sleep. My eyes closed, breathing slowed, heart took a second to catch up. Blackness took over.

I startled awake, limbs frantic, reaching out for anything to stop me from falling. I swallowed hard and flipped the covers off my head. The yellow light outside had turned pale blue, casting shadows over my room.

My eyes focused on a deep black figure in the corner. I gasped, and choked, and blinked at the thing. My stomach dropped six inches when the shape moved out of the shadow and I could see what it was.

Blood *whooshed* in my ears. "How?" was all I could say to

the dim shape of Rusty standing across the room from me. His face was clean, chest perfect. All he had on was a smile and a pair of jeans. For a long handful of breaths, he just stood there looking at me. I stared right back.

My chin quivered and my nose tingled and tears welled up at my lashes. I gulped over and over until I found my voice. "Why—Rusty, I am sorry," I croaked. "I was a thing, a beast, and I didn't know—I couldn't stop." I shook my head. "Forgive me. Please." I reached out for him and stopped myself.

"I know." His voice sounded like he was talking to me through a tin can on a string. "You gotta go now, Lynnie."

"What? I'm not going anywhere," I argued.

He ran his hand over messy hair. "Gotta go, Lynn."

"Where am I goin'?" I leaned forward onto my knees, sliding off the edge of the bed.

"Out." His smile dropped. "You got a long road, darlin'. Don't leave your soul behind ya'."

I reached out for him. "What?" And he disappeared into the darkest shadows. "No! Rusty?" I scurried to the corner, planting my hands on the wall where he'd stood. In a panic, I groped the dark for anything left behind. Salty tears pooled on my lips.

Bone-crushing pain curled me in half. I called out in agony. The sound of Garret washing up the dishes contending. The one damn time he decided to wash up his mess was the one damn time I needed him to be sitting on his butt drinking a beer in front of the idiot box.

Electric shocks shot from my head to my toes. I was gonna

be sick all over my ugly brown carpet. I looked down to my hands and watched my fingers curl and bend into beastly claws. Back arched like a cat, my ribs cracked and slid under my skin. Muscles ripped and reformed, bending my legs into inhuman shapes. Murky green fur pushed through the pores on my hands and arms. Shocks of pain popped in my ears, long sharp fangs erupted from my gums, swallowing up my human teeth with a sloppy slurp. I wailed and hollered and grunted in pain, but Garret never came for me. Fear desperately wanted his help, but logic said it was his only saving grace.

Slick, magical goo flung from my shaking coat. I caught the horrifying reflection of myself in the mirror hanging on the backside of my door. If I could have screamed out loud, I'd have broken glass. It—*I*—covered in a shaggy, dark green coat of fur with upward pointed, tufted ears, was a hulking beast. Not a cat or a dog, but some mystical thing in between. The tail, *my* tail, a thick, long braid or braids. Only, it was gnarled and snagged like something feral. Razor sharp claws curled from the ends of what used to be my fingers.

If I'd had human eyes, I'd've cried. Blazing high, hot and red, my monstrous eyes glowed, a fire freshly lit. My long mouth opened and out came a screeching howl. A sound I'd heard only one other time in my life.

Something moved down the hall. My ears perked. I could smell Garret's aftershave. *No.* Before I knew it, my strong animal legs carried me across the room. They leapt over the bed, and broke through the only window I had. I could still hear the glass breaking when Garret called out for me.

"Lynnie! Lynnie!" he hollered out the broken window.

Strong legs pumped, moving me hard and fast through the woods behind our trailer. I could hear him breathing, his boots—sounding sloppy, untied—shuffling the underbrush chasing after what he must've thought was a dog or maybe even a bear. Maybe the beast that'd killed his friend and left his only sister broken.

Panting huffs puffed from my snout. I scurried into a thick brush, hiding in the shadows. Garret moved through the trees. He was a varied shade of green like everything else. Like the rifle in his hands.

I knew he was my brother. I knew I loved him. But my animal mind didn't care. I only cared about hiding. Surviving. I knew he'd kill me in my current state. I had to hide. Hide or die. Or kill.

"Lynnie, where are you?" he damn near sobbed.

I wanted to run to him. Comfort him. The beast kept me hidden. I'd kill him before he ever got a shot off. Garret held his long rifle down at his side searching the dark woods for a dark beast. He'd never find me hidden inside my coat of green.

Inside my monster suit, I didn't have the same types of thoughts. I didn't really have thoughts at all. Just feelings in my gut. Like instinct. No thoughts, just knowing.

I was all alone in my emotionless new world. And I liked it.

WORDS WITH GOD

I woke up naked in the woods to the pure smell of dawn. And like the morning before, blood dried under my nails.

The last thing I remembered was Garret chasing me through the woods. I sat up, scanning the clearing for bodies or blood or parts or any sign of what I'd done. Other than the rust colored splotches on my hands and arms, no evidence of a massacre was left behind.

I couldn't decide if it was better not to know who or what I'd maimed to have blood dried under my nails. If the alternative was knowing I'd killed my only brother—I gulped back vomit at the idea—it was better not to know, even for just a little while. Living in denial was perfectly acceptable, if only to keep you sane long enough to stay alive.

I told myself I'd killed an animal. A squirrel or a rabbit.

I'd even go so far as to say a deer. Just dinner. My tattered heart couldn't accept anything more.

Hawthorn trees circled the clearing. Bright red haws hung from the branches like fat drops of fresh blood preparing themselves for the fall to earth come October. I'd grown up on tall tales of fairies that lived in those trees. If you weren't careful, weren't a good girl, they'd come steal you away to the otherworld and keep you forever. Those same storytellers would pluck those bloody berries by the handful. Best used for their *remedies*. Sounded downright stupid to say out loud, but that's growing up Southern. Old women, old ways.

I watched the sun come up, hoping to the heavens memories of my night out would come back to me like they did before. Nothing happened. The last thing I remembered completely after I'd changed was watching Garret cry while he walked back to the house. After that, it was like someone turned off a light. There was nothing.

Eventually, when it was clear I wasn't going to recall my night out, I started worrying about how I'd make it home naked as the day I was born, splattered with mystery blood. *Garret should be at work.* Unless he was so worried about me that he'd stayed home. Or I'd killed him. *No.* I shook my head wildly at the thought. *No,* I told myself, *no, it's just not possible. He's fine. He went home wondering where the hell I went off to and that's all.* I repeated the words over and over again until I believed it.

"Lynnie?" I damn near jumped out of my skin, clamped a hand over my mouth. "Lynnie, you out here?" Hattie hollered.

Where's Garret? Please have gone off to work, I thought. Hoped. Prayed. I sat still. Didn't so much as breathe. I knew there would be questions. Most of them I couldn't answer without inadvertently giving myself up to the law. Or starting a damn witch hunt. Or killing my brother with words alone.

"You see anything?" Garret shouted from further away.

Damn it. He's home. I thanked the Lord he was alive, twice, before I started worrying about what I *had* done. There was no telling what I'd gotten into after Garret gave up. Maybe I did something worse than kill Rusty. What if I'd sliced up babies, a bus load of senior citizens, devoured a litter of puppies while I was that damn green beast?

My heart flip-flopped in my chest, breaking and pounding in the same second. I couldn't imagine feeling any lower than I did sitting in the woods, filthy and naked, and questioning if I'd killed babies.

"Damn it, Lynnie!" Garret croaked, his voice warning the levy was about to rupture. I felt those words, that anguish, down to my blackened toes.

I thought maybe I could tell him. If Garret knew I needed it, really truly, he'd help me. But then he would know what I'd done to Rusty. He could never forgive me for something so awful.

I closed my eyes, the loneliness I'd enjoyed as the beast ripped through deep to where my soul hid. *Lord, I need you. Please help me. I don't wanna die. I don't wanna break my brother's heart. Please help me. Please, Lord*, please.

Silent tears rolled down my cheeks. I pulled my knees to my chest and buried my face into my legs and waited for a miracle.

It started in my toes, the heat of courage. A blaze gaining purchase, it moved up through my legs, flames licking my heart, screaming at me to get up and move. My eyes caught fire and I leapt to my feet. I ran on foreign legs, pumping silently over the earth—not so much as snapping a twig.

A drumbeat thumped in my chest—*bumpa-da-bump*— setting my pace. Ugly brown aluminum siding popped through the clearing. I ducked my head and pushed harder, feet slapping the paw tracks I'd left the night before. One solid push and I crashed through the fresh plastic covering my broken window.

I collapsed on my bed the second my feet hit the mattress. One breath, two. Garret and Hattie echoed through the woods talking back and forth from yards away. They hadn't seen me.

I swiped a pair of jeans from the chair by my closet and yanked a tank top from a hanger. I wriggled into my jeans while I ran out the front door. I'd gotten my keys from the table by the door before I let the screen door slam shut behind me. I didn't know where I was going, but I knew I couldn't stay there. Not until I had a damn good story to tell.

Dirt and pebbles kicked out from under my tires as I skidded onto the main road. I didn't have much of a plan, but my granddaddy always said if you're scared, go to church. Too many eyes, too many flapping jaws in Havana. My only respite would be in a place where I could get lost. Even if just for a little while. Just long enough to screw my head on right.

I caught sight of my face in the rearview. Yanking it for a better look, the sun glared, blinding me for a second. Dark red crusted over my chin, dried in drips down my neck. I gagged, scrubbing at it with a hand that wasn't much cleaner.

Ringed in purple circles, my eyes, wild, something feral, stared back at me.

I hadn't had a moment to consider that it'd happen again, that I'd be that thing again. When that woman sliced my throat, bled me into the fire, I thought I'd die right there. The beast tearing through my insides, I thought that was it, I was dead. My soul was ripped from my chest when I found Rusty—what I'd done—I thought I would die then too. The idea that I'd live and die night after night…

My veins froze, nearly icing over my heart. I'd cried so much in just a couple of days, I couldn't let loose any more tears. There was no time for it. I had more to manage than sadness. Staying alive. Keeping others alive. Unlike the beast, my thoughts were a jumbled-up mess. I couldn't pin one emotion down long enough to work through it before another one charged in guns blazing.

Instinct tickled my edges, warning me that survival would soon win out. Like a dog so hungry it eats its young. Maybe. I'd never been a furry, green beast before so I wasn't sure what I was supposed to be feeling. I didn't even know what the hell I was. How was I supposed to know how to feel? I didn't feel like me anyhow. I hardly even felt human walking around in my own body.

The only thing I knew, just knew in my bones, was that whatever I was, whatever they'd done to me, this was only the beginning. I needed to get to the bottom of things before it happened again. And I damn sure needed to stay as far away from Garret and Hattie as I could until I knew more. I'd already killed Rusty. If I lost Garret, I might as well kill myself right along with him.

The Baptist church in Danville was small, aging white with a brown roof and tall steeple that damn near touched the heavens. It didn't look to be open, but I knew it was. Church was always open. I didn't know if God was always in, but the building was always open to those folks who wanted to leave him a message.

I pulled the mirror and snarled at my crusty face. I looked like a maniac, or a vampire, or something. Desperate to clean the gore from my face, I scrubbed at it with spit, scraping with my already filthy nails. Eventually digging around in the glovebox for an old rag to finish the job.

I should've been scared, or sad, or locked up in a nuthouse, but I wasn't. All of that got shoved down deep beneath self-preservation to a place I was sure would eventually explode. My only concern was saving my soul. And stopping myself from tearing up any more people. And, if I could, never let that green beast out again. There was no time for crying and fussing, if I even had it in me still, to feel, to be normal. I'd use whatever I had left to keep my people safe or die trying. Let that damn creek rise.

My face wasn't Sunday supper clean but clean enough so as to not get myself locked up for cannibalism or something. I hauled myself up the steps, sore from the toes up. There weren't even a dozen pews on either side of the aisle. Metal folding chairs leaned against wallpapered walls in hefty stacks. Piles of Bibles teetered against the back of every pew.

I slid into the third row back. Admittedly, I hadn't been to church in what my nana would call a month of Sundays. Even Mama, in her strappy gold sandals and shimmery pink lipstick, rarely missed a service. It wasn't that I didn't have faith. I just didn't know why I had to do it in church at the butt crack of dawn.

I sucked a deep breath, pulling in the lingering scent of floral perfume and old book pages. Eyes closed, I laid down, curled up in the pew, and just about fell asleep. I hadn't done that since second grade. Nana singing, the preacher hollering and stamping his foot, the whole room in an all-out ruckus for the Lord. And there I'd be, struggling to stay awake. He'd deny it to this day, but I know Garret had trained himself to sleep with his eyes open.

A hot tear slid down my cheek and plopped to the wood under my head. So many tears for what I'd done, what I lost, my well ran dry. It wasn't that quiet, emotionless place of the beast. Just, empty. Exhausted. But survival, that burned hot in my gut.

No one came to check on me, laying there listening to the sound of the clock tick my life away. Even though I had the room and God to myself, I didn't risk saying my prayers out loud. Couldn't risk have anyone hear me ask God for forgiveness on account of becoming a monster and killing some folks out in the woods.

I should've been shaking in my boots, fearful of the thing I'd become. As the time ticked by, fear of the beast gave way to something else. I was still worried I'd killed children, but there was a part of me—an ever-growing feral place—that didn't quite care. The longer I laid there the harder it was to feel guilty over the damage I'd done—or would do yet—and it scared the panties off me.

The old clock in the entry chimed noon. Even the long late-summer day would soon run out and night bring with it the beast. I couldn't risk another night out without answers.

I swiped a hand across soggy eyes and sat up, thick blonde hair a nest on the side of my head. I'd given all the time I could spare. My kin before me would've likely sat in church day and night, laying hands, praying the evil away. I wasn't quite sure what I was belonged in the same world as God and church.

The beast was something wild, from an unnatural world. Needed otherworldly healing. There was only one person—okay two but I'd walk through fire to keep from involving her—who I thought could help.

I touched every pew on my way out. Praying for forgiveness. Begging for salvation.

FIRE BURN & CAULDRON BUBBLES

Witch.

Devil worshipper.

Healer. Medicine woman.

Most folks snuck around in the cover of night to visit Mama Lee, looking to heal what ailed them—heartbreak included. Likely the very same folks who spread ugly things about the poor old woman. My worn-out brakes squealed to a stop behind a thick of brush next to the aging white cottage in broad daylight.

Who was I to judge? At night, I turned into a big green beast and ate people. Let those ugly people see me. I needed help, didn't care how I came by it.

I pushed through shoulder-high sunflowers. Orange petals of butterfly weed tickled the tips of my fingers. Unlike every rumor I'd ever heard, I did not turn into a toad the moment I walked through her gate.

It was just a house. No sparkling magic swirling around in the garden or devils peering through the curtains. A white house with a couple of windows and a purple door, a nice old granny's house. If the old granny was a witch. A nice one.

Hanging from the eave, beads and charms spun on long strips of colorful ribbon. Drapes hung in a dozen patterns and sizes, some had drawings, symbols painted on them. Painted in black cursive, a wooden sign, *Cauldron Bubbles*.

"Well, looks like I got me a customer." A small older lady pushed through a tall patch of the sunflowers wearing ratty gardening gloves and a big floppy hat. She whistled. "And a doozy looks like."

I swallowed. *She knows. How could she know?* "What?"

She walked toward me, lifting short legs high over wildflowers, and I backed up. "Not yourself the last few days?" She nodded once, looking me toe to hairline and took a few steps closer, pulling her gloves off by the finger. I backed until I hit the porch railing. "Com'on, now. Let see what we can fix up for you." She walked past, up the steps, and through the hanging trinkets.

I stopped at the top step. *Please, Lord, protect me.* A

covered porch, stacked to the brim with old books, candles, bins of soaps and rocks sitting on every surface. Nothing looked to be for sale, but it was organized like a store with too much stuff in it.

"This like a store or something?" I asked, eyeing things in baskets and bins lined along shelves.

"Something."

On a small table in the corner a bowl like the one that caught my blood, some kind of sticks and leaves smoldered inside. Spicy smoke swirled in my face and I coughed, gutting the gag that came with it. A flash of the gash at my throat caught my breath. I choked, instinctively grabbing my neck, and the woman backed away, eyes wide, hand on her chest. Over her pounding heart, so loud and fast in my head. I shook it away but back it came. Beastly magic in my human body.

Mama Lee panted. "What… *happened* to you?"

An awkward half-smirk and a shrug came with my words, "What'd'ya mean?"

She closed her eyes, pulled in a strong breath and let it out slow. "Sit down." Her eyes opened and though her heart had slowed, they were still round and unsure.

I had no real idea of what magic felt like, but it was in the room. Welcoming warmth on my sticky skin. It wasn't anything like the night I was slaughtered like a hog—heavy, disruptive, unnerving. Here was… divine. If that was possible.

Brown eyes locked onto mine, she said in a low voice,

"You know who I am?"

I nodded. "Folks talk about you." I looked away. "Say you can help people. Cure people. Some say—"

"I'm a witch?" Her voice went up, but she didn't so much as flinch.

"Some people."

Mama Lee turned and spit on the floor. "Some people."

I swallowed hard. "My nana says you're a healer. Laying hands and all."

She nodded. "I do what I can." Her hand squeezed mine on the table. "Darlin', the kind of help you need…" She sighed. "It ain't gonna be easy. And it ain't gonna be free."

I sat up, desperate for her help. "I have money," I promised. "But I didn't bring anything. I left—"

"You left runnin'." She pulled a cigarette from a small leather case, lit it, and pulled in a long drag. Smoke twirled under her nose. "You never answered me." Slim, pointed fingers tapped ash into a green glass dish. "What happened to you?"

The truth will set you free they said. In my case though, truth might very well get me killed. "I don't know." Tears teetered on my lashes. It wasn't a lie. I didn't have one damn clue what happened to me. Just the aftermath. "Can you help me?"

Her cigarette bobbed in her lips. "Hold real still for me, sweet pea."

She pushed her leathery hands through my matted hair, running her nails gently over my scalp. My blonde hair fell over tan arms. She was not much taller than a kid, and skinny. Scrawny.

Those spindly fingers gripped my head, kneading like bread, coaxing memories direct from the source. I watched her, eyes following as she turned her head for better reception. Her heart thudded, echoing in my tuned ears.

Wrinkles creased around her eyes, crinkling in hard lines when she frowned. Her face, a crumpled old map of a life well-lived, showed every expression tenfold. I couldn't tell how old she was, but I'd heard she was *old*. Like ancient. If that was true, she looked pretty damn good.

Strong hands rubbed over my head, like jazz, no real beat, but a rhythm nonetheless. I closed my eyes, so weary. One big deep breath, and out.

Mama Lee shrieked. I opened my eyes and she tumbled to the floor, still entwined in my hair, yanking me down with her. We hit the floor and she backed away. Her dark brown eyes, round and wide, and knew far too much. The map on her face read clear. She thought I'd eat her up right there. Maybe she was right.

"It can't be," she said, so quiet most folks wouldn't have heard her.

Fear tipped the scales in my perfectly balanced emotional shock. "What? What'd you see?" I wasn't necessarily scared of what I might be, but what she might know. And mostly, what she'd do with that information.

"What'd you do?" she asked, fast and airy.

"I didn't do nothin'." I tried to stand up, but my butt was

tethered to the floor. Wiggling did nothing, I was glued to the spot.

"Claws, and teeth, and blood," she said through clenched teeth. I struggled to stand. "So much blood. A woman, with fire hair, a witch woman." She blinked. "A coven in the woods? Dark magic, blood magic. Death." She dragged in one heavy breath. "Oh, death." The woman rambled, but it was all true. Blood, magic, death, all of it.

"What am I?" I had to know, even though the thought of truly knowing brought puke into my throat. Even if that meant admitting to the old woman, to myself, what I'd become.

The woman's eyebrows turned in. Her eyes looked at me with total sadness and pity. And maybe a little bit of fear in there too. "Death," she said finally with a trembling voice.

My heart stopped. I'd been prepared for damn near anything, a werewolf, a monster, a demon even. But *death*, just death meant I was nothing more than a beast. A thing meant to kill. I wasn't ready to accept the fate of a killer.

Either she let me go or I got the gumption to break whatever spell she had over my hind end and pulled it up from the wood floor. "You—" I huffed. "Crazy old woman." I pointed my finger at her. "Don't you tell anybody I was here or so help me…" I leaned over her. "I'll come back tonight and you'll see death." It was a sin just to say it out loud but damned if I didn't give a shit.

I stormed off the porch with so much heat I might've impressed the devil himself. I was halfway to the truck when

I heard the hanging beads and charms clang against each other.

"You'll kill him, Lynnie Russell," she hollered from the step. My heart stopped at the sound of my name, but each breath still came thicker than the last. "If you ain't careful, you'll kill that strong brother of yours."

I didn't dare turn around. That fiery hate in me called to the beast inside. It was just waiting there to be unleashed.

My engine rumbled, puffing a cloud from the tailpipe. I risked one last look at the only living human who knew what I was—and *who*. She stood on the step, a string of beads clutched in her hand. Eyes closed, mouth moving at the speed of light. Praying, or chanting, or casting or whatever that woman did.

She opened her eyes and caught me watching. I tucked my chin and slammed on the gas. My balding tires refused traction and the old truck slid across the asphalt, leaving a nice trail of smoke when I took off.

It wasn't natural for someone to be able to rub your head and know your life. Your name, your family, your sins. It just wasn't natural. But then again, neither was turning into some kind of green hairy beast and killing folks out in the woods.

Rage tunneled my vision until only instinct kept me on the road. I'd near forgotten about waking up with blood on my face, about what I might've done. Memories dripped from my melting mind like wax from a long-burning candle. Consumed with rage, with that beast, with my sins. I'd talked to God. I'd seen a magic woman. I didn't know where else to go. Dusk was coming on fast. I was closer to becoming that thing. Becoming the beast that squatted inside me waiting to burst out with the force of death itself.

The narrow roads of Havana widened, becoming the highway. Through Russellville, I thought of Garret. Was he at work? Somewhere out there on the highway in that ugly orange vest. Or was he still out in the woods with Hattie looking for me? Rusty's bloody face popped into my head and I gasped, choking on whatever bile came up with it.

Cars honked, screeching around me at a dead stop in the middle of the road. Panic brought gasping breaths. I gripped the wheel, begging whatever would listen to let me be. The beast rumbled. Stirred. Promised it would take care of me and my humanity.

I blinked over and over until I finally saw the lines on the road. Slowly, I eased the truck off the highway and into the nearest parking lot.

"Fuck. This." I slammed my hand against the steering wheel with each word. "I can't do this. I can't." I swiped snot from my nose. "I can*not*," I whispered.

The beastly thing promised, *Oh, yes, you can.*

I leaned back against the seat and closed my eyes. "Here's

to Lynnie on her twentieth birthday," I said, repeating Rusty's toast with a shaky voice. "I want a refund."

Daddy's watch that always sat on the dash said a time I was certain was wrong. It couldn't be almost seven. How long had I been in that house? Worse, how long had I been driving?

The sun would soon set. I may not know what I was, but I knew what I was capable of. I wouldn't do it again. Couldn't.

The Ozarks were vast, easy to get lost in. And that's just what I planned to do. I picked up a triple bacon burger—extra bacon—from the *Best Spot in Arkansas*, or so the sign said, and got back on the road.

Orange, red, purple, the sky taunted me, daring me to drive faster. An hour, maybe less, I didn't have a beast timer. It was restless inside me. A child anxious to get out to recess.

True sunset was close; I'd gone as far as the night would allow. I parked in a clearing, deep as I could. Blue shadows painted strips of darkness in the distance. Magnified by whatever beastly magic rustled around inside me, the sounds of night critters clicked in my ears. Alone as I'd get I supposed.

In the thick of the trees, where the paint was darkest—as if night had already taken over. It called to me, yanking a string somewhere deep in my gut. *Long, deep breath in, back out.* It'd come. Whether I wanted it or not. Scratching just under the surface, the beast waited impatiently.

While I pulled my boots off, my head told me I should be afraid, terrified of what was about to happen. My heart told me I didn't much have a choice. Either way, I knew I was doing right by Garret to stay away, even if it was only for the night. Only until I could find some answers.

Mama Lee was right. I'd kill him. Sure as the beast was coming, if he was in the way, he'd be dead. I knew I'd change again. And again. And again until I either died or figured out how to stop it. The only help I knew had told me I'd do it and I hated her for it. I hated her for telling me the truth.

I tasted nightfall on my tongue like a sweet, chewy caramel, delicious, sinful. "Please, Lord," I whispered. "I'm no killer. I'm no monster. Help me."

A familiar pain swept through my gut, sending me to my knees. I groaned, eyes closed. *Lord, help me.* I knew this pain, the pain of death. It wouldn't kill me again.

My back arched, bones popped, crackling into place. A scream held tight in my throat. I wouldn't give it the pleasure of my pain. This soul was mine. It could have my body, but that belonged to me.

Great claws sprouted from the beds of my nails. Muscles ripped and tore and reformed around bones that shifted into the shape of the beast. With every tear, every crack, I begged God to save me. I begged Him to take me from this earth, to keep me from this torment. He never answered.

Swamp-green fur poked from pores along my skin. *No.* I fought, refusing to let it take me completely, willing myself to stay whole. I huffed a puff of air from my snout. Eyes, a red flame, saw the world in green.

We stood alone in the woods, my beast and me. Two beings alive in one creature.

PREDECESSOR

Heavy paws slapped leaf-covered dirt with a lazy flop. Brand new muscles shifted under a heavy coat. My body took up space, rustling bushes and kicking puffs of debris underfoot. Bigger than any dog, like no cougar I'd ever seen. Green, shaggy paws instinctively moved through brush, a clever dance between me and the universe.

Little light poked through the tops of the trees to the forest floor. Our feral eyes didn't need moonlight. The beast knew where we needed to be. The earth spoke to us. Or *it*, really. I was a passenger at the mercy of the creature at the helm, but I felt invincible. A superhero with no kryptonite. Or a villain. I could still be the villain.

I fought, kicked and screamed, pleaded for control inside that dark space but it didn't budge. When I killed, and I knew I would, I'd have to watch. Helpless. I regretted sticking around. No memory of the beastly things we did helped. It had to.

We moved into the darkest part of the woods. The earth sang her never-ending midnight serenade. How I'd possibly find my way back in the morning was a faint thought somewhere in the deepest parts of us. Instinct, a supernatural knowing, had her claws hooked deep in my core.

Lynnie, the girl who fell in love with a pigheaded cowboy on her twentieth birthday, was gone. Even when morning came, I knew she wouldn't be there waiting. I'd seen too much. Felt divinity in my soul. How could I be just a girl from Havana anymore?

We were old. Ancient. Centuries on earth. A purpose. I didn't know this as fact. We felt it as truth. Whatever I'd become she was mine. Her duty was my duty. Our lives, just one of many.

Clumsy, pointless human movement piqued my ears. I sniffed the air. Musk. Sweat. A man was in the woods with us. It could've been a hunter, or a camper, or hell, even Garret. She didn't care. We stalked toward the sound.

I held my breath, for whatever that was worth, begging her to stay back, hide. I didn't want to kill anyone else, but I sure as shit didn't want a buckshot in my ass either. She moved closer. *No. Stop.* A man stepped from a line of trees up ahead. A perfectly purple naked man out in the middle of the night, in the middle of nowhere.

Maybe she knew exactly who was in the dark with us all along.

Purple made up the shadows and light, creating a glowing figure shaded with the deepest color. He stumbled a few feet before he saw us. His heart raced, glugging blood through to his limbs.

I crouched, head down, eyes focused. My prey.

He stood, breathing slowly, heart betraying him. "I've been waiting for you."

He was there for *me*. I'd brought her halfway and she did the rest. Maybe she'd won the battle over my soul before I even knew the war had started.

Who are you? My voice was just a thought passing over instinct before it was gone again.

The man got down on his hands and knees, crawling toward me. Inside, I blushed at his naughty bits, but my beast watched in anticipation. Watched and waited for him to get closer. Close enough to eat.

The man bowed his head, offering himself up for slaughter. "I've been waiting so long," he croaked, choking back emotions the beast didn't understand.

In one swipe, purple blood shot out like a squirt gun, splashing in hot specks on our shared snout. My only grace was it wasn't red. The nightmares would be purple and that I could probably deal with. Another massive paw came down on him, a sprinkler of blood sprayed across my snarling teeth.

He rolled over onto his back, looking up at me. I stood tall over him, a beastly thing, probably the size of a bear. Maybe bigger.

"Weary. So weary." He choked. Death was coming. I smelled it on him. "Three days." His fingers attempted to show me but his hand didn't move. "So, so long." He closed his eyes. "Set me free. Do it."

He begged me to kill him. To relieve him of his life. I'd made that same plea to God. My plea wasn't answered. His was about to be.

Blood stained his lavender teeth dark violet. "Whoever you are, thank you." Purple spurts popped from his mouth when he coughed. "Your sacrifice freed me from that prison." He ran a single finger across our paw without moving. "Find strength. Accept it. Stay alive." I smirked at the idea of trying to survive and the beast snorted. "Make it quick."

We let out three long screeching barks—a desperate elk in heat. A release washed through me that'd been trapped inside, the powerful draw of a gun in a knife fight. One final strike and the last of his blood poured from his throat. A purple puddle spread from under him.

Rusty'd been green. Garret too. I wanted to ask the man why, what am I, what do we do? But he took his last ragged breath as we licked magenta spatters from his face.

I wished I could stop. I wished I could throw up, or scream, or cry, anything a human would've done. The beast didn't have wishes. She was doing what she was supposed to. What that man asked us to do.

As much as I felt for the man, I felt worse for me. The only human who knew what I was and I'd killed him. Unseen hands clawed inside that beast, desperate to escape. I kicked and scratched and screamed and all for nothing. I was stuck. Forced to wait it out until dawn.

My beastly eyes watched his blood darken to a deep

eggplant as it oozed from under his quickly cooling body. We licked his face and the zing of iron hit my tongue. Our snout nuzzled an apology, pushing his legs to a more modest position. She hadn't wanted to kill him, but like the sun set, it was just part of the gig. I prayed that God would take him, that his soul, and mine, were still pure. As pure as they could be considering.

She snorted and huffed, rearing on two strong back legs. We came down hard, leaves and dirt exploded under heavy paws. Our job was done. She didn't talk to me, my beast. But her thoughts—a knowing felt deep in my bones— seeped into my gut, leaving my human brain to interpret her ancient ways.

The sky was still dark, but the smell of dawn was in the air. A clean, new day scent. Like the lord Himself had come down from Heaven to pull the sun up over the horizon, leaving behind him a heavenly trail.

Soon, the day would show its first light and drag me back out of my nightly prison. I begged my beast to take me back to the truck, prayed she knew the way. We'd walked deep into the woods. So deep I'd have likely died out there alone, in the elements, lost.

She padded lazy paws through the forest. I couldn't tell if we were close to where we'd started, had no clue if we'd make it before dawn. But she did. We stopped in a small clearing and she laid us down in the cool dirt. Our heavy head plopped into a pile of leaves, puffing a few from their pile. She was tired. So tired.

Familiar pain wrenched my stomach. I had no control over my beast, but I sure as hell felt her pain. I wondered then how it felt for her to change. If she hurt like I did. If she dreaded the moment with every green hair on her body.

The sky lightened with the first show of dawn. *Here we go, girl. You ready?* Pain ripped through our legs. Muscles stretch and tore, human legs pushed in a wet slop through thick green fur. My toes—complete with blue polish—flexed, curling under the weight of agony.

Gooey, slick skin sucked shaggy fur into its pores and sharp claws shrank into their beds. My back arched, crackling as my spine found its place again. Boobs flopped through. Our muzzle morphed back to my human face. The beast let out one last howl—a dying elk blaring in the dark. She felt the change, just like I did.

Her howl bellowed from my lungs, ending with a weak human scream. I fell to the dirt in a heap of fresh pink flesh. Once again I was naked and alone in the woods.

Tears fell to the earth. Salty things meant for nothing and everything at once. A human thing, crying. Meant I had a soul, for that I was happy. But I cried for them, those I'd killed. I cried for myself, my beast, our prison.

I wanted to run back into the woods and find the man, see if he was really dead. Force him to wake up and answer my questions. I had to know what I was, how to fix it, how not to kill my brother. There was no point in it. He was dead. Very, very dead.

Hopeless, alone, feeling sorry for myself, I cried. My only allies, an old witch woman who saw in me only death, a now dead naked man, and a furry green monster that forced me to eat people.

I might as well take a flying leap from the tallest cliff. Knowing my luck, the beast was immortal, and I'd live on forever in that musky, green thing.

CRYIN' IN THE DIRT

Daylight hadn't breached the thick treetops, but slices of eerie white light cut through the branches like the fingers of God bringing the forest to life. It wasn't enough to help my human eyes navigate the woods, but true dawn was coming.

Soon enough, I'd stumble naked through the trees and back to my truck, my clothes. Shivering, covered in blood and dirt, streaks of tears down my cheeks. I curled into a ball at the foot of a tall tree, holding my shaking body, begging for day to come and show me a way out.

A gust shook leaves from their branches. Glittering dust swirled through slivered rays of sun. Small at first, a hint of what was coming. Wind blew my hair, tangling it around my face. A shimmering, gold dust devil tickled the earth, touching the forest floor, gathering up twigs and leaves. I sat up, blocking debris from my face. The sweet, familiar scent of pine and whiskey blew past and stopped my heart.

A croak of a whisper, "Rusty?" I peeked through my hands.

The glimmering dust settled. An angel in a pair of Levi's, Rusty Kemp stood a few feet away. A single beam of golden light shined over him.

"Well, hell, Lynnie. What a mess you got yourself into."

Gulping back a flood of emotions, I crawled on my hands and knees closer to him, bare boobs and all. "Rusty," I whimpered. "I'm so lost." I stopped in front of him, filthy hands clutched together, silently pleading him for forgiveness. Smooth skin and pale blonde hair glistened in his golden light—chest free from my death marks. Shame told me to look away, but I refused to miss even one second of this vision. "I prayed. I prayed so much." My voice didn't even sound like mine. Pitiful. Pathetic.

"Ain't God that's gonna help you, Lynn."

I let out a huff. "I even went to see Mama Lee."

A crooked grin pulled one side of his mouth up. "And she weren't no help neither?" I shook my head, tears rolling over my jaw and down my neck. "She can help. She just don't know how yet."

"What do I do?" I cried.

"You gotta know what the problem is before you can fix it."

"What?" I stood, giving no shits that I was naked. I was talking to a ghost in the middle of the woods, covered in the blood of a man I'd just killed. Nakedness seemed somehow less important. "How?" I stepped closer to him and he flickered like a candle. "Rusty, *tell me*," I demanded. "I'm scared." Shame finally won and I looked away. "I killed you. I killed you and I can't take it back, but I can save Garret. I have to. I can't risk him. How do I stop?"

He looked at me for a long few seconds. I didn't move, not a breath. "You can't stop what you are, Lynn." Air poured from my pouting lips in a noisy *whoosh*. "But you're not alone. You know what to do. You just have to think about it."

Wind blew through the treetops, rustling late summer leaves, flipping hair around my face. I swiped it away. Golden dust swirled between us. Rusty flickered, threatening to puff out altogether.

"No," I begged. "No. I need you. Rusty, I love you." I reached out for him, blood crusted under my nails.

He ran a hand through his hair and grinned. "I know."

A glimmering golden swirl twisted around his legs, up his body, and swept him away in a hundred million perfect pieces. I fell to the dirt, an agonizing wail popping from my lungs, carried away with the wind. With white-knuckled fists, I pounded the earth, damning the heavens for taking him away from me.

God won't help now, Lynn. I sniffed, reining in my tears. No time for crying. The day would pass and bring night and with it another change. There was no time for feeling sorry for myself.

"Carolynn Russell," I said aloud. "You get your butt up

off this ground and get out of these woods. You ain't doin'
nobody any good cryin' in the dirt." I was talking to myself,
but it was my nana's voice I heard in my head.

She'd been my guide, the voice in my head, since I was
old enough to have one. Nana would lay down her life to
help me, no questions, no judgments. She always knew what
was wrong and had some way of fixing it. Telling her what
I'd done, admitting what I was, terrified me. Downright
scared the beastly shit out of me. But losing Garret, that fear
burned scars into my soul.

Courage bubbled up inside me until I couldn't stop my
muscles from taking over and doing what my head couldn't.
I sat up straight, squared my shoulders, and stood. One long,
deep pull of air into my lungs, then out. I closed my eyes,
feeling the beast stir inside me. *Help.*

My feet moved on instinct alone, carrying me through
the woods. Strong legs pumped, an ancient tribal woman
moving through her territory: fearless. The chilly morning
wind in my face drew a grin across my cheeks. Ancient,
powerful blood thumped through my body, feeding even the
tiniest muscles—toes gripping roots underfoot, keeping me
upright.

It'd been days since my head was clear, solid. No mess of
worry or thoughts of who I was, what I'd become. What we'd
done. The beast was in me, guiding me, showing me the way
home.

My legs burned. Sticks and jagged rocks sliced my feet.
I ran anyway, pushing forward, knowing I'd be there soon.

Through a gathering of trees ahead, the worn-out green paint of my pickup.

One last shove of adrenaline, I burst from the woods. A woman, a beast, a warrior. I couldn't stop my momentum and I slammed into the side of my truck with an echoed thud.

Without thought, I slid into my dirty jeans and pulled the shirt over my head. Heart wild in my chest, my fingers stayed steady. I shoved the key home and fired her up. The old beast—my first one—roared to a start.

A maniacal grin shoved my eyes into squints. I shoved the mirror away so I didn't have to see myself, the wild thing I'd become. I had a few hours to put her to bed for the day, my beastly thing. We couldn't right scare Nana, now.

TELL ME I'M NO MONSTER

Nana's house—a small once-white shotgun two-bedroom—sat at the end of a long dirt road pocked with potholes and lined in weeds. Paint had been chipping off for years and the screen had holes in it, but it was hers outright and she was proud of it.

Granddaddy's hawthorn stood guard out front. My chin quivered at the sight, recalling Rusty's promise and our summers together. "Fuck," I hissed, choking on pity.

I swiped a hand across my filthy face, likely doing nothing to the mask of death I wore. The truck's heavy steel door clanged when I slammed it shut. There'd be no doubt I was out front. No turning back now. I stood on Nana's old porch, staring through the dusty screen door waiting for that divine providence to give me a push.

"Lynnie," she shouted from the kitchen, wiping her hands on a blue-checked apron tied around her thick middle. The sound of a ring on every finger clanking brought comfort, nearly sent me to my knees. "Your brother's been on the hunt for you."

My lip shook. "I know," I squeaked.

"You all right, sugar?" She pushed the screen door out my way to let me in. "Why you standing out there in the sun? Come on in."

Two steps in and my trembling legs betrayed me, sending me to my knees. My body hit the hardwood floor with a sickening thump. I stared at Nana's slim bare feet and skinny legs.

"Carolynn Russell, you get up off that floor. Ain't no reason to be on your knees in this house unless you're cleanin' or prayin'. I don't see a rag in your hand. You prayin'?"

Not anymore. I looked up at her and shook my head, tears pooling at my lashes. I'd left my warrior beast strength in the truck.

"Didn't think so. Now, you move yourself out of the way. I can't shut the door."

I nodded and scooted to the couch, slinking up the cushion without standing on two feet.

"Now, where in all of heaven and earth have you been? Garret's been calling here fussing about you for a full day. I liked to've come out there myself and look for you if he'd not asked me to stay put. Said there's an animal out there in the woods slicing people up. Oh, Lynnie, you're lucky he didn't call your mama."

I hadn't heard from her in a few weeks, but the phone call on my birthday. It wasn't like I'd expected much from her, but she could've called me when I got out of the hospital. My mom was a good person, but without a man around to hold her down, she'd flitter off like a butterfly. "Where's Mama?" Daddy'd been out on hauls all summer, no expectations there.

Nana sat beside me on the couch. "Garret didn't want her upset." My aching eyes didn't have it in them to roll proper. "You know how she can be." I did. She'd pack my bags herself and force me back home, shouting all the way how I was too young to be out on my own. Mama had always had the idea that I couldn't handle myself no matter how grown I was. Or how little she could handle her own self. She could run out on Daddy on a whim. She could be gone for days. But heaven forbid her baby girl wanted to be free to live her own damn life. Whatever that was.

I laid my head on Nana's overstuffed chest. "Nanny, I'm in trouble."

She ran her fingers through my hair without a snag. When I was a kid, I thought it was magic how all those rings never caught in my long hair. "I could tell that by the dirt on your face." Her heart thumped slowly, skipping half a beat then picked up again. "What's got you snarled?"

"Heaps," I whined. "Heaps and heaps." I pulled in a shaky breath.

She patted my head. The beating in her chest changed rhythm. "You ain't seen the start of trouble yet, girl."

I sat up. "What?"

Blue eyes watched my face, then looked down at her hands. "Carolynn Russell, you better keep your soul about you, baby. God's on your side, but He's not in control of this. You got a long row to hoe and it ain't gonna be easy."

I blinked. And blinked again. "Rusty…" I swallowed, vomit bobbing in my throat. "What's happening to me?"

Nana's milky blue eyes glistened. "I knew the day you was born you'd become something special. Something different. Something most folks wouldn't understand." I shook my head in disbelief. "Your brother didn't have the soul for it. Most men don't. But you, my girl…." She nodded once.

"Soul for what?" Worried thoughts flooded back in. "What the hell am I?"

"You watch that mouth, Carolynn." She took a deep breath and went back to her story. "Rusty came to me last night. Bless his heart." I blinked a thousand times, not comprehending what she was saying. "I was thankful for the visit, but I didn't need it. I knew, felt it in my heart, the night they made you."

In the woods I knew Nana would help me, even if she wasn't sure how. I'd never imagined that she'd known all along. "How— What am I?"

"Something ancient. Been around since man was throwing rocks at the moon." Her voice, sure as the day was long, sounded far away, like talking through a can on a string. The sound of my own heart threatened to drown her out. "It was only a matter of time. The changing of the guards I guess. It's been sixty years, give or take." She looked down at her well-weathered hands, picking beneath a curved nail. "How was he? Still as beautiful as I remember him?"

The thrumming in my head screeched to stop. *The man in the woods.* "Rusty?" I asked, hoping.

"He'd always been a sweet boy, my Percy. How was he?"

What could I say? "Naked." I'd killed that man. Tore into his throat until it gushed tangy blood into my mouth. "Young...."

"Handsome?" I nodded. She shrugged. "Before he died," she added. Shock hit my face like a back-handed slap. "You ain't the first, baby girl. You won't be the last."

My worry party'd been crashed by confusion and clarity swooped in with a sucker punch. It was a garish mess that would surely alert the law before long.

I sat back and stared at her. Tight white curls spiraled in tuffs from her head. Aunt Bobbi must've come by to give it a fresh perm . She'd sat there getting her hair done, gossiping, knowing full well I was about to become something *special*. That old woman had known all along this would happen and she hadn't said one damn word.

There was betrayal, pissing on the rug, puking in the roses.

"It would've been... forty-two? Yes. I'd turned twenty that year." She picked at the skin around her nail. "I'd worried for a year that he'd go off to fight in that damn war and I'd lose him for good." *Sniff.* "That night, under that damn moon, I left him. Alone in the woods with those... *women*. We should've never been out in those damn woods. Just couldn't help ourselves." She breathed soft, lost in memory.

"I ran so far and so fast I'd like to've never found my way to the highway. It was dawn before I came across a single soul out that night. By the time we found them again, they were already dead."

"The women?" I choked. "He killed them?" She nodded once. "You could've died, Nanny." I grabbed her hand. "I ki—"

"I know. I know, baby." Fear and sadness mingled at the tip of my nose. "Don't you cry, now. Ain't no time for it." She patted my hand once and let it go.

Nana's mostly blind cat slinked through the kitchen and into the living room, winding between her legs. "We'd looked for him, the whole town." Havana hadn't grown much in sixty years so I imagined a search party of twenty people, mostly all relation, shoving through the woods with torches. Pitchforks if they'd known the beast they were out hunting. "Our wedding day would've been three days later."

I made a sad noise in the back of my throat. Rusty popped into my head. "What'd you do?"

She grinned at me. "I went home, looked for *Mórai*, my granny. She'd had a secret too."

"I guess it runs in the family."

"In the blood." It'd been a joke. "Mostly. Percy took mine. My death." Heavy breaths heaved my chest. "The deaths I would bring."

"What am I?" I whispered.

Her face went still. "People around here call it the howler."

I blinked at her. "The *Ozark* Howler? I'm the *fucking* Ozark Howler? A damn tall tale?"

She snapped at me. "Watch your mouth, girl."

"That's a real thing? I mean, it seems so... *lame*." I'd been fully prepared for something you'd find in a dusty old book in the back of a magic shop. But a mountain myth?

"These old rednecks wouldn't know an ancient beast from the hole in their ass. That's just the name they gave it."

"*It?* Me."

"Do you have the marks?" I shoved my blonde brows into the middle. "On your body somewhere? Black lines, like tattoos. Percy had them on his arm." She pulled on both my arms, inspecting them for tattoos.

I yanked my arms from her grip, rubbing the idea from my tingling skin. "Maybe it's not real. Maybe I'm something else." That seemed worse.

She looked down her nose at me. "Haven't seen your mama yet?"

I shook my head. "Not in a while."

She nodded. "Mm."

"Mm? What does that even mean?" I groaned and flopped back on her couch. "Nana, I'm so lost. I need you to tell me what to do."

She shook her head. "You're gonna have to figure this one out, Lynn. I can't tell you what I don't know."

"Why didn't you tell me? You knew I'd become this beast." I jumped from the couch. "You let this happen," I shouted and stamped my foot with an echo.

Nana clapped her hands at me like I was a dog. I guess that fit. "You calm yourself now, Lynnie. You ain't getting anywhere being ornery." She huffed. "I know you're scared.

You ought'a be. Only idiots have no fear. Fear will keep you safe. But you gotta keep that under your hat. You hear me?" I nodded, lips pulled tight. "Be strong. Be with God."

"*God?* Where's God? He ain't here, I'll tell you that. He wasn't with me in the woods when I killed Rusty." I swallowed the word down like a bitter pill stuck on the back of my tongue. "When I killed Percy or those women. Where was God?" I waited a second for the man Himself to come down from the heavens and prove me wrong. He didn't.

Nana stuck her chin out. "You may not've seen him, you better believe He was there." She nodded, letting me know she was right and I damn well better get on board. "I'm sorry I waited. I'm sorry I waited even after Rusty. I just hoped… I hoped it wasn't true."

"I could've stopped it," I whimpered.

"No. Ain't no stopping it. Ain't no leaving it. You're no monster, Lynn. You're death for some. Vengeance for others. You'll kill. You'll hide." Her voice shook. "You'll leave. And you'll die. Young and perfect."

"I'll never get married." Rusty's face grinned at me. "I'll never have kids." I panted. "I'll never have a night to sleep in my own damn bed." White spots specked my vision.

My legs gave and I fell to my knees. I dropped my head into her lap, back-shaking sobs pouring out.

"You got two choices, Carolynn Russell. You can sit on my dusty floor and cry until you turn into that beast and gobble me up. Or you can get up, shake away those tears, and deal with your demons like a real woman should."

My nana had two ways of handling things. She'd either hold you and rock you until whatever was wrong went away, or she'd smack you in the head and tell you to shake it off no matter how bad it was. She was scared. I heard it in her voice.

"I ain't scared of nothing." She read my mind. Or maybe it'd been written all over my face. "Especially not a little green dog."

"I feel more like a cat," I said, muffled against her cotton dress.

"You better not run from me. I lived without Percy. I can't live without you." I looked up at her. She wiped wet cheeks. She'd lost two people she loved to the beast. It wasn't surprising she'd kept it from me. How could you tell a little girl she'd one day be a green monster of death?

"I am scared. I'm scared for Garret. And You. And Hattie. Hell, Nanny, the whole damn town." I snotted all over her blue-checkers.

"Don't you worry about this town. They've survived a lot more than an old green cat. If Percy managed to not swallow up the whole town, I reckon you'll be just fine."

Percy left. I blinked tears down my cheek that soaked into a wet spot I'd made. "What am I supposed to do?" Eventually, I'd have to leave too.

She sighed. "Well, baby, I don't know. But when you figure it out, you best come and tell me. I'd been waiting on Percy to come back and tell me all about it." Her voice got low, thick with sorrow.

"There's not a secret scroll hidden in an old chest in the cellar or nothing?" I looked up at her. Darkness moved across her eyes a second before laughter washed it away.

Her round belly shook. "Where'd you come up with that?" She had a silver tooth that flashed when she smiled.

I sat quiet, listening to the sound of her rings sliding

through my hair. "Nanny. Tell me I'm no monster." Glassy wet eyes, looking so much like Garret's, look down at me. "Tell me I'm just a girl." *Tell me it's all a nightmare.*

"You're something so much more than just a girl, Lynn."

I shook my head. "I don't want it. Take it back. I'm scared for me more than anyone, Nana. Scared that one day soon I'll just be the beast."

"You will always be Sharlene Carolynn Diamond Russell and I will always love you. Ain't no beast can take that away from you." She held my face between her two hands. Rough bandages wrapped tight around the bands of a few rings to keep them sized right scratched my cheeks. "My mama was *an fáidh.* Saw things, images from God, she'd say. Said it was in the blood." The gory face of the redhaired woman flashed in my memory. Her fiery hair the same shade as my great gran's before it went white. I swallowed back the sick that came along with it. "Ancestors were some kinda druids, you know. We come by it honest, some would say." She was smiling and showing off that silver tooth again. "But she was just an old Irish woman. Had superstitions for everything. Even said there were fairies out in these woods." Nana had retold those stories so many times I could say them backwards. "A family of divine women, I guess."

I thought about Mama. "Must've skipped a generation."

Nana raised her barely-there brows and stifled a chuckle at her only daughter's expense. She took one quick breath, nodded, and stood up. "You better get yourself on home to your brother before he comes out of his britches. You're lucky he didn't get the law after you." I'd have rather the law than Sue Ellen Russell. "You know he'd die right along with you if something ever happened."

Something did happen. "I have to stay away from him. What if I hurt him like—"

"Garret will just have to take his chances. Come on, now," she said, pulling me from the floor.

"What if—"

"No. You have no room for *ifs* anymore, Carolynn. Whatever your job on this earth, you've already clocked in. Get to it, girl."

I sucked back frustrated tears that hung on the edges of my lashes. My beast stretched inside me, content being mine. No room for ifs. My truth slapped me across the face with one clawed-paw. I was the beast. She was me. Whatever that meant, I had a true ally taking up shop inside where my have-to lived.

Without looking right at Nana, I wrapped my arms around her middle and squeezed until she let out an oomph. I buried my face into her chest and breathed the garden of fresh-bloomed roses. I loved that woman more than I could say in words. I hated to leave. I'd have laid down every tomorrow I had left to spend the rest of my life in her lap.

"You come back here in the morning. I'll have breakfast on the table for you. I want to hear everything about your night out hunting."

Nerves pushed vomit into my throat and I swallowed it back. Retelling my nights out was on the bottom of my list of shit to do. I was some kind of monster and Nana was proud to sit and hear about it. There's no one on the planet who loved you more than your nana. I could swear to that.

HOME AGAIN, HOME AGAIN

The sun sat dead nuts in the center of the sky on my way home from Nana's. I thumped a finger against the steering wheel, running through made-up reasons to have run off like I did. Ten minutes wasn't long enough to come up with a good lie to tell Garret about what I'd been off doing.

I had to figure out how to keep Garret safe without telling my secret. Keep myself safe. Not kill anyone else. And, this one was probably most important, not lose my ever-loving mind along the way.

Garret and Hattie stood on the porch when I bounced over the potholes in the gravel up to the house. "Shit," I hissed and slammed my hand against the dash.

I had half a mind to turn around. Let them watch me drive away. At least they knew I was alive. But I couldn't bring myself to turn the wheel.

I hadn't even put it in Park before Garret leapt off the porch and had my door open.

"Well, damn it, Garret, lemme get the thing parked," I complained.

He reached over top of me, shoved the shifter into place and pushed the button on my seat belt. "Where the hell have you been?" One strong arm wrapped around my waist and he yanked me off the seat. Just my tips of my boots dragged across the dirt as he carried me to the house. Hattie scurried to the truck and plucked the keys from the ignition.

Did they really think I was gonna run off? I bet they did. Could I blame them? Nope. Not one bit. Was I gonna get those keys back? You bet your ass.

"Sam's been calling here looking for you. You ain't been to work, ain't been home. Where in the holy hell—"

I kicked. "Will you put me down?"

"Lynn, I've been out of my mind looking for you." He let me slide until my feet hit the porch. "Hattie and me looked all over the woods for you. We called the sheriff."

Eyes wide, my hands flung in the air. "You called the sheriff?"

"Yes I did." He tipped his head in a dramatic nod. "He said you probably just need some time after…." *Ahem.* He couldn't say his name and it hurt my heart. I wanted to tell him everything. Tell him about Rusty, all of it. He had to know. I didn't keep secrets from Garret. Who was supposed to protect me if he couldn't? "I called Mama."

"You *what*?" I growled.

"What did you want me to do, Lynn? You were just gone." He looked at Hattie and back at me. "And there was this…" *Don't say it.* "Dog, or cougar, or something. I don't know. A *beast*." I stared at him, breathing as evenly as I could, begging him not to say it. "Lynn, don't laugh. I swear to the Lord almighty it was the damn Howler." Hattie rolled her eyes behind him. I didn't move. "I know it sounds stupid, but for a minute there, I thought you was ate up by the Ozark Howler." Hattie closed her eyes. I silently thanked her for being his voice of reason. Even though he was mostly right.

Mama pushed through the screen door as if someone had given her a cue. "My girl, there you are. Where'd you run off to?"

I didn't really look at her. "Hi, Mama." I let Garret think he'd seen the Howler and that I'd just run off to get my head on straight. As much as I wanted to, he couldn't know what I'd become. Liability alone was reason enough to keep him in the dark. "Where you been?"

"Oh, you know, just out and about." She admired her painted toes poking from the tips of her sandals. "Sorry I didn't come out and see you in the hospital, sweet pea." Her eyes slapped Garret with a switch that still made him flinch a little. "Nobody called to tell me."

"Out," I repeated and nodded. I knew what she meant. I loved my mama, but she had a man problem she couldn't quite shake. "I was out, too." I wasn't a big fan of my daddy, but I did believe in the bonds of marriage. It'd gotten worse since I moved out and she was all alone. It took me some years to figure out why she didn't just leave him. Mama liked men about as much as she didn't like to work.

"Thanks for coming out here to see me, Mama, but I'm fine. Honest. I spent some time with Nana today and feel a lot better."

Mama looked away and nodded. "Yeah." She clicked her tongue. "I love you, Lynnie. More than you could ever know. Why don't you come back home with me? You need looking after."

I'd been waiting for that. "I'm fine, Mama. I can look after myself. Besides, Garret needs someone here or this place will go to shit." I grinned at him.

"She'll be okay. It was an accident what happened to Rusty, Mama." Garret choked out his name and Mama winced. "I won't let anything like that happen again."

I begged the universe to make that true for himself. "We're fine here, Mama. Let it go." There was no telling what tonight would hold, and I damn sure wasn't going to get my half-brained mother involved in it. She'd surely have me in a nuthouse by morning. "I'll be by next week for dinner," I lied. I just need a few days to make a plan. To keep everyone safe.

She nodded, eyes focused on anything but me. "Sure thing, Lynn." Her hands balled into fists, then let loose again. Thudding in her chest echoed in my head. She turned to leave, stopped, and looked at me. "Happy birthday, my girl." A small bag made of old flour sack hung from her manicured fingers. "I know it's late, but it's yours. Should keep you safe." She dropped it into my open hand.

I gently pulled on the brittle string to open the bag. A leather cord spilled out with a jagged black stone attached with a silver wire.

"You didn't have to buy me nothing, Mama." It was pretty, heavy for how small it was, and not something my mother of all people would have ever given to me for any reason let alone my birthday.

"Of course I did. And I didn't buy it. It's sort of a hand-me-down. Been holding on to it for years for just the right time. It's a gift from all your nannies, and your mama." With tears in her eyes, she kissed my forehead. "Best be going." Mama patted Garret's cheek and touched Hattie's shoulder on her way down the steps. At her car, she stopped, hollering over the roof, "Keep your soul about you, baby."

It took a beat for me to catch up. "Mama," I shouted after her. "What'd'ya mean?" I ran to the car as it fired up. "Mama." I banged on the window and she rolled it down. "What does that mean? Keep your soul about you."

She breathed, a hot puff in the middle of cold air conditioning. "Just an old saying from my granny Maureen. Means don't lose yourself along the way. It's all you've got. It's all that matters." She put the car into gear. "Keep that close to you." She nodded at the necklace dangling from my clenched fist.

I watched her white car get smaller. Gray dirt clouds swirled and fell. "Everyone is so damn worried about my soul. They should be more concerned with my body." *Both of them.*

"I'm worried 'bout both." I jumped out of my panties.

"Hattie, you scared the shit out of me. How long you been standing there?"

"Long enough to see you get sad over your mama and start talking to yourself. You look like shit run over and smashed into the road."

"Thanks." I kicked dirt with the pointed toes of my boots on my way back to the house.

"You keep me around for the truth, don't ya?" She kicked a rock out of the way. "How long's it been since you had a proper bath?"

"A hundred years."

"Looks like." Hattie pinched a crunchy chunk of hair between her fingers. "Is that blood?"

I jerked away. "Uh, must be ketchup from that new diner in Russellville. Best burger in Arkansas." I cleared the steps in one long reach. "Thanks for being there for Garret. But I'm fine. You can go on home."

She scoffed. "You're fine? You ain't fine. You're about as fine as a cat in a snare. I don't know what kinda mess you're in, but you better get yourself out of it. Your brother's half gone crazy and he's taking me with him."

Garret banged pots in the kitchen. There was no way in hell I was cleaning up whatever mess he was making.

"He won't talk about Rusty, but I will." His name was a poison arrow shot through my heart. "I'm sad. Stupid sad. I can only imagine what you're feeling."

"He told me he loved me," I said without thinking.

"Finally." She raised her hands to the heavens. "Took him

long enough."

"I'll slap you if you knew about this and didn't say shit, Hattie."

"Would you have believed me?" Probably not. "That boy's been in love with you for years. You must be as dumb as you are filthy." I glared at her. "Rusty Kemp would've walked off the edge of the earth for you." She pinched her lips between her teeth.

She was right. He would have done anything for me. Even die for me.

Garret pushed open the screen with a handful of cold beers. "Ladies," he said, handing us each one.

Hattie looked at him, then at me, and back again. She pulled in a deep breath. "I actually think I'm gonna head on home."

Eyes bright as a spring morning, a grin tugged the corners of Garret's mouth. "All right." He swiped a wet hand across his jeans. "Thanks for comin' out, all your help. I really appreciate'cha." They looked at each other for a few seconds, then Garret leaned in and wrapped both arms around her. I watched, brows at my hairline, icy bottle clutched in each hand. They'd known each other as long as I'd been in school; they'd hugged before. This one was different. Longer. More handsy.

A sickening weight I hadn't known I carried lifted from my chest. The idea that if I left, by will or by kill, he'd be okay. Someone would look after him.

One day Nana would be gone. Probably sooner than later, in fact. Mama had her life she was living. If Garret and Hattie paired off I'd be alone. My person, the one who would've looked after *me* was dead. I'd killed him.

I walked past the two, waving lazily. "Bye, Hattie," I said, hoping they didn't hear the crack in my voice. They really were right for each other. Hattie the mother and Garret the man child. Inside somewhere happiness shined bright, but that bright shiny place was hidden in the shadows of the beast. No. Not the beast, me. What I'd done. What I'd taken from us all.

Bath water filled the tub when the screen door finally creaked open and slammed shut. Garret didn't come knocking like I thought he would. It relieved me more than hurt that he hadn't. I wanted to sulk in my misfortune, sink into the steaming water and wash away the death that clung to my skin.

The house was hot, sticky humid, and I was chin deep in a steamy tub. Suds floated on the surface and I blew them away. The overhead light painted my shiny wet knees white. I ran my hand over the semismooth skin and considered swiping a razor over them. They'd just be coated in green fur come nightfall. What did it matter anymore? Things like shaved legs were for the girl I was before. This girl, the one desperately trying to hold it all together, had bigger fish to fry.

I pulled my fuzzy pink robe tighter around me, tying the knot at my hip. Wet hair made the collar of my shirt soggy before I wrapped it up in a band and the fabric stuck awkwardly to my skin.

Garret stood in the middle of the living room, staring at nothing. Lost in his own head. "Aren't you burning up in that thing?" he asked when I walked past him to the kitchen.

Chilly mountain air had sunk deep, rattling in my bones since the first morning I woke up in the woods. Still, sweat dripped down the middle of my back. "Just looking to feel cozy."

He nodded, accepting my bullshit. "Hungry?"

Starved. "I could eat. But I really just wanna sleep for a million years. Feels like it's been a week since I laid in my own bed." *Give or take.*

Bright summer sun poked him in the eye through a break in the front curtains. He took a breath to ask me why I'd be sleeping at noon but stopped and thought of a more important question. "Were you out drinkin'… er?"

I sighed. "Garret. I was just out. Thinkin'."

"Thinkin'?"

"Yeah. With my brain. You know, that thing between your ears." It wasn't his fault I had to lie. Not *all* his fault.

"You really not gonna tell me where you been?" His chest heaved under a tight gray T-shirt.

I swallowed, one big gulp of prickly lies. "Not on your life."

He moved into the kitchen to stand close. "One day, doesn't have to be today, you're going to tell me what happened in there." His eyes shifted toward the back of the house, my bedroom.

Those lies clawed their way up my throat and out my lips. "I was just drunk, camping. Thinkin'." I could've added the R word, forced Garret out of the conversation. A secret weapon I'd use when there was no other choice.

His eyes played over that night, what he'd seen. "Sandwich?"

I watched his face, waiting for him to force me to fess up. "Tomato?"

One nod and he was off into the cabinets for bread. He'd ask me again. If he didn't, he was dumber than I gave him credit for. What I'd say when he did depended on things I wasn't even sure existed. Like my future.

Garret'd cleaned up the glass and taped a piece of cardboard over my escape hatch. I'd have to rip the tape off to get out this time. Long before the beast popped out.

I flopped onto my bed face first, burying my face into the pillow. "He washed the sheets?" I mumbled into the pillow.

I slid off the bed, crawling a few feet to my balled-up jeans on the floor and pulled Mama's gift from the pocket. A small purse made from flour sack and old twine. Using my nails, I picked the knot until it came free. I dumped the necklace into my hand. I slid the leather strap over my head. The weight of it was strangely familiar, comforting.

A rolled piece of old, leathery paper was stuck in the

bottom of the bag. I plucked it out gently, the brittle fabric one quick move from ripping. Written in aging red ink, a poem scrawled in jagged cursive.

"*By the Moon*," I read. "*Power in thee, this stone charged in protection be.*" My fingers traced the edges of the stone. "*Who wishes harm render still, not spoil a soul nor bid thy will. Hear my plea on this night; impart protection to this bringer of right. By these words power show, grant your guard upon this stone.*" The thing around my neck started to warm between my fingers. "*Wholly in power and divinity, by these words, so mote it be.*"

"Now you're gettin' somewhere."

A squeaky yelp popped out of my throat and I dropped the piece of paper. I searched the darkened corners for my boy. I'd heard him clear as day. Scurrying to my feet, I ran to his corner. Nothing. Not even a spark of magical energy left behind. "Come back," I whispered. "Come back."

Light caught my eye in the mirror on the back of the door. The black stone glowed vibrant purple. Brighter than the blood I'd spilled.

My eyes refused to move, locked onto the glowing thing, terrified to look away, refusing to let fear rip it from my neck. It burned, hotter and hotter the longer I stared. I stood there, silently waiting for it to burn me up like the abomination I was.

Searing pain hit my spine. Not the pain of the beast, a scratching, claws from the outside instead of in. I gritted my teeth, gutting any sounds of pain that would bring Garret. My knees shook, but I wouldn't let them take me down. I had to watch it happen, whatever it was.

The stone flared to a white blinding light. Like a balloon pumped till it popped, the pain burst, instantly cooling in icy strips down my back. A force of air filled my lungs and the stone flickered to green.

Holding myself up with hands planted on either side of the mirror, I panted, "What. In. The. Hell." Eerie lime green light cast villainous shadows over my face.

Prickly heat crawled up my spine, sending chills over my body. I checked the time in the mirror. Hours still until the beast clawed free. I shrugged out of my robe and ripped the soggy shirt over my head.

My stomach hit my toes. "It's real." Black slashes cut across a long line down the center of my back. Were these Percy's marks? *My* marks. "I am the beast."

The necklace dimmed until it was mostly black again. I thought about taking it off, burning it, refusing the change. My gut promised I was an idiot.

I'd live in that body, under those marks, sharing my space with a big green beasty until I didn't. Until someone came to take my place.

I looked at my naked twenty-year-old body. It would never grow a big pregnant belly. Or get wrinkles. It'd look like that when they came. "When they eat me up."

My radio popped on to an old country song when the alarm

went off an hour before sunset. It'd been a restless, dreamless type of sleep. I thought about letting the beast take me to that quiet, emotionless place tonight. Wasn't sure if I had it in me to do it again just yet. To remember the beastly things we did.

I stuck a note to my mirror for Garret. *Had to get out. I'll be back. Don't worry about what I'm doing. I can take care of myself. Love, me.*

The tape peeled back easily but I had to jimmy the cardboard to stay closed from the outside. I put the truck in Neutral and pushed the old beast—the other one—down the driveway, starting it up only when I thought Garret wouldn't hear.

Warm sun hovered over the mountains, one last tease before dusk. The beast yawned and stretched inside. Soon she'd pace, antsy for her night to come.

BECOMING

I watched the sun set through my dirty windshield on the bank of Blue Mountain Lake, in the spot where Rusty had parked that night. Some weird place inside me thought he'd be there waiting. Grinning, shirtless, beer in hand, waist-deep in the water. I was alone. Even the cicadas had gone quiet for the night.

She stirred inside, my beastly thing, ready for her turn. I pulled my boots off and set them on the floorboard, stacked a clean pair of shorts and a shirt in the seat before shutting the unlocked door, keys in the glovebox. If someone came all the way out there to steal my shitty old truck, then let them have it.

Cool, soft soil squished around my feet. I pushed my toes into it, feeling the earth squeeze between them. Tiny *plips* echoed off the water, fish popping through the surface to snag their dinner. Life went on living around me. And it would. Whether I wanted it to or not.

I made my way around the lake to the cove where I'd decided I loved Rusty Kemp. The ghosts of us lingered behind, splashing and laughing and living and loving without even knowing it. It's a sad truth, the saying you don't know what you've got till it's gone.

The stone around my neck warmed, flickering a low green light. Over the top of the mountains the sun blazed one last fiery farewell. The beast rumbled.

Fear had taken a break in my soul, making room for things like acceptance, peace, and a hint of pride. It may have been the stone or my new tattoos. Whatever the cause, I was ready for the night, for what it would bring.

I closed my eyes, shot a single prayer up to the powers that be. *Don't kill anyone.*

"Rusty… let me see you one more time," I begged, gut churning.

"It's not his turn, *deirfiúr.*"

I jumped and lost my footing in the muddy bank, hollering loud enough to rustle birds from a tree. "Who the hell are you?" I scrambled up from the dirt, keeping my eye on the small woman. "And why are you wearing a nightgown?" It wasn't the strangest thing I'd seen in a week, but it also wasn't every day that a woman in a sheer white dress sneaked up on you in the middle of nowhere.

Dark brown hair flittered around her face in the windless night. She circled slowly around me, her gown blowing in the unseen breeze. "This visit isn't about who I am. It's about who you are." Her accent softened the syllables into one long word—speaking in cursive like the redhaired woman had. White-blue eyes locked onto mine while she made her first round.

My heart thudded, adrenaline pumping. "What am I? Just tell me. I've been waiting, beggin', praying."

A smug grin pulled the corners of her mouth up. "Gammy, Cu," she grumbled. "My name is Avery." Her circling was starting to spin my head into knots. "I've been charged as your guide." I turned with her, untying her knots, and tangling more.

"Will you stop that?" I shouted.

She sucked air in through her nose, pulling her soft features in with it, wrinkling porcelain skin into a sagging, soggy mess. Her eyes flashed pure white. Billowing brown hair flipped around her face in dense, dripping snakes. One long, piercing scream heaved from deep in her lungs, blowing me over. I toppled to my ass, moist dirt soaked through my jeans.

As the echoes of her screech faded, so did the haggard woman she'd become. Smooth skin rounded out her cheeks and her white eyes shifted back to blue.

"What the hell was that?" I asked, looking up at her from the ground.

She brushed make-believe dust from her arms. "Just a parlor trick, deary."

"Are you like… me? A beastly thing inside of you

too?" She raised her brows. A cocky expression half-closed her eyes. "You're supposed to help me?" Pain in my core doubled me over. There were just minutes left before she would burst free. "What am I?" I asked through gritted teeth.

"Godshite, girl, get up off the ground. I can't talk to you down in the muck."

Shaky legs forced me up from the dirt. "Hurry, I don't have—" I groaned, holding my aching sides.

Her eyes shifted to the setting sun behind me. Without any more urgency, she said, "You are Sidhe." Curled in on myself, I blinked up at her. She sighed. "An ancient sect of fae."

I blinked again. The beast went silent—maybe she blinked at the woman too. "I'm... a *fairy*?"

Avery groaned and turned away from me, plucking a leaf from a low branch. Her hair blew in waves down her back. "American. Not a fancy thing with wings and a wand and all tha', flittin' about in the woods." She spun the leaf in her fingers. "Some are rotten little mogs, causing mischief, havoc. Some are like you. And me. Sidhe have a purpose. A job. And you, my *beastly* little thing, are one of a kind." I swallowed, choking on my truth. "The only living breathing Cu Sidhe in this dimension." She roared inside at the sound of her name and an unexpected tear fell down my cheek.

"Don't I feel special," I slurred, wishing I was back on the ground, knowing full well my knees would soon give way and take me down anyway.

"I don't have all night, and clearly neither do you, so shut up and let me finish." She lifted the stone from my chest. The green glow reflected in her eyes. "Where's your Ogham?"

Fresh fur tickled under my skin. "What?"

"You're really gon' have to keep up. Your markin's. You have the Black Sentry." She dropped the stone. "And the *geas*? You read it?" Words refused to leave my tongue. "Sealed the deal."

I huffed panting breaths. "*I* did this? I could've stop it?"

Her head flipped back and she laughed one loud bark. "There's no stoppin' it. You were born Sidhe. You will die Sidhe. Accept it."

Trembling legs finally gave out, sending me to the earth on my knees. I looked up at her. "But the women. In the woods."

Her dress billowed around her legs before she squatted to meet me. "Ghosts of a curse long past." She watched my stone brighten; it heated my skin. "Listen to my words." An inch from mine, her lips moved quickly, pushing each lazy syllable into my face. "You will bid the will of death until another takes your place." Cold breath filled my lungs. "The bearer of vengeance, justice, punishment."

I sucked in air, taking in her chilled breaths. "I am vengeance." I winced, my voice sounding hollow, far away.

"You are Cu Sidhe. You are death."

I met her eyes, squared my shoulders, and said the words

from deep in my soul. "I am death." Pride filled me to the brim. "I am Cu Sidhe." The beast stretched her monstrous paws, kneading claws against my insides.

Avery sat back and smiled. "There you are, love." She stood, her dress flapping around my body. "If your granny'd accepted who she was, if she hadn't let her fear win, poor Percy would've died an old man." She picked another leaf and watched it twirl in her fingers.

A scream popped from my gut. The sun was gone. And so was I. Legs pulled to my chest, I rolled to my side.

"Damned humans have no business in our world. Don't have the soul for it." Bare feet stood a foot from my face. My back arched, popped. "There you are," she sang. Cold hands ripped at my shirt, pulling it up over my head. She ran a finger down my spine, sending a chill over my already humming skin.

I opened my mouth to ask her about Nana, to force her to tell me everything before the beast took over. A screeching howl came out in its place. A true gust of wind kicked up leaves and dirt, swirled Avery's hair around her face, and swept her away.

We were alone, my beast and me. One being. One mind. One soul. I'd sealed the deal. Accepted my truth. My purpose.

Vengeance. Justice. Punishment.

I was death.

On the bank of Blue Mountain Lake, I was born for the second time. A beast. Cu Sidhe.

And this is the part of the story where the action begins.

GOOD MOURNING

Heavy paws slapped the soggy bank. A huff shot snot from my muzzle. My long braided tail whipped the thick night air—wet, humid, it matted my fur into pointed tufts. She shook it straight, my shaggy body flopping back and forth. The glowing stone swung at my throat, the strap tight.

It'd been a long time since she'd worn it, the weight of it was cumbersome. Would take some getting used to again. I'd have to loosen the strap when I had thumbs again. This body was hers to control, but we shared knowledge, cunning. She didn't think in words, or pictures, not that I could hear or see. What the beast knew, what she understood, I'd know. When I needed to, apparently.

We stalked the woods, moving freely through thick trees, pushing past brush. The world a lush green. Death was my job. Righteous kills. I was vengeance, but for who? How many people needed justice in Havana, Arkansas? Percy hadn't left just to keep Nana, or the town, safe. Work sent him away. And soon, it'd send me away too. Walking the night, fighting crime. Or something. Alone.

The day Garret moved out, Mama came into my room crying. When I asked her why she was crying, she ran her hand over my head, looked me dead in the eye, and said because now she'd be alone. I told her I'd be there, that she wouldn't be alone. Mama just shook her head and said one day I'd know what lonely felt like. Hindsight being what it was, she should've been more specific.

I should've gone deeper into the woods, somewhere I wouldn't be caught. Desperation hoped he'd be there, my shimmering angel—which was peculiar since he'd never been angelic in his life. If I was going to survive this new life, I'd have to start thinking like the beast. My stupid, reckless human heart had taken me back to that place. And the beast had found what I was looking for.

She snorted and sniffed the ground, dragging in his scent. Our heart sped, thumping a hopeful tune. *Rusty.* He was everywhere. And nowhere.

We moved quickly through the line of bushes to a place I recognized even through my mystical night vision. *No.* I wanted to see him, but not like that. Not *that* Rusty. The tangy, sweet smell of him lingered on every leaf, the rocks that circled the now dead fire pit, soaked into the earth itself. Blood I'd spilt.

My beast whimpered, unseen sadness from my soul to

hers. Even animals mourned their dead. As much as I was becoming my beast, she became me.

Dry dirt puffed around my heavy paws as she paced, drawing in Rusty with each panting huff. For the first time, her thoughts—what they were—raced.

She'd found what I'd come looking for. Like a VHS tape finding its track, Rusty's limp body flickered lime green into the scene and back out. *A ghost of curses past.* My sorrowing cry of solace howled, echoing through the still night.

With a weighted flop, we fell to the forest floor. Defeated. Wholly ready to be done with it all. Another whimper, and a huff.

Wailing wind ruffled my shaggy fur, swirling leaves and dirt. Avery's bare feet, almost covered by her billowing dress, touched the ground feet from me.

"Oh, love, you have much to learn, yet," she said, sitting on a fallen log.

Avery ran her hand over my head, scratching a spot I wouldn't have thought was itchy. "This place has no power for you." My fiery eyes looked up at her. "Your love is gone." *Huff.* "I will never lie to you, so ready your heart."

Petting me like a dog—which I wasn't convinced I was—should've been a kick in the shin, but we liked it.

"Rest yourself, now. Let go of who you were. That girl, she died in this place. Mourn them both tonight, wake in the morning knowing who you were born to be, Lynnie Russell."

Avery said my name for the first time and the beast's heart warmed. Like she'd been waiting to know who she was too.

She traced her thumb up and down between my eyes. They slowly closed. "Mo ghrá den chéad fhéachaint thú, 'Eleanóir, a rún," she sang. Her song, in a language like the one that revived me from death, warbled in her throat, echoing back on itself in the trees.

A long, exhausted breath pushed from my snout. I wanted to go home. Sleep in my bed. Storm into my nana's house and ask her every question expecting every answer. Go back in time and do that night over.

Nana survived because she'd ran. Whatever that meant for Percy, well, that's how she goes sometimes. If Rusty had ran, left me there to meet my fate... I hadn't believed in fate. A series of poor choices was usually the culprit for wrong turns in life. This thing I'd become, it'd been waiting for me at the end of a cul-de-sac.

Pain woke me. A sharp, searing poker in the gut. Dawn was on the horizon. Fire deep in my body blazed and shot through my furry limbs. Each hair along my rough hide retracted, fangs on a venomous snake. Together we endured the torture of trading places.

Day broke, washing shimmering light over my tan skin, grotesquely reflecting off the gooey remnants of my beast. The last howl of transformation scratched through my human throat. I panted, an animal recovering from pain, welcoming another morning with a hardening heart. Birds sang from their perch nestled somewhere in a nearby tree. If I'd had a rifle, I'd have shot those birds. What did they have to sing about?

I sat up and shook leftover beast from my skin. Avery's lullaby had given us a reprieve from our endless days and nights. In the sunny light of day, the weight of my future hung heavy.

She'd gone with the night, my enlisted guide. Leaving me with more questions than answers. If Avery was truly meant to help me, she needed better time management.

Without my beastly body, the scent of Rusty was gone. But the ghost of my death, theirs, was burned into the very earth. Red specks dotted rocks around the fire pit. I closed my eyes, pretending it was paint, or animal blood at least. His face flashed in my mind, sickly dark, crusted blood caked the creases of his skin. My eyes popped open and I gasped, sucking in a painful gulp of air.

"Fuck," I screamed, hefting one of the rocks and hurling it a few yards away.

The universe, and the heavens, and the magic that made me what I was could downright go fuck itself. My beast rumbled, sharing in my misery.

The walk back to the truck was longer than I'd expected. It was hard to believe that poor deputy had carried me all that way. Granted he'd been wearing boots. And clothes.

When my truck came into sight through the trees, I stopped, knelt behind a shrub, and listened. I'd be exposed for a dozen yards and couldn't risk being seen by some lone fisherman out for an early morning bite.

Water lapped sluggishly against the bank. Those brainless, cheery birds sang on. No footfalls moved through the woods. I closed my eyes and tugged at the beast, listening for the faint sound of a human heart glugging away. We sniffed the air—my nose not nearly the power of her snout—hunting for the scent of a human.

Clear of any accidental peepers, I scurried from the forest to the truck. Early morning light danced on the lake. Beauty sent down from God. A gift to heal my tattered soul. *Go.* My heart sped and without another thought, I ran into the water, splashing through the cold chest-deep.

Golden sun warmed my cheeks. I leaned back and let the lake carry my body. Floating, tits out for the world to see, my wet skin soaked up the sunshine right down into my soul. Avery's song played over in my head, calming my fiery heart. Her words meant nothing to me, but my beast knew it was a song about love.

My body was calm, still, but my heart waited for something that would never come. A silent tear rolled down my cheek and plopped into the water. "Rusty, you shithead, how am I supposed to keep on this life without you in it?"

A long, flittering whisper floated over the lake. "I'm here."

Hands flapped hard against the water. I righted myself, covering my boobs, standing waist deep in the water. "Hello?" I scanned the bank for Avery, hoping that I was otherwise alone.

When no one answered, I waded back to the bank, hustling to the truck. Hiding behind the open door, I pulled a clean pair of skivvies over my butt and slipped into a white top.

"Hurry."

I spun around, searching for the owner of the ghostly voice. "Who's there?" I swallowed. "Please answer me."

Still as stone, I stood and waited. Even my heart stopped to hear the voice I desperately wanted.

"Home, Lynn. Go home."

I didn't wait around to ask questions. I knew that voice by heart. I poured my legs into a pair of shorts. My muddy feet kicked boots away from the pedals.

"I'm coming." I promised.

Trembling hands refused to work the key. I closed my eyes, filled my lungs with cleansing air, and blew it out slow. *Get it together, Lynn.* I shoved the key home and cranked it over. She roared to life. Inside, I burned, desperate to get home.

"Wait for me," I begged and yanked the shifter into place. "I'm coming."

LOVING THINGS'LL KILL YOU

I barreled toward home, cramming my foot against the brake feet from the porch. A trail of dust swirled up the driveway behind me.

"I'm coming," I panted under my breath. "I'm coming."

The door was open and I was tumbling out before my fingers found the buckle release. "Fuck." I fumbled with the button and it finally came loose.

Dried mud flaked off my feet as I stomped up the steps. The porch echoed back at me. "I'm here." Shaking hands hardly managed the key. I shoved through the door. "I'm here."

Dead space. Hollow. Empty. "No." I shook my head. "No, no, no, I'm here. I came." My voice cracked. I tore through the house, checking every darkened corner. "Rusty,"

I called. Nothing.

The house was silent. Garret wouldn't be home for hours yet. "Damn it."

I huffed, pulling in more and more air until white spots popped in my vision. "One thing. That's all I asked for." I pouted, storming off to my room.

I slammed the door behind me even though the only person who heard it was me. It didn't help. "Look," I said to whoever or whatever oversaw my existence. "I'll do the thing—the beasty thing—but I want one damn thing. One." I stopped and thought. "Two. Two damn things." The bed squeaked under my butt. I folded my legs in front of me. "Keep Garret safe, from me at least." I closed my eyes. "And let me see my boy one more time." A hot tear streaked down my cheek.

Warmth filled my soul—a pitcher running over from an over-pumped well. My heart stopped. The world stopped.

"Where you been?"

My breath let out, a smirk tugged at my lips. "You really askin'?" I opened my eyes, ready to look into a perfect set of baby-blues I'd ignored until it was too late.

Nothing. My chin quivered, sobs bounced my chest. "Can't I see you? Can't I at least have that?" I begged.

Like a thunderstorm in August, the air shifted, charged. It crackled on my skin, pulling each tiny hair on end. "Damn it, Rusty Kemp. You get your white ass in here," I demanded.

Warmth hugged me, swirling with a frosty chill, an icebox left open on a hot day. Only just gone to rest, my beast stirred. The ghostly magic called to her. She lived there too.

I dragged in a deep, ragged breath. "Rusty," I said, searching for the magic that lived inside me. Thick enough to cut with a knife, electric air crawled over my skin.

The stone at my neck glowed, a pale, soft white. My eyes burned, but I refused to close them. I wanted every second. Needed it.

Gold shimmering dust floated in the slim beams of light that poked through the cardboard window. Heavier, more willful.

A shift in the universe. Salty drops both happy and sad slid to the crease of my mouth. Bright blue eyes creased at the corner. He smiled. I smiled.

I reached out to him sitting in front of me, wrapping my arms around him. They fell right through. It was a tease. A universal "April Fools." Here's your love, back from the dead. Look upon him with magic eyes. But you can't touch him. For eternity.

"I'm sorry." I didn't know what else to say, but sorry didn't even cover it.

"I love you, Lynnie Russell."

That was all my heart needed to break right in half. I couldn't talk. Could hardly breathe. I wanted him to stay with me forever. I wanted him to love me forever. I wanted more than anything to take it all back. To go back to that night, the night I became that thing. My beast. I wanted Rusty Kemp more than I wanted anything in my whole life. He'd been right there all along.

"Shit," I hissed. "I was a stupid kid. I didn't know." I shook my head. "Please. Stay with me. I don't care that I can't touch you. Just stay." The desperation in my voice annoyed the beast. She turned and grumbled inside. "Tell God to save my soul. To let me into heaven." My blubbering even started to irritate me.

"I can't tell God nothin'. You got things to do here, Lynn. Things I can't. Things not even God can do. You're one of a kind, kid."

Tears flowed into snot on my lip. I swiped it away. "No." I shook my head like it'd make a difference. "You can't leave me. You can't. I need you. I got nobody."

"Well, I can't right stay here." His smile stretched wide. "You got special things to do, Lynn. Go on, do 'em."

"Damn it, Rusty, listen to me. I can't. You hear? I can't."

He closed his eyes. The room went still, no crackling magic on my skin, no puffs of golden dust. Just him and me. "You got my heart, Carolynn Russell. Always have." His eyes opened and the world stopped. "I'll be here when you're ready."

My heart punched a hole in my chest. "I'm ready now. I'm ready."

"Nah, silly girl. Go get your shit done. I'll see ya in a bit." His voice echoed, bouncing off even the trees outside. He leaned close. I waited for him to poof right through me. Soft lips pressed against my forehead. Instantly addicted to his touch.

Icy air flittered over my face. He was gone. Swooped off to wherever southern ghost boys go. I flipped through my pillows, flopping Nana's old quilt onto the floor. Searching every inch of my room for one more taste of him. His scent lingered on the linen where he'd been sitting. I shoved my face into the blanket, sucking in a gulp of what was left behind.

My dying heart ached for him. For myself. For what could have been. What a cruel universe to entangle two souls destined to spend life apart. Even if he'd lived, I couldn't be his. This was a fate I'd never escape. A curse that killed my soul.

They say love hurts. No one ever said loving things would kill you.

OLD WOMEN HAVE OLD WAYS

The front door slammed and I startled awake. "Lynn?" Garret hollered, home for lunch.

I didn't move. Hadn't in hours. The spicy smell of my boy had faded and with it the last of my tears. My pity party had officially been shut down. Rusty was gone, real and truly. I'd begged for one more time. I'd asked and I'd gotten. Figured the universe didn't answer prayers twice.

My door flung open. Garret let out a quick, heavy sigh. "Damn it."

Face pressed to the pillow, I mumbled, "What?"

"Where you been? When'd you get home?"

I lifted my head to look at him. Met with puffy eyes and a red nose—and surely the traces of murderous guilt across my face—Garret dropped to his knees beside the bed.

"What in heaven's name…?"

I bit my cheek, refusing to let his name leave my lips. "Rusty," I whined.

Garret pressed his forehead to mine and breathed softly. "I know." His breath shook, but he didn't let his tears loose.

"I just wanna stay in this bed until it stops hurting." It wasn't a lie. I'd lay there for the rest of my life if the powers would allow it.

He swallowed hard. "His mama called this morning, said they're releasing his—him to the funeral home in Danville tomorrow. Asked if I'd help. With the arrangements and all." I nodded, wanting nothing more than to crawl into a deep pit and never come out. "I told her I would." I like to have come out of my skin waiting for him to let out the breath he held, the words constrained in it. "He was my brother, Lynn." He swallowed again, but it did nothing to the knot at his throat. "My best friend and now…" Cheeks wet with fresh tears, he whimpered, "He's gone. Just gone."

Not gone. Not really. *Wasn't*, anyhow. "I love him, Garret."

He looked me square in the eye, suddenly remembering what happened that night. My birthday. "I know you do. Knew it all along."

"Liar."

One shake of his head. "Nope. Not a liar. A truther. And I'm telling you that was your person. And damn it, I miss him every second of every day, but if I'd lost *you*…." Another swallow. "I'd've died right along with you."

All the air shot out of my lungs. I couldn't look him in the eyes anymore. He'd know. He'd figure it out just looking at me that I was the monster who killed his friend, his brother.

He couldn't know. Not just about Rusty, but about all of it. Me, Nana, the beast. It'd kill him. Nothing in this world or the next could've made me break his heart again. I'd keep that secret to my grave. Or his. Whichever came first.

"I'm gonna go see Nana for a bit. You be all right?"

He sat back on his heels. "Where you been, Lynnie? You all right?"

No. Not one bit. "Fine. Why don't you call up Hattie to come over for dinner later?" I wiggled my eyebrows. "She'll keep ya company."

He pinched his lips. Guilt washed over his face, turning his cheeks pink. Like he'd done something bad. Like he wasn't allowed to be happy. Garret would've walked off the end of the earth for me. I had half a mind to do the same. If only just to not have to see that look on his face again.

"You can be happy, brother." I sat up and clapped a hand on his shoulder. "You have my permission." *If nothing else, please just be happy.*

Garret was my person, would be as long as he was alive. My brother by blood and soul. The tether holding me to earth. A rock steadfast in my whitewater river.

"I'm sorry I told you all that stuff, Lynn. I should've—"

"I don't damn think so, Garret Llewellyn Russell. You're not gonna apologize for telling the truth." A knot caught in my own throat, the balled fist of hypocrisy. "Listen to me." I grabbed his chin. "Until I die, I'll never, ever blame you for one bit of what happened." *Please don't blame me either.* "Live life. Be happy. Have babies."

He blushed, looking down at his hands. "How can I do that without my brother?"

The truth, hot on the tip of my tongue, almost spilled out

into his lap. "He'll be here when you're ready," I repeated. A promise I prayed with all of my soul he'd keep.

Garret nodded, accepting my nonsense. "Yeah." Swallow. "You gonna be home tonight? Have dinner at least?"

I hoped Garret really thought I'd been out drinking at the lake every night. Or finding a new man down at Maldoon's. Anything but howling at the moon. Although, I hadn't done that yet. "Will do," I lied. "Now get your ass up off my floor, ya big ol' pansy." He kissed me on the head on his way out. "Call Hattie," I demanded.

Garret stopped at the door. "We're gonna be all right, Lynn."

He'd be all right. I'd be whatever fate allowed.

Nana sat in her rocker on the porch shelling peas. Her fingers worked quickly over the shell, shoving each little green bead from its home in one swoop.

"Hey, sugar," she said into my ear when I leaned for a hug, her knees held tight to the old metal bowl between them. "How'do?"

"Oh, fine," I said, plucking a loose pea from her chest and popping it in my mouth.

The record player crackled inside before a new song started. "I guess we're tellin' lies today." She looked up at me over top of her glasses, one thin brow arched.

I brushed twigs and leaves off the swing on the end of the porch where I'd spent most every summer night of my childhood. "Well, Nanny, I think you and I both know I'm not the only one lying around here." She blinked at me.

For once in all of my twenty years, I felt like a grown up. A real adult with real adult things to say. It wasn't the beast; it was realizing the people I thought were adults were no better than me. We all lied when it suited us. We all had secrets.

She set the bowl of peas on the table next to her chair, pushed the bucket of shells from between her feet. "I prayed you'd never know the word unpleasant." Thin, strong fingers pinched tobacco from Papa's old pouch, stuffing into his dark wooden pipe. "I prayed you'd grow up a willful woman. Marry a good man. Give your mama beautiful grandbabies. Die a nanny in your own bed." Flame crackled to life at the end of a match. She puffed, slowly lighting her pipe. "God had a plan for you, darlin'."

"God," I scoffed. I'd come to learn God had no power in my world.

Smoke rolled out the corners of her mouth. "I promised your mama I'd let you live what life you had ahead of you." *Puff, puff.* "She thought if you didn't know…. Knowing or not knowing, fate comes anyway."

I'd never thought my nana would've lied to me my whole life. And yet, there she was, pants on fire. "You gotta tell me now, Nanny, I gotta know. Why did Percy become the beast? Why wasn't it you?" I leaned forward, elbows on my knees, desperate for anything she would give me.

"My story is a long one, Lynn." She sucked her teeth. "It ain't fair. It ain't right and it ain't the way it should've been, but there's nothing I can do about it now."

I slid off the swing and to my knees. "It's my story now. Make it right *now*. Make it fair *now*. Help me. Why not you?"

Musky pipe smoke swirled in golden sunlight. I breathed it in, falling into the distant memory of Granddaddy Higgins. She'd picked it up the day after he died. I was certain she'd done it to live in his memory as often as time would allow.

"Divine Providence."

I sat back on my heels and looked over my shoulder at the hawthorn, bright red berries ready to burst.

She swallowed. "I loved him so." A finger poked at the ash inside her pipe. "He loved me right back." I looked up at her, watching her eyes focus on long gone memories. "I knew what I'd become. Granny Gwen came for me when I was a girl, like I should've come for you. My daddy thought he could stop it, pray it away." She looked down at me. "Ain't no stopping fate."

I closed my eyes and pressed my forehead to her knee. Her hand ran over my hair without a snag.

"Percy succeeded where Daddy failed," she finished.

I looked up at her. Blue eyes flashed dark and back again. "I know you ran. I know you left him there."

She puffed on that pipe until I knew it had to have been ash. "We shouldn't've been out there. We'd've been married in just a few days. But we were young, not kids of course. Twenty wasn't the same as it is now. Two young people in love, off in the woods for a night alone on a long summer night." Smoke had stopped rolling out; she still puffed. "They were there waiting. The women."

I nodded, seeing the scene again in my mind. "Ghosts of curses past," I whispered.

"I ran that night. I left my love behind. Never did I think *he'd* become Cu Sidhe. I thought he'd be spared and my fate'd be changed." She tapped the pipe against her chair, ash tumbling to the porch. "I begged Granny to fix it, take it all back." A long, ragged breath heaved her chest. "Two days later, Percy came to me. Filthy. Black markings on his arm. Dressed in damp laundry he'd swiped from a line. Granny's blood dried under his nails."

I gulped back vomit. "Oh, Nanny," I breathed. I'd killed Percy. He'd killed Granny Gwen. Who'd likely mauled the one before her. One day someone would meet me in the woods and continue the cycle. "Changing of the guards," I repeated her words.

"I should've known it'd come one day, her death, my birth—or what should've been. She told me as much. My mama was an infant when Granny Gwen became the beast, left her babies, her husband. I was almost an adult when she finally came back for me. When I didn't change, Daddy thought he'd won. He praised the lord it'd spared me. Mama knew better."

"Nana Maureen," Nana's mama, "told me once before she died I had the blood of a warrior. I thought it was just the crazy talk of an old woman on her deathbed. She knew what I'd become."

"Like my daddy, your mama thought we could stop it. Hoped it was just a tall tale come over from the old country. I knew it was true. I'd seen it with my own eyes. Granny Gwen, my fiery-haired twin. Rounded cheeks, hair like flames licking her pale face. Two years she walked the Arkansas woods, waiting for the day I'd take her place. Mama told everyone she was my cousin come to visit from Ireland."

I stood, paced back to the swing, and plopped. It creaked under my weight. "You lived your whole life knowing this was coming," I said mostly to myself.

"Hopin' it wasn't." She pinched more tobacco from the bag, packing into her pipe. "Your granny Maureen told your mama what you'd be, warned her, told her to find you a proxy—your very own Percy." *Rusty.* "Men folk don't have the soul for it. Too wild. Too uncontrolled."

"Human folk," I said, remembering Avery's words. "I won't change. The rest of my life I'll just be… this." I dropped my head to my hands. "Until someone kills me and takes my place." Not *someone*, my kin. My great grandbaby. Or their poor human proxy.

Smoke swirled over her curly white hair. "Accept what you are, Lynn." I had, honest I had. "Be Cu Sidhe. Be fair. Be righteous. Be with God."

"God? Is God still with *me*?"

She plucked the bowl of peas from the table and went back to work. "God never left you, baby."

"How did *He* let this happen to me? To Percy? To all those before us." There was nothing in the Bible about green fury beasts coming to take unjust souls.

"God lets what needs to happen, happen. It's people who label it good and evil. Divine. Providence." She ran her thumb over the pod, sliding peas out into the bowl. "By the time I met your granddaddy, the whole town knew what'd happened with Percy. They called me a miracle. Said I'd survived a bear—hell, some even blamed the howler. Morticae Higgins was one of them. Eventually, I told him what we are. That my blood is cursed." She watched a welcomed breeze rattle haws loose from their branches. "He chose this spot because of that tree. Fairies live there, he'd say. The day he carved into it, your granddaddy touched my big round belly, and swore he'd be whatever the heavens needed him to be. Let what is to be, be, Lynn."

My head dropped back to rest on the swing. "I hate to break it to you, Nana, but there's no God in what I am."

She scoffed. "Fine, no God. Divinity isn't a man up in the clouds wearin' sandals and a white gown. It's everything that holds the worlds together, baby. It's in your blood."

I let out a heavy sigh, rubbing my burning eyes. "What am I supposed to do about Garret?"

She nodded, grinning around the pipe held in her teeth. "Your great protector," she said. "All that boy needs is a solid woman to keep him grounded, wash his britches, fix his lunch. Love him until the end of his world. He's a good man, Lynn. You've seen to that."

I sat up right and looked at her. "I took his brother from him, Nanny." It hurt to say the words out loud.

She nodded. "You're no monster. I can't tell you what happens next, how to live, how to be the beast you've become. I missed that part. All I can do for you now is be here when you need, love you for what you are, and have breakfast on the table in the morning." She nodded.

"What if I hurt someone I love?" *Again.*

"You are part of Earth's balance. That bit around your neck will keep you safe. Your pure soul will keep safe those you love."

I held the black stone in my hand. "Where'd this come from?" *How'd Percy survive without it?*

"A magic scroll in a chest in the attic." She grinned, her silver tooth shined. "Blood of my blood, you are Cu Sidhe. Your life will be lived keeping the balance of justice. A bringer of death to those deserving. You are not *a beast*. The beast is you. Existing in unity for the greater good."

JIGGEDY–JOG

Hattie's feet bounced against the hand-me-down wicker chest that doubled as a coffee table. "Hey, Lynn, where you been?" Garret clanked around in the kitchen, his new favorite place to let out aggression. *Channel 12 News* played quietly in the background.

"Vistin'." I nodded, no energy for anything else. Summer nights shortened by the day and with each one the beast sank deeper into my soul. It made interacting like everything was normal horrendously difficult.

"Lynn," Garret said, stopping in his tracks to stare at me, two icy bottles clutched in his hand. The sight reminded me of the night of my birthday and my gut fell to my toes. "You staying for dinner?" He swallowed loud enough to hear.

My brother could've busted my nuts for being gone, for not keeping up my end of the bargain to make sure he was fed and his house was clean in exchange for free rent. He didn't. My protector.

"Yeah," I choked, gulping back the idea of Rusty and the memory of that night. "Sounds good."

He grinned, pushing his eyes into crescents. "Great. What'cha makin'?"

"Hilarious." He handed Hattie her beer and me the one meant for him. "I'm really not all that hungry." My stomach rumbled, setting my lying pants ablaze.

"Yeah." He eyed me. "Sandwiches?" It was too damn hot to get the stove going anyway.

I nodded once. He grinned all the way to the kitchen. I sat next to Hattie on our itchy, dated couch. "Thanks for keeping him company." I clanked my bottle to hers.

"Y'all are family." She swigged her beer. "Of course I'd be here."

I raised my brows, a sly smile tugged at my mouth. "*Family*," I joked. My heart soared at the idea that Hattie could one day be my honest-to-goodness sister. Even if I wasn't around to see it.

"If it were me on the dead end of things, Rusty'd be right here where I'm sitting doing the same thing." Always trust Hattie to be brutally honest. No matter how much it hurt. The world could use more people like that. "We're all we got, pumpkin. It's how it's done."

My cleaned plate sat on the edge of our makeshift table. Hattie laughed at something Garret said. Their voices warbled, a station coming through from another dimension. My head trapped in the world of beasts and magic and dead things.

The day had almost passed, and oncoming night stirred inside me. Ancient blood filled my heart with purpose. Sitting in my mostly secondhand living room with the people I loved most in the world, my skin danced with the need to run. Hunt. Kill. A deep yearning to fulfill the one task I was on earth to do.

Gut churned, spine straightened. Purpose tugged at every cell in my body. Yanked my soul to its feet.

"*Authorities are still searching for two missing girls last seen near Cove Lake early this morning...*" I sat forward. "*...leaving a campground with what witnesses say was a park ranger.*" Panting breaths puffed out my nose.

"Lynnie," Garret said, sitting up, brows pulled tight in the middle. "You okay?"

Hattie stared at me like I'd just grown a long wooden nose. "You don't look right."

I turned to look at her. Blinked. Blinked again. Their shamrock faces blinked right back. I shook my head, desperate to rid myself of the beast's vision. "Fine." There's that wooden nose. Heart punching its way from my chest, I took off into a full sprint from the couch. "Not now," I breathed.

"Where you going?" Garret called after me.

I snatched my keys from the table by the door. "Out,"

I said without turning around. "Not. Fucking. Now," I growled when the door slammed shut behind me.

The truck door rattled back at me when I heaved it closed. Garret's old brown trailer washed in mint. "Damn it." I slammed my hand against the wheel. "How am I supposed to drive like this?" I pleaded with whatever would listen.

You must, a stronger version of my own voice echoed in my head. "Where do I go?" My real voice shook. *Drive.*

Knuckles white, wrapped tight around the wheel, I drove as fast as I could up the 309, deep into the hills. Trust was a dangerous thing. Under the right circumstances, it could get you good and dead. Trusting the instincts of the mythological creature stuck inside me brought sweat down my spine. Any more nights like the ones I'd been having and it'd bring shit to my britches if I wasn't careful.

Fear rolled off my skin. I talked to it like it was a living thing. "We're doing this. Scared or not. Scared keeps you safe," I repeated Nana.

Blinding lime-colored sunbeams poked through thick treetops that covered the narrow access road off the highway. A police helicopter whirled somewhere overhead. They wouldn't find them. They couldn't. Not in the thick of those trees. Even the search crew that I knew what was out in those woods hunting wouldn't. Not that I wanted the job, I really didn't. But I knew like I knew how to breathe, I could.

Would.

I parked off the road as much as possible, mostly hidden from view by bushes. "All right, girls, where are you?" I whispered.

No beacon shined from the deepest parts of the forest calling me, pointing the way to them. Electricity danced on my skin, standing tiny hairs on end. It wasn't the girls I was there for. It was *him*. I wasn't the savior. I was vengeance.

I closed my eyes, listening. Not to the birds or the bugs or the wind. I listened to the earth, the universe, the magic that sat inside me anxious to break free.

Run.

Without thought, I tore off, kicking through decaying leaves and twigs underfoot. Supernatural senses picked up the sweet smell of lilac soap among the trees. Followed by the sticky, sweaty stench of a man, a predator. I pushed my legs to move faster, stronger.

Get there. "I'm coming," I panted.

Blood, a coppery scent I could taste on my tongue. A low growl rumbled in my chest. My beast flared to life. The sun still shined, but she clawed her way free. Determined to complete her mission. Our destiny.

I'd find those girls. I'd kill that man.

I couldn't stop. Couldn't slow. Not one second could be wasted. Sharp pointed claws stung my insides. I swiped my shirt over my head, letting it fall to the ground as I ran. Boots slid off easily, slowing only long enough for one swoop each.

A grin curled the corners of my mouth. Crackling over peach fuzz, a vibrant current of magic rolled through to my fingertips. Skin, and hair, and teeth, and bone burst free in one slick slop, spattering the nearby trees with bits of me.

Heavy paws hit, sending debris into the wind. Huffed breaths puffed from my snout. I was death and it felt good.

We ran. Close. So close.

I smelled her blood before I saw it, emerald and coagulated along violet arms. A small body lay in the leaves at his feet. An older girl cried, huddled against a tree, waiting for her turn to die.

Lime drips of blood hit the forest floor. Still as the dead, the girl laying in the dirt smelled like the man more than the blood drying on her little body. He'd been all over her before his blade did its work.

He turned slowly, the shiny tip of a long, sharp knife glinted at me. If my beast had the means to laugh, she would've. Lilac skin stood out like a beacon in the sea of green. My target. Sights set. Fight initiated. My lungs filled and three sharp howling barks shook the earth to its core. *Death's come calling.*

Heart steady. Even breaths. Focused. We stalked. Pacing around him. The true monster. His hand was steady, prepared to kill. Soulless eyes locked onto mine, reflecting back my raging fire. Piss trickled down his leg, soaking through aged-denim jeans.

Strong legs heaved my heavy body from the earth, colliding before he had the chance to turn and run, taking him to ground. He flailed, desperately trying to free himself. Two large front paws stood on his chest. I snarled, snot and spit sprayed into his face. Terror sent his heart into somersaults. Crackling waves of magic drew squiggly olive lines over his skin. Could he feel judgement coming?

One last rally of strength, one moment to save his life. Strong and steady, he slid his knife into my side. I yelped, pain seared through to my core, but the beast didn't waver.

My massive paw swiped across his face, blood spurting feet away. Gurgling screams bellowed from gnarled lips, echoing the agony of the damned. I roared toward the sky, rearing back on powerful hind legs. Long, deadly teeth sank into his throat. Copper filled my mouth.

Not Percy, or the witch women, had tasted so sweet. So sinful.

In that moment he knew pain. We hovered over him—my beast and I—fiery eyes piercing through to his soul. All the deaths before were practice for this moment. What I was born to do. Vengeance.

Blackness, pure as the night sky, poured from his mouth, his eyes, through the hole I'd ripped in his throat. Like a swarm of flies in a vat of oil, slick and endless.

All that darkness pooled into a swirling black cloud above him, dripping sins in long gooey strings. We reared again, one long, piercing shriek. Magic crackled around him, zapping the ends of each of my murky green hairs. His cloud of sin, that filthy black soul, shivered and shook and sucked in on itself. A sickening slurp and *pop*. It was gone. Sent to hell or limbo or wherever we shipped assholes like him off to.

I am vengeance. I am justice. I am death. I am Cu Sidhe. I am the beast and the beast is me.

SAVING GRACE

Soft footsteps moved quickly beside me. Fearless, angry.

The older girl—maybe ten with long brown hair—clutched his knife in her small hand. Her eyes met my beast's golden flames. She didn't look away. Didn't run. I wasn't the monster she'd feared.

Steady, true, the girl held the knife with two small hands, raised it high above her head, and plunged it hilt-deep under his sternum. Her scream, a cleansing, pure thing, rattled heaven itself.

The man was dead, I'd seen to it, but she didn't know that. She needed to see it through.

A tiny heart thumped, faint chugging only I could hear. The little engine, unmoving, but still alive. *Save her.*

We scooped up her limp body in gentle teeth. Let out one snotty huff, preparing our legs and the wound at my side, for the run. We were off.

Dangling from my mouth, the girl's soft, chubby legs dragged along the earth beneath me. There was no choice. Even if I had the power to change back, use human arms to carry her, I'd never make it to the road in time.

It was worth the risk of scraping up her legs. Of getting caught, being seen. To save an innocent. In my soul, I knew that was *me*—little ole Lynnie Russell—running the show. Saving the innocent.

The older girl kept up as best she could, but her breaths were ragged, legs wobbled. We passed my boots, spread feet from each other. My shirt and what was left of my shorts. I'd need them, wanted to stop and add them to the bundle in my jaws. No time.

Instincts sharp, the girl slowed and scooped up my things. We acknowledged her spirit and trudged on, leaving the little one trailing yards behind.

Boots. Voices. Guns clanking in holsters.

I stopped, heart at a full gallop. They'd find her. If I left her right there, they'd come. I'd be gone. I'd be safe. And so would she.

Gently, I lowered the girl to the ground. My wide, rough tongue swiped across her face. Nudged her legs with my snout. Blood still swooshed through her veins, but she didn't move.

Go. Hide.

Brut and shoe leather wafted from not too far off.

Escape.

I huffed, searching the forest for the men who'd come for

them. Back arched, ready to run.

Little Miss Fearless caught up, running to the body on the ground. She dropped my stuff at my feet, sliding on her knees. "Don't go," she begged, holding the girl's head in her hands.

Run.

"Don't leave us." She looked up at me, eyes wet. "Stay."

I couldn't leave them. The beast couldn't get caught. Men with guns would come. Someone would die.

Way down deep inside, I lit the match. *Change.* Churning, rolling, forcing myself from the beast. She'd clawed herself free, I'd do the same.

I'd accepted my fate as death incarnate. I'd done my job. Night would come soon, her time to walk, but it wasn't now. This was my time. And I'd take it by force.

Energy charged through the earth, up my limbs, crackling in my center. The fire inside me roared to life. *My turn.*

Claws, and teeth, and bones, and fur slurped and cracked and popped. The poor girl watched in horror as my shaggy green beast slopped into a naked blonde girl.

I panted, hands gripping the earth, clenching twigs and dirt in my fists. Sharp pain shot through my ribs. I hollered and fell to my side, clutching my ribs. Skin stitched itself together, healing the bone-deep knife wound from the inside out.

Hands shaking, I lifted them from the once gaping hole. Blackened purple speckled a fresh, deep bruise over my kidney. I could've died. *Should've.*

Day changing. Healing fatal wounds. Questions piled one

on top of the other and not a soul in godforsaken Havana could answer them.

"What… are you?" asked the tiniest voice.

I laid on my back, watching fluffy summer clouds float by. Death. "I'm a warrior," I finally answered.

"A warrior," she whispered, soul ignited in strength. The girl would grow to fight her own battles, the demons that would follow her out of the woods and those that'd cross her path later. She'd fight, survive, and win. Without a green beasty to tie her down.

I slid into what was left of my shorts after my change and pulled my shirt over my head, wincing just once when the pain in my side hit hard.

With wimpy human arms, I lifted the little one from the ground and slung her over my shoulder like a bag of dog food—easiest way to carry fifty pounds running.

"Keep up," I said over my shoulder.

We shuffled as quickly as I could manage through the woods. They'd find us. The men. They'd find us and they'd save her. It was a hope, a prayer, more than a knowing.

A man hollered, "Grace?" It echoed, shaking birds from the trees surrounding us. "Hope?"

Breaths heavy, almost not enough to shout. "I've got them," I said. "We're here."

White speckles filled my vision. I needed my beast, her strength, our power. *Help.* I fell to my knees, cradling the lifeless body in my arms. "We're here," I panted.

The older girl shoved through, disappearing into the bushes toward the sound of their footsteps. "Help," she shouted. "My sister is dying."

Dying. Not dead. Not yet.

They barreled through, two men and the strongest little girl I'd met in my life. "Oh my... Lord have mercy." The men stared at us for a heartbeat. Two.

"She's alive," I breathed, the world turning gray.

The guy in the Brut plucked the girl from my arms. Free from her weight, they reached for her. A motherly instinct I didn't know I possessed. He left us there, running as quickly as his boots would allow, shouting to whoever could hear him that he needed help.

I fell to my hands, sucking in air, willing myself to stay conscious. Adrenaline was fleeting, leaving me spent, half dead myself.

"You're a hero," the man said, resting a hand on my shoulder.

The little girl squatted down beside me, looked up at him and said, "She's a warrior."

HOPE RESTORED

Machines beeped from rooms down the hall. Dehydrated. Worn and tired and ready for sleep. Sunset was only hours off and there I sat, yet again, alone in a cold hospital bed.

"You're lucky you're not dead." The officer's radio squelched and he turned it down.

I looked out the window at the evening sun. "Yeah." *Heard that before.*

"You're a hero. Hope survived because of you." He shook his head. "A downright superhero. Little thing like you overpowering a grown man." His head shook over and over, trying to make sense of it.

It wouldn't make sense. Not really. Not without the cold hard truth and I wasn't about to hand that over. I needed to get out. I needed a lie. A hideout. Anything.

Eventually someone would realize I was the very same girl they'd plucked from the woods bloody and dirty and lucky to be alive—not unlike another young woman sixty-odd years ago. Questions would come. I'd need to drudge up some answers.

"Hell, I wouldn't be surprised if God Himself came down from heaven to shake your hand." Highly doubted that. "You're no hero. You're an angel come right down from heaven. Saving the innocent. Smiting the wicked."

Damning the unjust, all in a hard day's work. *I'm no angel. I'm death, baby. Ain't no doubt about that.*

"I'm really fine." I sat up, thinking twice about yanking the IV from my arm like they did in the movies. "I don't need to be here."

The officer stepped forward with his hand out. "Now, miss, you need to stay right there until the doc comes in. You've hardly been conscious since they found y'all out there in the woods." He watched as I eyed my arm, ready to yank. "Just calm down. You're not in any kind of trouble."

Yet. "Yeah. Yeah. I just… I don't like hospitals." My name echoed through his radio, so low I wondered if he heard it himself. The jig was up.

I wrapped my fingers around the tube in my arm and jerked. Pain whizzed up my arm. White specks were back. Bare legs swung off the edge of the bed, my head swimming.

"Miss, sit down, you're going to fall, now." The officer's face washed white.

"I'm fine," I growled. Legs wobbled.

"Miss Russell. You're back." The handsome doctor flashed

his white California grin. "And just as quick to leave." His dark eyes moved to my arm.

I clamped my hand over the stream of blood that leaked from the new hole I'd made. "Just wanna get out of here, Doc."

He nodded at the officer to leave us alone and pushed the door shut behind him. "Let's just have a seat so I can check your vitals and you can be on your way." The doc laid a warm, reassuring hand on my shoulder.

I huffed—not nearly as menacing as the beast—and slid back onto the bed.

"I'm fine."

"Mm." He listened to my heart, watching my face for every terrifying second. He'd hear her in there, my beast. I knew it. Maybe he'd missed her the first go round, but there was no way I'd get out free twice.

He lifted my shirt, touching my back with a cold instrument. "Breathe deep." Not a mention of the new, fully healed ink I'd acquired since he'd seen me just days ago.

I pulled in a gulp of air and winced.

"This happen today?" Gently, he prodded the bruise on my side.

He'll know if you lie. "Yeah."

"Looks painful."

Should've seen how it started. "I'll be fine."

"So you've said." He leaned close, looking at my eyes with a penlight. He smelled like molasses and sunshine. "Having vision problems?"

Fuck. "Nope." *I wouldn't call it a* problem.

He nodded. "Mhm."

"Can I go now?" Sticky blood dried in the crook of my arm.

"So eager to get away from me?" Shining grin flashed again and he ran his hand through wavy dark hair. A gesture that burned my throat with guilty bile.

"It's been a long week."

"I'd say. From miracle to hero. You've been busy."

A smile crinkled the edges of his eyes, putting him closer to thirty than my twenty. Handsome, young doctor just a town away. Mama would've kicked me in the shin if she knew I was ready to walk away from such a catch.

I breathed. "You have no idea."

He leaned against the counter. "Why don't you tell me?"

I slid off the bed. "You wouldn't believe me if I did." It slipped out. I hadn't meant to say it. Secrets can only stay in for so long before they squeaked out. Like a fart that way, I reckon.

His hand fell heavy on my shoulder. I shot him a look that I worried might've lit my eyes aflame. He blinked at me. "You'll need to sign this release?" The doc lifted the stone at my throat—examining it before letting it fall to my chest. "And let me clean up your arm."

The clipboard he handed me had my information on it. "What's this?"

He swiped a cold cloth down my arm. "A release. Says you're leaving against medical advice." A cotton ball pressed to the spot, he pulled a bright cartoon bandage across it. "And when I call you later, you'll answer."

That's a good man, Lynnie Russell. Mama's voice rang in my head. But Rusty Kemp had my heart and it ached to imagine another man taking over.

"I'm out tonight." *Every night.*

He sighed, sucked his teeth. "Well… a deputy had offered you a ride to your vehicle."

"Where'd they take my truck?" I'd been in no state to drive and got to the hospital riding passenger in a cop car.

"I'd assume it's where you left it." He stepped close enough only I could hear him. "They didn't realize who they had when they found you." Glad he couldn't hear my racing heart anymore, I stared at him. "Odd, right? A little thing like you…," he repeated the officer.

"I need to be getting on, now."

"Let me take you." He raised his brows. "I assume you'd rather not sit in another police cruiser for the ride home?"

He assumed right. "I'll call for a ride, thanks."

Dark curls bounced on his head. "No time." I glanced at the clock. "The sheriff is on his way here now. He'll be here any minute."

I stepped back. "Why are you helping me?" The beast perked up.

"I've never met another like you."

That's an understatement. "It's likely you won't."

"Is that a yes?"

"How are we getting outta here?"

"Let me deal with that." He pulled a small white pill from his pocket. "I brought you a pill and not a needle. You're welcome." I looked at it, then at him, and back again. "It's for your side. It hurts like hell, right?" I nodded. "This will make it all better."

Nothing could make any of this *all better*. "What is it?"

He handed it to me and poured water into a small plastic cup. "I'm a doctor, Lynnie. You can trust me."

"Not as far as I can throw you."

"He's a good man, Lynn," Rusty's voice warbled through the ether.

Deep brown eyes sparkled. "Good girl. I'll make you a hot deal. You take that, and we can leave right now." Heavy boots and police radios echoed through the door. "It's a simple painkiller. To take the edge off."

"Trust him." I spun around, expecting to see my boy leaning against the wall in his faded blue jeans.

Voices whispered my name outside the door. I turned back to the doc, pinched my lips between my teeth. "Shit." I popped the pill in my mouth and swallowed it back.

The doc shoved me toward the closet and pushed me in, closing the door.

"Sheriff Crocker," the doc said, voice muffled through the thin wood.

"Doc. Where's our girl?" His voice was gruff, and the way he said girl made the beast roll over twice.

I breathed heavy, sucking up the oxygen that small space allowed. My heart should've been pounding as fear tickled along my skin, but it slowed. Beating sloppily in my chest.

"Ah, just missed her. Off in imaging." Long, awkward pause. "But I think there's someone else you'd like to meet. Hope is out of surgery. Grace and her parents are with her on the second floor." Their voices moved away. "Let me take you there."

Ear pressed against the flimsy wood, I waited for the door to shut. "Rusty," I whispered and waited in breathless silence for his response. "Rusty?" My voice caught in my throat, squeaking at the end. "Come back," I breathed, forehead pressed against the closet door.

Church bells in the distance chimed six o'clock. Time was quickly running low.

On suddenly wobbly legs, I shoved from the closet, nearly falling to my knees. The world shifted, turning crooked then back again. I blinked it away, steadying myself.

I looked down at my bare legs. "Pants," I slurred.

They'd been mostly shredded when I changed, but they were enough to cover my ass so I could make my great escape without drawing too much attention. I tore through the blankets, in the closet, under the bed.

"What in the—" I swayed.

The door popped open. "Ready?" My grinning doc stood behind a wheelchair. A pair of blue cotton pants folded neatly in the seat. "I'd suggest you slip into these." He tossed them my way and I missed them completely. "Oh, that's fun." His grin widened.

I leaned against the bed for balance, sliding my numbing legs into the pants. "Where's the sheriff?"

Doc held my arm, helping me to the chair. "Don't worry about him. Let's get you out of here."

My head flopped back and I watched his Adam's apple bounce when he said goodnight to the nurse at the station.

He wheeled me to the elevators and right out the front door.

"How are you feeling?" he asked, clicking the seat belt into place.

I giggled, looking him in the eye an inch from my face. "I've been building some thoughts and I'm thinkin' there just might be something wrong with my head here." I patted my head, smashing my wild hair. "What's wrong with me, Mr. Doctor?"

A dimple dug deep into his cheek when he grinned. "Puck."

"What now?"

He shut the door and walked around to the driver side. "My name is Puck." The engine roared to life. "Not *Mr. Doctor*. And I do believe that's the medication taking effect in your system."

I breathed through my nose, heavy and loud. "You said… I just took that."

"The effects of the sedative I gave you typically take thirty minutes, or roughly the time it takes for it to metabolize. In *humans*."

Breath ceased. My gut dropped right to my ass. *Sedative? Humans?* "If I ain't human, then what am I?" I laughed like I wasn't filled to the brim with terror. "An alien?" I rolled my heavy head to the side, watching his dark eyes.

Mr. Doctor Puck didn't look away from the road. "An alien you're not." My chin quivered. "You're no angel either." Vomit bobbed in my throat. "You're not a miracle or a hero." *Don't say it. Don't say monster.* "You're death." A painful breath burst from my lungs. "You are Cu Sidhe."

WHAT'S UP, DOC?

Trees whizzed by out the window, spinning my already swimming head into a tizzy. Words came in jumbled letters, a tornado of senseless lines and curves.

"Who…?" Blood whooshed in my ears, slow, thick, an engine desperate for fresh oil.

"Who am I? I am an ally. A friend."

Friends don't secretly drug each other. "Drugs…." Forcing my eyes to stay open, I fought sleep—refused to let myself be taken without a fight. It was a losing battle.

"How's the side?" *Ironically, pain free.* "I'm so very sorry about the ruse." He gave no more explanation.

My eyes closed against my will. I fought the drugs dragging me deeper into darkness. Focus. Feel. Search for the beast. She was there, waiting, trapped in my fog. I needed her. Needed the magic that bound us. Without it I was just a little thing.

Falling jarred me awake; my limbs jerked. I blinked the world into focus. Puck leaned into my window; his ridiculously white smile glowed in my face.

"Good morning, sunshine. Welcome back."

Wordless grumbling proved I wasn't quite back.

He opened my door and unclipped my belt. "Let's go. We're here."

Regardless of what the deputy may have said, I wasn't *that* little, but Puck hauled me from my seat and tossed me over his shoulder like I was. He pushed the door shut with his foot. I watched helplessly as the car got smaller and smaller, bouncing against his shoulder while he bounded up steps.

Cedar, sharp and pungent. Wood floor. A cabin. "Where?"

"My home. For now." His voice showed no sign that he had a hundred-some-odd pound woman slung over his shoulder. "Here we are, a nice comfy place to relax." He laid me down gently on a couch with a scratchy cushion that reminded me of home. "You'll be feeling more like yourself soon, I'm certain, so let's get this show on the road."

Puck sat at the end of the couch, lifted my limp legs and laid them across his lap. My blue cotton pants—property of Danville Hospital—clashed with worn leather boots. Mystery stains marked the front of my white shirt. He pulled my boots off, exposing sweaty feet tipped with month-old blue polish.

Strong hands squeezed my toes together and stopped. "Hm, let's just dry these off for you," he said, wiping a wool blanket over them and between each toe.

Weak, I lifted my hand and raised a middle finger.

"I like your enthusiasm." He worked his thumbs into my arches. "Now, time is of the essence, so I won't waste it." Fingers pinched and wiggled each little piggy. "I need you. And if you're honest with yourself, you need me too. I think the fact that you've already got the attention of local law enforcement proves that theory."

I couldn't keep my eyes open. If he wanted me conscious for this chat, he'd need to stop rubbing my feet. Even the beast had mellowed.

"I've been waiting a long time for you, Carolynn Russell."

I groaned. "Lynnie."

"Cute. One of the most powerful beings on Earth... Lynnie." He sighed. "You and I are alike, Miss Russell. It wasn't chance running into each other. I knew you were coming. It was just a matter of time." I needed my voice, trapped inside a chemical cocoon. So many questions. "Not like Percy. That, my dear, let me tell you, was the work of serendipity." *Percy.* "Nice fellow, but not what I needed. Human, I'm sure you know. He did the best he could under the circumstances. They are *not* built for even temporary immortality. There is definitely a reason the universe made them finite." A quiet sigh and silence. "Anyway, I waited and you came. I didn't know it would be a beautiful blonde. I'm going to call that a win."

One eye opened a slit. "Bite me," I slurred.

"Maybe later. Right now, I need you to hear me. We belong together." *No, I'll bite you. Hard.* "Not a sex thing—unless you're into that—but a partnership. Two immortals—

mostly, on your end—doing the best they can under the circumstances."

I shook my head once. "Nope."

"I can teach you how to control it." I swallowed. "It's confused. Right?" How was I supposed to know? "Coming out at sunset? Rumbling, pacing, clawing to be free? Not quite yours and not quite its own." Nod. "Cu Sidhe is fae. A beast not fit for man. It's spent decades trapped, sharing a human existence. Bound by the lunar cycle like some meager werewolf. You are where it belongs. It's home."

Huff. "She."

"Yes, right. Silly me. *She* is remembering who she is, learning who you are. Give her time. And my help."

I smacked my dry mouth. "I'm listening." Not that I had a choice in the matter.

"You need a friend, Miss Russell, and I am here to fill that position."

I had a friend. Hattie. And Garret. Nana. Even if they all knew my secret, how would they ever understand? How could I expect them to?

"Let me help you."

Gulp. "Why?"

He ran his hand up my pant leg and squeezed my calf. Tension released, warm tendrils swirled under my skin.

"Because we are the same. Fantastical beasts so far from home."

"Be happy." Heavy lids popped open, scanning as far as my eyes would reach for him. For Rusty.

"I can help you keep them safe." I looked at him, waiting

for him to say his name. "Your family. Your brother. I know what you fear. And rightfully so. Garret means so much to you."

Adrenaline cut through the fog, zapping the magic that swirled inside me. I sat up, pulling my feet from him. "How do you know about my brother?" *My fears?*

He rested a hand on my leg. "I've been around for a long time. Longer than your beast even. I know of fear. I know too how to read a patient file." His head dropped into my lap and he looked up at me, white grin shining. "I have a feeling you're going to learn to love me." He booped my nose and I jerked away in slow motion.

"I have a feeling night is coming and you're about to get real dead real quick."

He chuckled. "I'm fairly certain—at least I hope—that Xanax I gave you will keep your beasty at bay for a little while longer." Long fingers twirled my hair. "Quicker in, quicker out. That hardy fae blood. You can thank your human parents for the receptor." He laughed.

I flopped back against the couch. "A fairy doctor," I garbled. "What's next? *Leprechauns?*"

He stood up. "We are not going there." Hand on his hips, he leaned over me. "It's all part of the game, babe." He winked. "Mr. Doctor." One loud bark of a laugh burst out and he planted his hands either side of me. "You need me. You need what I am. What I do."

Wind kicked the door open to the wall. I jumped. He dropped his head and inch from mine and groaned. "Fuck."

His hair flittered around my face. Soft brown curls twisted

together. Wailing echoed off high ceilings and up the stairs to the second floor.

White sheer fabric billowed in through the doorway, flapping against the jamb. Long, wet snake-like tendrils whipped in spiraled pieces.

"Damn, Bean Sidhe, mind your affairs," he grumbled, still leaned over top of me.

Avery's contorted face, mouth stretched into an oval, eyes white, shimmered, shifted, and morphed into the blue-eyed girl I remembered.

"Padraic O'Kain," she said, her thick accent rolling his name like a perfectly executed smoke ring.

He closed his eyes, breathed deep, and stood. "Yes, Satan?"

She scoffed. "Right. Come, Lynn, you don't belong here." A slender hand reached for me.

He cupped a hand around his ear. "I think I hear a Milesian taking his last breath." And shooed her with both hands.

Her eyes flashed white. "After all this time, you still think you can tame this beast? She is not yours to toy with."

Puck let out a rumbling huff. "Neither yours."

She stepped closer. "For generations I've been charged with guiding the Cu Sidhe through the transition. For generations I've protected it from the likes of you. It is not my toy. It's my duty."

"Ha! Duty? It didn't take long before Percy—the human—was out in the world all alone. This *duty* is your punishment. Don't pretend it's anything more."

Eyes white, she seethed. "Come, girl, night approaches."

Avery reached out for me one last time, never taking her eyes off Puck.

He crossed his arms over his chest, white smile smug. "She's broken the lunar tether. Cu Sidhe is fae again. No thanks to her Bean Sidhe fairy godmother."

One solid huff puffed from Avery's nose. "Does she know?" Puck tilted his head. "Who'd you use, eh? Someone she loves? Her brother?" She stopped, looked at me and back to him. "Oh, you… godshite púca."

"I'm right here," I said, finally sitting up. Chemical fog still weighed heavy on my head, but I'd gotten my wits about me. *Quick in. Quick out.* "Stop talking about me like I'm a damn child."

Avery jammed her fists to her hips. "Did your boy come to you today?" *Rusty.* I nodded. "Say nice things about your old friend Puck?"

My heart flipped twice. "Yes."

Avery looked at Puck, eyed him as if to force a confession. Puck shrugged, a sly grin curling his lips. "It's what I do. It's harmless."

"Harmless? He's a trickster, Lynn. He lies. He swindles. It's what he does."

My beast rolled and stretched. Still with some time left before true sunset, she stirred as fear and anger boiled inside. "What're you sayin'?"

"Never trust a púca."

Puck threw his hands in the air and groaned. "Oh, cry me a fucking river and *drown in it*." He glared at her. "Too late."

Avery's hair blew back from her face, phantom wind

billowing her dress around her legs. "Padraic O'Kain is a liar," she declared like it would send him straight to hell. I had it on good authority that wasn't how it worked.

A knot clenched in my gut. I looked at the clock. Hardly seven. Late August sun still blazed outside. She'd break out on her own soon if I didn't willingly let her free. "Guys," I croaked.

"Your duty is done. Mission accomplished."

"She doesn't belong to you."

"You're right. She's a free agent."

They argued. Bickering as if I wasn't about to burst slimy green fur from my skin. "Guys," I said again, louder this time.

"No, not free. She also has a duty. A *mission*," Avery hissed.

"Death dog, got it. All I want is to be her friend."

"Friend? Right. How'd that work out for Gwen?"

"What?" Pain stabbed through my center, doubling me over. Magic crackled over my skin. If I didn't run, I'd be trapped in that house with those... people and there was no telling what I'd do to them. Immortal? I wouldn't stick around to find out.

A whining growl rumbled from my throat. I jumped from the couch, shoving past them and out the front door. Bare feet slapped warm earth. She stretched, filling me to the brim.

Avery's wails echoed among the trees, off the jagged rocks that lined the trail. She wasn't far behind. Galloping followed. Heavy, quick. Hooves beat along with the pumping of my heart. My beast reared inside, recognizing the sound. The scent.

I looked back, desperate to see the animal that tracked me. A shining black stallion. Eyes, yellow lightning bugs. Its breaths came hard, steady. I'd never lose it at my pace.

The earth stopped underfoot. My legs cycled like in a Wile E. Coyote cartoon. Water rushed below. Hundreds of feet to fall, I'd never survive. My back arched, fingers splayed. Skin and hair and teeth erupted. Free from her human cage, the beast readied herself for impact.

We sunk deep, claws disrupting mossy soil as we shoved back to the surface. Strong, relentless, we defied the current. Sure strokes paddled the surface, hind legs propelled our weighty body to shore.

Alive. Both in nature and in spirit.

Golden sun spilled over the tops of the cliff, one last grab for daylight. The black steed stood at its edge, looking down at me. Avery's screeching song called to the beast. She ignored the banshee's words, staring up at the horse, daring it to jump.

"My apologies, old friend." Puck's ghostly voice floated across the water.

The beast dipped her head and let out one grunted snuffle. Indifference. She didn't need Puck, or Avery; her burdens had been longstanding. Lynnie Russell, on the other hand, dreadfully needed an ally.

To be Avery's duty, her penance for some unknown crime, or Puck's friend, his pupil—his plaything. A choice I'd need to make fast. With the sheriff sniffing around my crotch—so to speak—I didn't have time to weigh the options.

ALLIES

Always out yonder, never close enough to see her, Avery's keening echoed. An eerie soundtrack for a green beasty stalking by silver moonlight.

We'd left the horse high on its perch before the sun was completely gone. Nothing to hunt, no wicked to be smote—smited?—we walked, padding lazily downstream, noticing the cooling soil squeezed between our toes. Night birds whistled, harmonizing with croaking frogs squatted on the bank. The wails of my Bean Sidhe guide faded, a distant rhythm lost in the raucous choir.

No longer bound by our lunar tether, according to Puck, my beast could come and go as she pleased. Which clearly wouldn't do being that she was a big green monster. I'd live my fate, bear the burden, but I'd do it on my terms. Control was what I needed. Precise, concentrated control.

Inside my beastly prison, I breathed, focusing on every otherworldly cell from the tips of our fuzzy ears to the ends of deadly claws.

Stretch. Soft soil crumbled underfoot, claws curling into the earth. Back arched, ass in the air, our tail whooshed, slapping the water. Match struck.

Focus. One at a time, each clawed toe popped, pushing slender fingers from wooly paws. Fire ignited.

Change. Micro jolts of electricity zapped beneath our dense skin, tickling the barrier between us. Our long, thickly braided tail whipped around my front legs in defiance. *Its.* Ribs spread. *My.* Slick, slimy skin stretched. Tail retracted, yanking me from hands and knees.

I fell, face in the dirt. "Shit," I cursed. Tingling crackles zipped across my toes, remnants of magic well spent. A grin spread wide. I rolled over to my back, staring up at the moon. "Hello, old girl. Miss me?" She stared right back.

Bathing in moonlight, I laid there, dreaming of the day I could come and go at will. Puck's promise to help me learn who and what and how played in my head.

Rustling behind me caught my attention. I sat up. Naked, I crouched on one knee as I waited, watching the brush line.

The pain in my side was gone. I twisted to see, the black bruise had faded to a pale pink. Shoved out with the beast.

Twigs snapped in the darkest shadows. Yellow eyes glowed. Too small to be my stallion. I crept closer, inching toward it. "Come on out," I called, curiosity a beast of its own taking me over.

I'd never been fearful of critters, big or small. As a beastly thing myself, I was anxious for access to their world.

"I ain't gonna hurt you."

A long black snout pushed from the berry bush. Two round puffs for ears. A bear cub. No bigger than a hound.

Smile wide, I couldn't help but crawl closer. "Are you lost, little one? Or you got a mama out here somewhere waiting to gobble me up?" Could I call on the beast in time to protect me from Mama Bear?

The cub wiggled through the brush. I sat in the dirt, legs folded under me. Still. Waiting. Fearless, his little legs trotted to me. Slowly, I reached out, swiped a hand over his head. Wiry fur rougher than it looked. He moved closer, nuzzled against my chest, and plopped down in my lap, belly up.

"You're certainly brave." I scratched his belly, giving it a sweet, hollow pat. "I can't wait to tell Garret—" I stopped short. He couldn't know. I'd never be able to explain how I come up on it in the first place. "Guess you'll be my little secret. One of them."

He looked up at me, deep brown eyes locked onto mine. *"My apologies, old friend."*

Waves of silvery light surrounded the cub. My heart stopped. I shoved it away, scurrying back until my hands hit the water. "What in the—?"

The light warbled, shifting, a blob taking no shape, but equally many. A single breath in time and *snap*.

"Are you fucking kidding me?" I jumped to my feet.

Puck shook tufts of black fur from his shoulders. "That was an adventure." White grin, hands planted on his hips. Also naked. "I thought we'd never ditch the harpy."

"You're," I panted, "a goddamned *bear*?" The beast shouldered my insides in agreeance.

He tipped his head. "I'm a lot of things."

I took a step back. "You're the stallion."

"You better believe it."

Red flushed my cheeks. I wrapped my arms around my bits as much as I could. Puck didn't. In fact, I think he poked it out toward me just a smidge.

"What do you want from me?" I moved into a shadow, away from the telling moonlight.

He shook his head. "Just to be your friend. It's lonely. Earthly life. You may not feel it yet, but you will." Blue light cast shadows over his face. Sad, longing.

"Why me? Why not... Avery?"

He laughed, one loud belly shaker. "You're young so I'll let that one go. Just know, we're not close." His bright grin glowed.

"Do you ever not smile?"

Shrug. "Why? Don't like smiling?"

I did. Who didn't? Just didn't have much to grin over as of late. "Why'd you drug me? Trick me?"

Long legs stepped closer. "I couldn't risk the dog getting loose." I snarled at his remark. "And I'm sorry. I needed you to trust me and that was the only way."

"Why him? Why Rusty?" His name hardly squeaked out.

"He was there anyway. He was easy. And you'd follow him off the end of the earth." The last was cold hard fact.

"What'd'you mean he was there?" My somersaulting heart did a handstand.

"He's always there. Just under the surface. Or is it above it? I'm not sure which. I digress." Puck held his hands out in surrender. "I borrowed his voice, but I did it for you. If you hadn't trusted me, you'd be in county lockup tearing the heads off those innocent deputies."

More truth. I swallowed hard. "Can you see him?" The desperation in my voice made me cringe.

He raised his brows, creasing deep forehead lines. "Oh, Rusty, no. He's just… there." Puck shrugged, an exaggerated movement that wiggled most everything that was loose. I looked away. "Before we can do anything, you're going to have to get quite used to your own body. All bodies, actually. Clothes are manmade; they won't shift with you." He chuckled and strolled around me. "In fact, once I had to walk naked through— Another day." His hand swiped the idea away. "For now, this. You need an ally. A true guide. Not some keening woman pretending she's something she's not. You're getting stronger. You'll outgrow this place. When you do, where will you go? Who will be your people?" He stood behind me, resting his chin on my shoulder. "You are the most coveted creature in both worlds. Cu Sidhe hasn't seen her home in centuries. I could make that happen for her. For you. I could show you the wo—that movie really undid that whole phrase." His breath soft on my neck, he added, "There's so much you don't know. Let me show you."

"How can I refuse an offer like that?" I breathed, slow and steady. Emotions controlled. Beast at ease. "What about Avery?"

"She'll move on to more pressing matters."

I chewed on my cheek. "Why does she hate you?"

He clicked his tongue and stepped away. "Hate is a human emotion. Loathing is a burden on a timeline such as ours. Indifference is far more palatable." My beast knew that

well. "Besides, her only reason for hanging around has little
to do with you and me, and everything to do with saving her
own ass. Meeting her quota. Doing her time, as they say."

I was her punishment. "What was her crime?"

He sighed, looking up at the moon. "You know, it's been
so long, I'm not sure I recall. Perhaps one day she'll spill
those proverbial beans over a glass of rosé and girl talk." He
took two confident steps toward me. "Let me take you out
of here."

"I can't leave. My family." I let my arms drop.

He shook his head. "If not now, when? When you're still
twenty years old in ten years? After you've been caught, shot
in the ass by a hunter or worse?" Hand wrapped around my
chin. "After you've hurt someone you love?" I jerked my head
away. "You can't hurt me. Try as you might, babe. No man or
beast. Not." He tapped my nose. "Even. You."

Losing Rusty should have killed me. Surviving after
that was my penance. If something happened to Garret...
I couldn't stay in Havana. Loving them meant letting them
be.

"No more lies." I met his eyes. "No more bullshit. Truth.
Loyalty." He nodded. "I may not be able to kill you, but I'll
bet I could hurt you real, *real* bad."

A cocky grin carved dimples in his cheeks. "Deal." He
spit into his hand and held it out to me.

I sucked my teeth. Choice? Did I ever really have one?
Our spitty hands slapped together in solidarity. "Deal."

Window-shattering, screeching howls silenced the night
creatures. Glowing white fabric whipped, winding through
trees, flapping over shrubs. "You've made your choice, Cu.
Live in it," Avery chortled, a sinister brook, bubbling over

smooth stone.

I spun, searching the darkness for her. "I had no choice. I have to survive. They have to live," I shouted.

"And live they shall," she wailed, the last trailing off with the breeze.

"Shit. Shit. Shit." I stamped my foot, slamming my heel into a jagged rock. "Fuck."

Puck's hands gripped my arms. Soft brown curls fell over his forehead. "Dra-ma-tic." I scowled at him. "The banshee," he assured. "Look, I can't promise the decades will be easy, but they will certainly be entertaining. What more could you ask for?"

A normal life as a normal girl. "I'm not sure I even like you as a person just yet, Doc."

Dimples. "The first thing we need to get very clear, don't call me Doc."

My eyes narrowed to Eastwood slits. "That was a lie too."

"A suggestion. To live. To survive. Lies become necessities. The world's changed over the course of my existence. We can't hide anymore. We're not feared anymore."

"Maybe not you."

Dark eyes moved over me, glancing down and back up again. "Touché. Like me or don't tonight. I take time to grow on you."

"Like a fungus."

He closed the gap, lips an inch from mine. "Like a pair of perfect breasts."

Breaths swirled between us. One. Two. "I'll eat you whole."

"Promise."

"Dare me."

LONG GONE

Puck's T-shirt hung loose around my shoulders. He didn't have a pair of pants small enough for me, so I wore a floppy pair of drawstring shorts and my beat-up boots. I'd whipped my uncombed hair into a knotted bun.

My rusty, steel truck bounced along the potholes that dotted Nana's dirt drive. Clay dust billowed out from under my tires like muddy fog. It was hard to see which way was up, but I knew where I was going. Stopping a few yards from the twisted old hawthorn, I put her in Park. When the dust settled, Garret's motorcycle sat in front of Nana's porch.

"Shit on a hot shingle," I mumbled and considered backing out and screeching away.

The ratty screen door flew open and out popped my spitfire of a brother. His white undershirt made his bare arms look darker than they really were. Faded Levi's and boots, he looked like my damn daddy barreling out the door hollering at me, except Daddy was usually hollering at Mama.

"Sharlene Carolynn Diamond Russell, you get your butt outta that cab and in this house, *now*. I been all over this county searching for you. You know you got the sheriff out looking? They're wantin' to talk to you about those girls up at Cove Lake." Garret shouted all the way to the truck, flinging open the door. He grabbed hold of my arm, pulling me from the seat.

"I got it, Garret. Let me free." I jerked my arm away. "Just 'cause you're older than me doesn't mean you get to play Daddy." I was death incarnate; who the hell was he to boss me?

The loose bolts rattled when I heaved the door closed. Shoving past him, I stomped up the steps. His boots echoed behind me. He let the screen slam behind us.

"Lynnie, you better have a damn good story." He spun me around by my arm and pointed a calloused finger in my face.

"You better believe it." I grinned, calling on Puck's confidence.

"I sure would like to hear it." Nana wiped her hands on her apron. "Coffee's on." Calm, collected, she hadn't been worried. She knew where I'd be, that I could take care of myself. Mostly.

"So would I." Garret folded his arms across his chest. Biceps flexed, tightening his shirt sleeves.

"Don't you have a sweetheart waiting on you somewhere?" I hadn't truly been talking about Hattie. Garret always had *some* girl waiting on him.

"Hattie's gone off to work." The fact that he thought I meant her wrapped my heart in hope. "I called in sick on account of you. Where've you been? It weren't no joke about that law. I wouldn't play around with that sort of thing. They're looking for you. Said you saved those little girls from that man. Said you're some kinda hero, or maybe something else. What'd you go do?"

A lump of a lie bobbed in my throat. I'd thought it over and over on the drive from Puck's to my truck, dug through each word on the way to Nana's. It still stuck behind my tongue. "I had to do *something*," I croaked. "Those girls… after Rusty… I couldn't let my saved life go to waste. I just got lucky, Garret. Maybe it was God, I don't know. But they're safe and that's all that matters."

"And the man?" He stepped forward until we were nose to nose. "There's something ain't right about all this. That sheriff came to the house this morning with some wild stories and you're at the center of all of them. Did you know those women in the woods with you and Rusty?" He didn't let me answer. "Well, every damn one of them is missing. Yeah, *missin'*."

Ghosts of curses past. "What do you want me to do about it?"

"Sheriff's department can't make heads or tails of it. Bodies don't just up and go missing." He paced away from me and back again. "They want to know why you lived, why you lived and they didn't. They wanna know how you found those girls in the woods." His voice got louder until it was an all-out bellow. "They said you killed that man that took 'em. They're talking like maybe you got something to do with Rusty," he screamed in my face.

Jaw tight, I said through gritted teeth, "I suggest you get outta my face, brother."

He huffed once and spun away. "And where you been for the last twelve-odd hours?"

"I just drove around. I went to the lake."

"We searched the lake." He squinted.

"Well, I wasn't there the whole time. Garret, can't you just let me be? God, you're just like Mama."

"Well," he planted his hands on his hips and shimmied his head, "somebody's gotta be. She'll be here just as soon. Her shift ended about an hour ago."

I stepped back, mouth wide, betrayed. "Garret Llewellyn Russell, you did not call our mama into this! You son of a—"

"Carolynn, you watch that mouth in this house," Nana scolded me from the kitchen.

"You bet I did. You're just plum out of control. I love you, Lynn, but I can't do this. I can't control you."

I slammed my fists to my hips. "You're right. You can't because I'm a grown-ass woman, not a child, and I can come and go as I please. You need to worry about you and Hattie, and your life. Stop fussing over me, so help me."

He stuck his chest out and leaned into me. "I'm supposed to be taking care of you."

"Damn it, Garret, you get your nose outta my business or I'll bite it off," I shouted, spit flying across his face.

"Get your butt in line or I'll kick it straight."

We squared off.

A growl rolled out my throat. "You have no idea what you're getting into."

His eyes went wide. An audible gulp bounced his Adam's apple.

"Oh," Nana wheezed from behind us. "Oh, Lynnie." Her voice just a smidge above a whisper.

I glared at Garret a second longer before I turned away to see what Nana was panting about. One ringed hand clenched her apron, the other pressed against her chest. Her face as white as Avery's gown. In the time it took for me to take a breath and lose it again, she toppled to the ground. Her thin legs gave way, top-heavy body falling forward. She didn't so much as reach out to brace herself. I lunged to catch her and missed. She hit the hardwood with a thud that brought bile up the back of my throat.

I was at her side and rolled her over before Garret even knew what'd happened. "Nanny, Nanny, are you okay?" She wasn't okay. Nothing would ever be okay.

"What is it?" Garret's panicked voice boomed over the top of me.

"Open your eyes, Nana. Look at me."

Her lids fluttered and hazy blue eyes rolled, no focus. Breaths came ragged. I closed my eyes, concentrated on the sounds of the room. Under the whir of the swamp cooler, her heart slow, out of time. Dying.

Shit. Fuck. Shit. No. No.

I opened my eyes to meet their reflection in her milky blues. Fiery embers. Garret leaned over behind me, heavy breaths heating my neck.

She grinned, flashing her silver tooth one last time. "Oh, there you are," she said, hardly even moving her lips.

The hairs on my arms stood on end, sending shivers down my spine. She breathed, letting out a lot of air, more than she took in. Her smile faded. A quick breath rocked her chest. A long exhale followed.

"Nanny." The tiny voice coming from somewhere far away was my own. "Nanny?" I gripped the front of her dress. Under the whir of the swamp cooler, my heart shattered.

There were no more breaths. No more smiles. No more Nana.

Shaking hands refused to touch her lifeless skin. Deep, agonizing wails poured from my lungs. Garret whined, a sickening sound, high in his throat.

She died in her living room while I argued with Garret. She stood behind us scared and alone.

I shook my head, over and over, demanding the universe bring her back. The broken pieces in my chest sparked to life. Eyes blurred with tears, I reared, and a howl burst from my lips, spilling a rage more wild and untamed than the beast itself.

Garret fell backward away from me, thudding onto the wooden floor. His eyes, dinner plates, filled with terror, watched in breathless horror.

In a single beat of his heart, the beast broke free. Slopping green fur burst from my skin. Limbs flailed a moment before snapping into place. Sharp, deadly claws spread wide, swiping directionless. Lime blood shot from Garret.

"Holy God!" Garret shrieked, holding a bloody arm to his chest.

The screen door slammed. Mama screamed.

My nightmare come to life. I knew the day would come. Wild. Unkempt and uncontrolled. I couldn't stay. They had to survive.

Garret tried to stand but stumbled back into the wall. Mama ran to him, clearing the doorway. Four strong legs barreled out, right through the screen door. Mama's screams echoed long after I'd gone.

All peace I'd mustered had been snatched away. Any control I'd gained, gone. I'd become what I'd worst feared. A monster.

Havana wasn't my home anymore. My people needed me gone. And I'd go. First, I'd have to find myself again, lost inside my beastly prison.

REFUGE

I raced through the back roads and ditches of Havana. Escaping, running until my beastly legs carried me to a familiar garden on a corner lot. In broad daylight, I galloped through pastures, over fences, stopping only when I found the person my beast had sought out.

Exhausted, I collapsed on Mama Lee's back steps. Hard, panting breaths heaved my chest. We'd come for sanctuary. For solace.

Thud. The sound of Nana's body slapping the hardwood floor played on loop, rattling the tiny hairs in my tufted green ears. My nostrils flared at the imagined scent of Garret's blood, pure. His torn flesh forever engrained in emerald. Rusty. Nana. Garret. Mama's sorrow. My penance.

"Well now," Mama Lee said quietly above me. "You sure

are a ballsy little thing, aren't you?" She looked down from her top step. "If I invite you in, are you gonna play nice?" I snorted, no energy for much else. One corner of her mouth tilted a smirk. "Come on then." She stepped back and held the beaded curtain.

No eyes to pour tears over downy cheeks, a whimper, high, tight rattled from somewhere deep. In the place we share. My beast and I.

We fell in a heap at her feet. Agony, a blanket tucked too tight, held me inside her. I could stay there. Escape into the magic of my beast. I'd forget soon enough about my people. The longing I already felt for them would go and I'd live my mystical existence until my time was up.

"You thirsty? I'll getcha a bowl of water." Tiny feet carried her out of sight. A minute later, she was back with a bowl and a bit of raw meat. Rabbit from the scent of it. She set it a few inches from my head. "Get your sea legs back. I'll wait."

I needed legs—real ones. And hands. Words. I needed out. Escape from my prison of suffering before I let her keep me there for good.

"You came all this way. You must need something." The beast lifted her head, lapped at the water, pulled a piece of rabbit from the plate. I screamed and prayed she heard me. "How do I get that little Lynnie Russell back with us?" She squinted, thoughts churning.

Slender legs bent at the knee, she sat on the floor by my side. I laid my head against the cool tile. Mama Lee curled up next to me and ran her hand along the top of my furry head.

Her brown eyes held mine. She didn't say anything, raking slender fingers through dense fur. Traced a finger up my snout, drawing my eyes closed. Even, tranquil harmony hummed in her chest. My tail, thick as a fence post, lifted and flapped to the floor. Breaths slowed. Racing heart came to rest.

Sharp, stinging pain—splintered stones in my soul—smoothed. It didn't go away. Those jagged rocks just didn't slice at my heart with their edges.

"There you are," Mama Lee said softly.

Nana's last words rang my ears. Wailing sobs burst from my lungs. A salty waterfall streamed across my nose, plopping to the floor. Rough edges cut deep, churning the muck that'd almost settled. I slapped the tile, stinging my palm. She'd found me, brought me out, but at a cost.

"Just rest, child. You're beginning to shut down. We're not going to let that happen." Mama Lee didn't play with words or lies. She just said it like it needed to be said. I appreciated that.

I had so much inside that needed to find a home. So much pain. And sorrow, and guilt. Any hope I'd found standing beneath that silver moon with Puck was gone. Not gone, just buried under twenty tons of horseshit.

Gently, she whispered, "Would you like me to smooth out those edges?"

I nodded, doing everything I could not to erupt back into my fur suit. "Yes, ma'am," I croaked.

One quick nod and she hopped up from the floor. Mama Lee was no spring chicken, so whatever she was doing for herself was working out fine. "I'll getcha something to put on while I'm up," she said over her shoulder on her way out.

She talked to me like we'd known each other for years. Like a dear old auntie there to help when help was needed, love when love was needed, and fight when a fight came about.

Puck'd been right. I'd been naked more than I was clothed in one day, lying there with all my bits and pieces out didn't bother me as much.

She padded on swift legs back into the room. "Pull this on and wait there on the floor. Mama Lee'll fix you right up." She nodded once and went to work.

Swiping snot and tears from my face, I sat up. My head felt two sizes too big. Eyes puffy. Nose surely contending with Rudolph. The cotton flowered dress slipped on easy enough. It was the cleanest, best fitting clothing I'd had on in more days than I could track. A size too small, I was grateful for even the slightest give in the fabric.

Mama Lee pinched and mixed spices and powders in a pot no bigger than my head—when normal sized—that rested on little clawed feet. She moved like a cat, never stopping to think of what she was doing, all instinct.

She struck a match against the table, lighting a single flame burner beneath the cast iron pot. Steam puffed from the top, and she pulled in a long sniff, adding one more thing. A dried chicken's foot replaced a stirring spoon.

It bubbled, boiling the brew. Speaking in cursive, Mama Lee whispered what sounded like one long word. She looked to the sky, then leaned over the pot and spit into it.

Before it had any time to cool, she tipped the liquid into a round, clay mug. "Now, gulp this up fast. It's hot, but it has to be. Don't let it cool. Drink it all in one breath." She handed me the mug. "Put the soles of your feet flat on the floor, push all the air from your lungs, and chug it like you're out at Maldoon's."

I did as she said, planting my feet flat on the floor without moving my butt. Spit or no spit, my soul couldn't withstand another sharp shard of despair. I gulped it down and begged those edges to lie down and rest quiet for a while. They'd resurface in time, that I was sure of. Smooth or sharp, a steady stream bares its stones. Sharp rocks cut the flow of the water, chopping it, making it wild and unpredictable. Eventually, that water wears those edges down until it runs level again. I'd run level again. I just needed time to wear those edges down under the surface. And as it appeared, time was the one thing I had in abundance.

It tasted like soap and burned my tongue. I swallowed the last bit, gulping a full breath of air. With it, hope flooded in. My pain hadn't gone. Sadness still shrouded my heart. Hope wrapped it all in its loving arms and held it steady for me. She hadn't taken away anything. Mama Lee'd just made room for hope to find its way in.

"There now." She smiled. I almost expected the glint of a silver tooth. "Feeling better?" I shrugged, nodding once.

"I can't…" Tears welled. "She's gone. Just gone. Like that." I closed my eyes and saw Nana's face. Scared, confused, seconds before she hit the floor. Choking on the lump in my throat, I sucked back sadness. "Garret's gonna—he was so angry. I should'a just let him holler and be done with it. He's never gonna—how will I ever—even if I could, my brother is never gonna wanna see the likes of me again."

Well-weathered hands gathered what she'd pulled out for my elixir. "Oh, that boy'll get glad in the same pants he got mad in." Shuffling off into the kitchen she said over her shoulder, "I suspect this'll be the last time I get to see you."

I closed my eyes and leaned my head against my knees. "I can't stay."

"You gonna say goodbye?"

I shook my head. "What's the point? They'll miss me either way. Might as well not give them the chance to fuss over it." Callousing took time, which I had, but I'd already begun.

Mama Lee swept through the doorway, a wide-brimmed hat in hand. "Well, it's no glasses and big nose, but it'll at the very least keep that sun off you." She plunked the hat on my head. "Hope you're all right walking. I don't drive."

I'd walked there, I'd make my way home. I pushed myself from the floor on bare feet. "Thank you. Thank you for everything. Since… thank you for being so kind when there was no good reason to be."

A tight grin turned her lips white. "Happy to have met a girl like you. Lynnie Russell." She handed me a pair of thongs—the sandals, not the underwear. "Might be a nip small, but it'll keep your feet from burning on that hot asphalt."

I pulled her in and hugged her tight. We weren't kin. Hell, we hardly knew each other. But she'd been inside, in our shared place, the spot down deep where the beast lives. That bond would never break.

"Do you have a plan?" She kept her hand on my shoulder while we walked to the steps.

I looked up at the bright morning sky. "I have a friend."

"That's a start."

JUST ONE BAG

Garret, for all he was and wasn't, would be my brother until the day I died. After, even. Seeing his face, that horrible look when he saw what I'd become… I'd leave and they'd be safe.

Mama Lee's woven straw hat did indeed protect me from the blazing morning sun. The sandals were too small, my heels hung over an uncomfortable inch. Her white cotton dress, specked with tiny lilacs, hit just at my knee and stayed relatively cool on my walk home.

I couldn't right go back to Nana's for my truck. They'd be there. Police likely. Home wasn't too far off. I'd make it. Just had to suffer through small shoes and no underwear. And pray Mama, or Garret, or the damn sheriff didn't roll by and catch me.

Clomping horse hooves beat the road a way behind me. I

moved out of their way, walking along the gravely shoulder.
Head tilted away to better use my hat disguise, I waited for
the rider to pass. Clip-clopping slowed to match my pace. I
braced for the sound of a police radio.

"*Hello, old friend.*"

Beside me, a black steed glistened under hot summer sun.
"How in the holy hell did you find me?" I breathed, mouth
wide.

"*Luck.*" His mouth never moved, words just popped right
out of his head and into mine.

I nodded once, eyes in squints. "Right."

Puck lowered his head, kneeling to offer me a ride. I
groaned and hoisted myself onto his back, tucking what I
could of my dress under my lady bits.

"*Hang on.*"

I leaned forward and wrapped my arms around his neck.
My body was tired. My soul was tired. I could've fallen asleep
right there on his back. Puck took off into a sprint, headed
toward home.

A shapeshifting fairy doctor—or at least he played one
on TV—had sought me out. Followed me. Found me. Saved
me. For his own gain, I reckoned so. I needed him too; there
was no denying that. I'd stay sharp, vigilant. Watch my six,
as they say.

When folks talk about making good choices, they never
mention good options. Sometimes it comes down to picking
the better smelling shit.

Puck's blue sports car was parked in Garret's driveway. He'd come for me. "This is gonna need an explanation." Puck lowered himself so I could slide off. The back of my borrowed dress caught, flashing likely pale cheeks.

Shimmering silver light waved around him. Like his bear, it shimmied a breath before popping back into Puck. He shook leftover magic from his hair. "I'd gotten to the main highway when I realized," he sighed, "leaving you alone would be reckless." He leaned into the open passenger window, exposing his full backside. I didn't look away. "The bear is a proficient tracker. The best in the animal kingdom. Did you know that?" He spun, a neatly folded stack of clothes in hand, and caught me looking. I blushed but refused to turn away.

"I couldn't right ride a bear down 7th Street."

He clicked a finger gun at me. "Bingo." Khaki pants slid effortlessly over his hips. "Clearly I was correct. Yes?" One at a time, he slowly buttoned a lightweight cotton shirt.

I looked down at my too-small shoes. "Yes."

"Right." He slipped his feet into a pair of blue canvas sneakers and wiped sweat from his brow. "This heat. It's the humidity, really." He sounded like a true southerner. "I cannot wait to get out of this swamp. Ever been to Oregon?"

My breath caught. I'd been trying to escape Havana for years, the reality of it was more painful than I'd anticipated. "No. I've never been outside of Arkansas."

Puck stood up straight. "Say what? Oh, baby, I really do have things to show you." He pushed his arm under mine, hooking our elbows. "Pack light, but be sure to bring long pants and a sweater. Something with a hood would be beneficial."

He walked me up the steps to the door. My mind played Garret's face over and over. The sound of Nana hitting the floor made me jump.

Puck stopped, put his hands on either side of my face. "It's for the best. I can't promise it's going to be easy, but I can tell you that you've got magic inside you. It won't stop. It won't quit. It'll be you until you die. Accept what you are or it'll eat you alive." He shrugged, brows raised. "What I can promise is my allegiance." He bowed. "Until the end."

Dark eyes, nothing like the lightning bugs of his stallion, locked onto mine until I finally nodded. Better smelling shit.

I pushed open the door that was never locked. Silent. Empty. We were alone, but surely Garret or Mama or both would be out looking for me. I just hoped shock kept them put until I could get outta Dodge.

Puck moseyed through the living room, looking closely at the few pictures I'd hung on the wall. He grinned at one of me standing thigh deep in a mud pit. Rusty'd taken it the summer the creek behind the Kennedy farm flooded damn near half of Havana.

My room, filled with things I'd collected over my two decades, seemed hollow. Useless for all intents and purposes. I hadn't slept in my bed in too many nights. The idea of knickknacks and old love notes was just so damned *human*. More human than I'd ever be again. *If I'm being honest, probably more human than I'd ever been to begin with.*

Pack light. I fingered the stone that hung from my neck.

It'd be with me, my Black Sentry, my guard. The small cotton bag that it'd come in sat on my night table. I grabbed it, plucked a few photos of me and Hattie, Garret, and Rusty from their home on my mirror, and slid it all in the side pocket of my duffle bag—which I hadn't used since grade nine camp.

I'd laid Mama Lee's dress out flat on my bed. If she decided to come looking for it, I thought it best if Garret could find it easily. I pulled her hat on. It'd be my something borrowed—or however that worked.

My favorite boots were gone, laid to waste in Nana's living room. I closed my eyes and tried to see her face, smiling, happy, not on her hardwood floor. It wouldn't come.

Bag slung over one shoulder—Huckleberry Finn, all I needed was a handkerchief on a stick—I stopped at the door. One last look.

The cardboard that Garret put up after I'd crashed through the window was still pulled back from the night I'd squeezed out. I'd made my bed, closed all my drawers, left it clean for him. Easy. I didn't truly need anything in that room, but I sure as hell wanted it. Given more time, resources, I'd have packed that whole damn thing.

If I could fit a massive green dog inside my body, I could certainly find a way to pack an entire room into one bag. Right?

FAREWELL

We hit Louisiana by dusk. I'd sat in the passenger seat, silent, hands trembling, since watching Garret's shit brown house get smaller in the side-view mirror. The empty pit in my stomach grew deeper with every mile marker. A cavernous hole I'd never fill.

"If you'll look out your window, you'll see Shreveport. A bustling metropolis filled with people and places to get lost in."

I pressed my forehead to the glass. "It's so big."

Puck chuckled once. "That's what she said," he murmured.

I scowled at him over my shoulder. "Aren't you, like, an ancient being?"

Heavy sigh. "I've been away from *Cnoc Meadha* for

centuries. This is what living among the masses has done to me."

"Knock-what?"

A dimple poked into his cheek. "In English, Knockma. It's my home. *Was*. Your home too. Although, Cu Sidhe hasn't stepped foot in the realm for *eons*."

"Two homeless fairies. What a world." I let out a hollow laugh. "Why *was*? Almost kill your brother too?"

Sidewalks crowded with people whizzed by. "Daddy kicked me out." He snorted. "That is a story too old and too long to tell. Today is your day."

Certain I'd be saying the same in a few decades, I let it go. We'd have plenty of time for long, old tales. I had bigger questions burning a hole in my head. "What do you know about how I came to be? More specifically, the ritual, the women?"

Quiet for enough breaths, I wondered if I'd broken him. "They disappeared?"

"Yes," I squeaked. "Four dead bodies just walked right outta the morgue in Russellville."

He shook his head. "They didn't *walk*. Just..." A warbled whistle pushed through pursed lips and he wiggled his fingers. "Vanished. They're ghosts, Lynn."

Avery. "Ghosts of a curse long past," I repeated under my breath.

"Precisely. *Croí na Tlachtga* is one spoke in your wheel, babe. The magic that binds you and your feral beasty. When the time comes, they'll come."

"And I'll die."

He nodded. "The cycle continues."

"Why? How?" Tense hands scrubbed down my face. "Is there a book on this or somethin'?"

"Not on earth."

"What about Avery? She's my guide—*was*—she'd know, right?"

Silent, Puck watched the road. Orange tinted his face as the sun set. "Possibly. If you could find her, convince her to help you." Fingers tapped the wheel. "Tell me to kick rocks," he added, heartache in his voice.

Admittedly, I didn't know either of them well, but Puck had been there when I needed him, when Avery wasn't. I couldn't right walk away now, sitting shotgun, my only belongings in his trunk.

"No, no that's... that ain't who I am. Never was. Just scared is all." Lavender clouds streaked across the reddening sky. "What about Knockma?" I turned to look at him. "That's our home, right? We could go there and—"

"No," he protested. "You can't—not yet. When you're stronger, more controlled... I'm sorry I can't give you the answers you're looking for."

Hand wrapped tight around the Black Sentry, I closed my eyes, searching for any help it'd give me. My beast rumbled, stirring, preparing herself for impending freedom. "Where will we go? How do I... hunt? What if the old girl busts free in the middle of a shopping mall?" Thoughts spun loose, spilling in one long stream.

Puck laid a hand on my leg. "Take a breath. In and out."
I pulled in one shaking breath. "You're still new. It's going
to take time. Percy was… inept. His vengeance was poorly
reaped. You, my dear, sweet girl, were born for this. The Cu
is stretching her legs, feeling you out. Every day is easier,
yes?"

"More and more."

He rubbed my leg. "You'll get there. Give her time. She
knows what to do. Listen, she'll tell you."

"Until then, how do I keep from killing people?"

He held up a finger. "Ah, how do you keep from killing
the *wrong* people?"

That was the sixty-four-thousand-dollar question.

The more days spread between the man with the girls, the
more the beast longed for something I didn't have to give. I
couldn't say it wanted blood, because that'd be inaccurate.
It wanted vengeance. In a world as unjust as ours, surely
there was someone out there in need of smiting.

Thick woods blocked the half-moon high in the sky.
Holding my girl back took everything I had in me, but to
save the innocent I'd hand over my last breath.

Puck pulled off his jeans and T-shirt and stood with
his rounded backside facing me. I'd brought a change of

clothes to avoid being naked in the woods another damn night.

"Are you ready to get started?" he asked, turning around, his frank and beans on display for me and the world to see.

Looking anywhere but at him, I asked, "What is it that I'm doing?"

"You're searching for the catalyst that sparks your beast."

"All I have to do is let her loose."

"Exactly," he said, nodding his curly head.

My beast rumbled in her hiding place, anxious to break free. "You really don't know what you're talking about, do you?"

"Look, I'm sorry Avery left you." She hadn't left me so much as let my choices be what they were. "But she's not like me—not true Sidhe. All Bean Sidhe were once human like you. Their place here is a curse more than an inherited trait. Avery, in her death, just so happened to be chosen to guide you, Percy, and Gwendolyn, until you're able to get out there and do it to it."

"But—"

"I don't know why so don't ask. I've been away from *Cnoc Meadha* for a very, very long time, and as such have not been in the loop." He sighed. Still quite naked.

I let it go. We all had our demons, and judging by Puck's reluctance to spill the beans, it seemed his were the kind with teeth and claws. I could relate.

"I'm just going for it then." I changed the subject, anxious in my own right to escape into my beast's world.

"Keep your mind open to what the beast needs. Don't lose Lynnie, but allow yourself to *be* Cu Sidhe. Remember, you're always Cu Sidhe. The beast is merely a symbol for what you are."

I dragged a deep breath through my nose—sucking in the awkward scent of the bayou, part sweet, part dank. Teal slivers of moonlight cut through shaggy trees. She was there, waiting, just beneath the surface. Free-flowing electric magic danced down my arms, crackling in my palms.

With a crooked finger in my mind, I beckoned her. *Come on, old girl. It's time to play.*

In an explosion of fur and bone, my body burst at its core and the beast came to be. No time to feel joints crack and bend. Not a moment to savor the sickening sensation of my teeth shifting to make room for fangs. No time for slopping crackles of magic.

Puck stood naked with his hands on his hips like Peter Pan. "Well, that was unexpected."

I panted, specks of snot popping from my snout. The change wasn't easy on either one of us, no matter how fast or mystical it became. I shook my heavy coat and the last bits of human slop flung off and into the dirt. Once again, the world was bathed in shades of green. I longed for that devilish violet that meant I let loose to reap revenge. Puck reached his now emerald hand out and scratched me under the chin.

"Pretty girl." He patted me on the head. "Of all the

creatures on this earth, you are the only one I cannot become." Puck pressed his forehead to mine. "Extraordinary little beastie you are."

Glimmering silver lights shivered around him. The world shifted and Puck snapped from existence. The shiny black steed took his place.

Kisatchie Bayou, thickly covered in underbrush, seemed cumbersome for a horse to get on to a full gallop, but I wasn't the one on four hooves so who was I to call it a problem. Puck's firefly eyes glowed in the shadows beneath the tallest pine. He whinnied, flipping his glossy mane, taunting, calling us out to play.

Like old friends catching up, Puck's steed and my beast stalked the night, splashing over the bank of the bayou, bathing in moonlight. I caught and all but devoured a rabbit, like things with sharp teeth and claws tended to do. It wasn't enough. The beast had a quota to fill and weren't a hare nor varmint on that list.

The moon high in the sky, Puck clomped through over a fallen log, pushing through brush back to the bank where we'd left our clothes. Lichen dangled from his hind end, clung to his shiny mane. Midstride, the universe flickered. Puck's bare feet padded over rocks and twigs, swamp mud stuck to the soles.

I fought and tugged at my own soul to pull the human back out, but it wouldn't budge. My human-self tossed and turned inside me mirroring the sensation of the beast rolling and rumbling when she wanted out. I struggled, pulled, yanked at my own humanity locked inside the beast. Puck had told me he could help me train the beast to cooperate like it had for centuries when it belonged to my ancestors. The only thing Puck had done was get me stuck inside myself. My shared heart raced and the beast started to pant. Panic washed over us.

"Come on, babe. You're in there somewhere. Come on out," he coaxed.

Mama Lee's low, even hum played over in my head. I forced myself to calm down and focus. Nana's smiling face popped in and I almost lost it, but I let the image stay, appreciated it for what it was and ignored the feeling it left, like an oil slick in my soul. My heartbeat slowed, steadying. Calmly, I called at my human, trapped and scared deep inside me.

Puck ran his hand over the top of my furry head. "It's time to come out."

I agreed and the fur along my arms sucked back into my skin. I wondered where it went once it wasn't covering my body anymore, got a little grossed out, and decided to forget about the technicalities of it all.

Instead, I focused on being human again.

Puck grinned, looking down at me, deep lines carved his cheeks. "There you are."

"Here I am," I panted and swallowed back vomit.

"You did it. The moon is high in the sky and you forced yourself in and out of Cu Sidhe at *your* will." He looked at me for a bit. "Does it hurt?"

I shook my head. "A scratch," I joked.

He nodded and his fluffy hair bounced. "Are you okay?"

I wasn't. I shook my head a second before I upchucked on Puck's naked lower half. I clamped my hand over my mouth. "I'm so sorry," I muffled through my hand.

Puck laughed and the night echoed with delight as if he'd forced it to be joyful right along with him. "Well, I have to say, you sure keep things exciting." He put his hand on my shoulder and let it slide down my back.

I did my best to cover my parts and scooted to my clothes that sat in a pile just a bit from me. "I'm sorry," I mumbled over and over again.

"It really is okay, Lynnie. It's just partially digested food and stomach acid." He shrugged, rubbing dirt over his legs, soaking up the wet bits that hadn't fallen off when he stood. "It'll wash right off." I shook my head and pulled my jeans on. "Look, I'll be right back." The air shifted. He was gone by the time I turned around.

"Real damn nice, Lynnie. Go and puke all over the one person still on your side. Stupid," I said to myself.

I pulled on my boots and kicked dirt over the patch of my partially digested food and stomach acid that was left behind. Rustling in the woods behind me caught my attention. "Puck?" He didn't answer. I waited for an animal of some kind to come scurrying out of the darkness but nothing came.

Feeling sorry for myself, I shoved my hands in my pockets and kicked at the leaves and brush. My head jerked and looked over my shoulder when a screeching wail echoed through the night. It sounded like a woman. I thought for a second I'd lucked out and stumbled on another bad man doing bad things. No fiery instinct sprung loose in my gut. Another screech floated over the swampy creek.

"Avery?" I called out, listening for more familiar shrieks. No more screams or any other sounds came from the night. "Avery?" I cupped my hands and hollered with all my might.

"She's not here." Puck stepped into the clearing, naked and free of vomit.

I swallowed, embarrassed I'd puked, but more so that I'd hoped my keening friend had come back for me. "What was that shrieking?"

He shrugged, slipping pants over his ass. "Possibly Bean Sidhe. Avery isn't the only ghostly woman floating around." He turned to face me, pants undone, a dark line of hair poking out the top. "Most likely a fox." White teeth bared bright against the darkness. I didn't return the grin. He pulled a shirt over his head, moving close enough to touch. "She's not coming back." Hands wrapped around my arms. Dark eyes glanced down at my chest and back up. "I'm sorry."

I covered bare boobs with arms across my chest. "I don't know if I can do this, Puck." It wasn't Avery's disappearance that weighed heavy; it was the idea that everything I'd known was gone. Right and truly gone. I could never show my face in Havana. Never look my brother in the eye. Never look myself in the eye.

Strong arms pulled me in, boobs pressed against his chest. "You can, because you must."

OLD FRIEND

Long days flew by, quickly becoming weeks. Havana, my time of innocence, seemed like a past life, recalled only in dreams. It was in those vivid dreams that I lived. I had it all again. It was mine.

Like a lost limb, a ghost unseen but felt in prickling tingles, I missed who I was in Havana. Just an American girl, *raised on promises*. Just a little thing. I yearned for her like a lost lover. The frantic pleading of a sinner for forgiveness.

Limbs don't grow back. Lovers tend to stay gone. And sinners, well, sinners went to hell. I was the one who sent them there.

I'd assumed bringer of death would be a more active position. The beast had been edgy, nights out wndering, no hunt, no target. We'd made an excited emergency stop in

Texarkana. My emerald vision alerting a false alarm.

Most days, I slept. Finding solace in the memories of home. Puck dragged me through towns and cities—filled with people, and coffee shops, and buskers, and bike lanes—one after the other, searching for that violet beacon. It'd come so easy that day at Cove Lake. Finding those girls, hunting that man. Three weeks on and the beast grew restless.

Puck was just happy being among people. Watching, talking, touching, he was at home in a crowd. Hospitals were a favorite of his, undoubtedly, but since I'd have rather had oral surgery, we settled on travelers—bus stops, airports, train stations.

Kicked back on his end of the wooden bench, making a mess of peanut shells at his feet, he grinned at every person walking by.

"You plannin' on cleaning that up?" I asked, nodding at the mess, arms folded over my chest.

He split a shell and let it fall to the floor. "Squirrels will get it." He popped the peanut in his mouth and nodded at a woman who passed.

I closed my eyes and leaned back. "It's an indoor station," I grumbled.

Puck poked me with the toe of his sneaker. "Turn that frown upside down, pumpkin. Today is an excellent day."

Eyes grudgingly open, I watched mamas scold their children. Watched men and women hugging and kissing, and refusing to let the other go. Pretending it wasn't goodbye. I watched people hustling about, rushing to their next destination. A place of sadness. Rushed, forced life.

A child no bigger than a peapod trotted, her little sandals slapping the tile floor. She carried a rag baby and a confidence I wished I could borrow for a while. No mama or daddy, just the little girl running along.

I sat forward, senses on alert. Ears perked. A tall man in heavy boots scooped her up in his arms. On my feet, adrenaline engaged, I charged forward, the savior.

"Daddy," she squealed.

He buried his face in her neck. Chest-rattling sobs bounced his shoulders. Stopped in my tracks by pure, true love. Mama caught up, belly round, grinning to each ear. Daddy rubbed a circle around her bump.

My chin quivered. I'd see sadness in a newborn baby or a gaggle of puppies. Too broken. Too damaged. So many things unsaid. Goodbyes ignored. The beast wasn't alone in her frustration. I grew restless too. For a time I was desperate to forget. For a future I couldn't imagine.

"You left me!" a woman screeched, the sound echoing off concrete.

Hattie's sandy ponytail sat high on her head, and her big brown eyes glared at me. She stomped, boot heels clicking against the floor. "I'm liable to rip your hair right outta your head, Lynnie Russell."

I looked at Puck. He winked, pointing a salty finger gun at me.

Fuck. "Hattie." I had no lies for her. No energy to make any.

She punched me in the shoulder. "What in the holy hell, Lynn? How could you leave me like that? Leave Garret?"

Tears welled at her lashes. Hattie looked over her shoulder at Puck, who grinned and nodded. A tear escaped when she rolled her eyes at him.

Silence as my lips refused to move. All those things unsaid tangled on my tongue. "I was scared, Hattie," I croaked. "So fucking scared I ran through town as a fucking green beast to find a witch's magic for help." I clamped my hand over my mouth.

She shook her head. "You could've told me. You didn't have to lie. Not to me." She swiped away a stray tear. "Mama confessed everything to Garret the day after you left. He swore he'd watched that monster swallow you up. Was set out to kill it. *You*. Why didn't you tell me?" Her voice thick with sadness.

I swallowed the lump in my throat. "How?"

Quietly, she looked away, searching for words I knew didn't exist. "You don't have to be scared anymore. You can come home now."

Over her shoulder, Puck watched, pinching his lips into a frown. I couldn't. Havana was a place of dreams. I was the ghost. "I can't, Hattie."

"Sure, yeah, you can. Garret hasn't touched your room. It's all still there. Like you left it. And the sheriff… well, the sheriff just wants to talk to you. Just talk, is all. It's just too weird for Havana, the deaths, the missing bodies, those girls, but that's your home, Lynn. You *have* to come back," she rambled, desperate.

"I'm not that girl anymore, Hattie. I miss who I was, and you and Garret and Mama and—" I couldn't choke out her name. Or *his*.

"Her service was beautiful." I closed my eyes, a tear fell, curving into the corner of my mouth. "Headstone'll be in by Christmas. You could come… for Christmas."

I forced a breath. "Love him, please. Love my brother for me."

"You'd leave us just like that?"

"Hattie, Nana died. I hurt Garret. I ki—" I bit my lips, holding my unforgivable sin. I wouldn't say it. The words would not touch my tongue.

"It was you, wasn't it?" She swallowed hard. "You killed Rusty when you were… that… *thing*?"

All systems stopped. Breath clung to my lungs. Blood no longer pumped. She knew. Wouldn't have said it out loud if she didn't. She just needed to hear me say it. I quivered, "Yes." I needed to hear me say it too. "On the first night I became Cu Sidhe, Rusty tried to save me and I killed him along with the others. I hadn't meant it—even my beast doesn't kill the innocent. He just got caught up in the middle of a battle no human belonged in."

"Jesus, Lynn." She shook her head like the good Southern woman she was turning out to be. "I'm so sorry, baby." She pulled me in to hug. I didn't have my nana or my mama, but I'd take my best friend.

Sobs bounced off high ceilings, clanging against cement walls. I had too much time ahead of me to fuss over the embarrassment of crying in public. It was in me and needed out. "I loved him. I *love* him. I miss him every day. I was so stupid, Hattie. Not knowing. All that time. How'd you let me be so stupid?"

She kissed me on the head. "Ain't nobody telling Carolynn Russell what to do. Not since the day she was born. You think I could've changed that?"

"Garret did."

"Well, Garret is a soul very dear to yours. There'll never be a day that boy can't turn your heart."

"Will you take care of him?" I asked, wiping snot on my sleeve.

She looked down, corner of her mouth turned up. "Am I that obvious?"

"Like a damn full set of teeth on a Baker brother." She laughed at our inside Havana joke and covered blushed cheeks with her hands.

"He stole my heart, Lynn. It's so stupid, but I'm ass over teakettle for Garret Russell." She sighed. "Is that okay with you?"

It was everything I'd dreamed. "I need you to promise me you'll take care of him. Be good to Mama and try to keep my daddy in line as best you can."

"How am I supposed to do it without you? How am I supposed to be a Russell without you?"

A wide grin pushed my puffy red eyes damn near closed. "You're gonna be a Russell *for* me. I need you to be a wife to my brother, a daughter to my mama, and a mama to my chubby nieces and nephews. I need you to live a life I can't." Sometimes saying words out loud helped the healing along.

"Lynn, how am I supposed to live *any* life without you?"

"The same way I'll be living lifetimes without you. Faith.

Hope. Knowledge that the universe holds more than flesh and bone for the likes of you and me. It's all I have. No better choice in life but to live it. Best get on with it." Nana's wise old voice come through mine.

"When did you get so wise, Lynnie Russell?" She grinned at me like a proud mama.

"The moment I realized I didn't have any other choice but to be everything the universe has in store for me."

"Havana, Arkansas is never gonna forget the likes of you."

"I'd like to hope not." I looked on my old friend with new eyes. A mother, a grandmother, a wife, and a corpse in a box surrounded by crying people mourning her death. In that morbid way, I envied her. I'd die alone in the woods at the hand of an unknown green beastie just as lost and scared as I was.

After a long, easy few minutes of silence, Hattie asked one more time with tears in her eyes. "You really not coming back?"

I wrapped my arms all the way around her and squeezed. She buried her face in my neck. Apple shampoo. She'd used it since we'd started high school. I pulled in as much of the scent as I could, storing the memory in a safe place. Sucking back tears, I whispered, "I'm sorry, old friend."

MENDED IN GOLD

I stood on a cliff edge, looking out over never-ending spread of green—true, earthly green. Treetops so thick, a soul could get lost in them. Yellow, orange, and fiery red dotted the landscape. Autumn leaves swirled through the ravine.

"Don't jump."

I shook my head. I hadn't jumped the first time. I fell. "I ain't gonna jump. You thinking of pushing me off?"

Puck's hand rested on my back. "Why would I go and do a thing like that?"

I didn't look at him, but I knew he was smiling. He was always smiling. Every day was a terrific day. Or an excellent day. Days weren't anywhere near.

"Do you like it here?" It was the same question he asked

in all the other cities and woods we'd visited in our weeks together.

I nodded. "It's nice." I hugged my arms around my chest to block the cold.

"Not Havana, but it'll do?" he repeated the usual answer he'd finally drag outta me.

I'd been a mess, a mean, ugly old trash bin and I knew it wasn't right. It wasn't fair to Puck. Whether for his benefit or mine, he'd lived up to his promise to be my friend, an ally. It didn't really matter either way. I was happy not to think about it. About being truly alone. Thinking about Garret and Nana and Mama, and my life before the beast, wasn't doing me any good either. That wasn't fair to me. There was a life to be lived, and it was time I started living it.

"Would you ever go back?" Puck asked.

Hattie and Garret would hide me away, put me in the storm cellar at Nana's, out in the shed at the Kemp's. Until the day the beast slopped from my body and killed one of them, if the law didn't find me first.

"I don't think anyone in Havana wants to see Lynnie Russell's face again unless it's to lock me up or burn me at the stake." As far as Havana knew, I was a ghost. "Let them think this monster gobbled her up."

We stood shoulder to shoulder, surveying our temporary home. Marine fog swallowed hills in the distance. I huddled in my sweater.

"So, now, what do you think about Oregon?"

I looked at him, hardly moving my head. "It'll do."

Bacon. Coffee. Beautiful morning—or late afternoon in my nocturnal world—scent washed through the room. Cuddled under two quilts and a crisp white sheet, I wiggled my toes, stretched long.

Every single day for nearly two months. "Good morning, sunshine." Like clockwork. Puck pushed through my door carrying two mugs—the only houseware item he insisted on toting from place to place. White cotton pants hardly clung to his hips. It didn't catch my second glance. He'd been right, shifter types lose any and all modesty eventually.

"Mornin'," I croaked and took my cup.

He laid on his elbow across the foot. "What are we doing today?"

Living with Puck was nothing like living with Garret. Puck was clean and generous. Every day he brought me fresh ground coffee, topless—it was Puck so I was certain that was intentional—smiling. What idiot would say no to that? Inside, I wished he'd go away. I couldn't properly wallow in my grief with him around. Which was surely part of his plan.

"Actually, I'm feeling a little beastly today." She yawned and stretched in her hidden space. It'd been weeks—hell, months—since she'd gone to work. I let her out to play every night—the safest time of the day—but chasing Puck and hunting deer are things for animals, not death, not Cu Sidhe. It kept her strong, but she wasn't satisfied.

He wiggled his brows. "Titillating." A deep draw of steamy coffee warmed my face. "I want you to be happy with me," he said all of a sudden. "Are you happy with me?" A chestnut curl sprung out and fell over his forehead.

For a second, I thought about a movie Garret took me to see when I was a kid. A woman had her favorite writer locked up in a guestroom. She played nice and all, but really, she was crazier than a shithouse rat. I wondered if Puck had a big sledgehammer hidden in his pajamas. You know what I mean.

"I ain't even happy with myself." That was the God's honest truth. It hadn't taken long for my heart to harden and my head to soften after I left Havana. It was a miracle I wasn't a big green beastie roaming the streets, clawing up unjust assholes and gnawing on the bones of philanderers everywhere I went.

He scratched over his floppy hair in a way that made me sneer and swallow back sorrow. In my head, only Rusty could muss his hair. Only Rusty could make me happy. And Garret, and Hattie, and Mama, and Nana, and hell even Podunk Havana.

He huffed, letting out a noisy sigh. "Get dressed. We're getting out of this house today." He held up his finger and pointed it at me like a daddy to his daughter. "You're not arguing either."

"Puck."

He pursed his lips and cocked his head, a gesture I was learning meant he anticipated something shitty.

"I'm happy you're my friend."

A grin pulled wide, he flashed white teeth, carving lines around his mouth. "I'm happy you're my friend, too." He stood and gulped the last of his coffee.

"Do you think I'll ever stop breaking?" I asked, sorrow sagging my eyelids.

He watched my face, something he did often, before answering. "I think before long you'll be too strong to break."

I thought of decades waking up in the morning with

jagged stones in my soul. I should've died right along with Rusty and Nana. Saved myself the torment.

Puck sat on the edge of the bed in front of me. "Did you know in Japan, when a dish gets a crack in it, they fill that crack with gold?"

I didn't know why in the world he was talking about cracks in Japan, but it stopped me from counting the days until I died.

"It's called *kitsugi*. When a piece of pottery is cracked, or broken, instead of throwing it away, they repair it with gold. Gold strengthens the bonds and highlights the damage as a proud remembrance of impact. They embrace the change and boast its effect on the life of the piece. Repair yourself with gold, Lynnie Russell. Embrace the changes in your life. Claim your damage, remember its impact. Don't allow it to end your existence."

He leaned close, touching the tip of his nose to mine. We shared a handful of breaths. A hand wrapped around the back of my neck, Puck pressed his lips to my forehead. "Get ready, peaches. We're going out," he said, and left me to sit alone in my rented room to think about golden cracks.

Accepting my fate as a mythical creature had been a simpler task than accepting my future as a broken human. I owed it to myself, to the women—and Percy— who endured this life before me to live every day. Not another soul on the planet could exist like I could. The ghosts of Havana would haunt me until death, but it was time to let their rattling chains be silent.

BACK IN THE SADDLE

"*Pull* off up here." I pointed, pushing the tip of my finger against the glass.

"*Here?*"

"Yeah, right here!"

Puck whipped the wheel, pulling into the lot at the last second, and parked his car in the gravel to the left of Ray's Tavern. Dust swirled up from the tires. Neon beer signs blinked in blackened windows through the haze.

"This isn't exactly what I had in mind for a night out." He looked through the back window, lip curled. "Dinner. Dancing…."

I didn't wait for him, shutting the door behind me without taking my eyes off the glowing letters perched on the roof.

"No, this is perfect." We longed for that devilish magenta, my beast and I. Weeks of catching rabbits and chasing Puck, practice for what I knew I'd find in a place like this. On a night like that. "He's here," I breathed.

Puck stood next to me, looking up at the sign. "You're sure?"

My girl roiled, anxious to be free. "She is."

"What an excellent day for a reaping." He wiggled his brows at me, trotting off toward the door.

Chrome-spotted bikes leaned on kickstands out front, lined up one after the other. In the gravel lot, a handful of rigs parked side by side. I shook away the thought that my daddy was in that bar drinking himself stupid and shoved through the door.

Only big enough for a pool table and a jukebox, the small space inside overflowed with people wearing worn leather dotted with stitched patches. All but a handful of heads turned and looked my way.

I ignored their stares, letting my eyes fall intentionally unimpressed but interested over each of them. A trick I'd learned blending in at Maldoon's. Can't be too eager. Can't look like the wide-eyed kid I was.

"Howdy." I leaned on elbows. "I'll take a bottle of your finest piss water." I winked at the bartender—a man old enough to be my granddaddy, gray beard skimming his round belly.

"Where'd you come from, sweetheart?" He grunted and pulled a bottle of beer from an ice box behind the bar.

I snatched the bottle, tipping it back, guzzling it dry in a single run. Slamming the bottle back, I looked him in the eye and let my accent do the talking. "Yell County, Arkansas." Sudsy beer settled in my gut. My beastly girl rumbled, unsure but familiar.

"Well, then. Welcome to Oregon." I fought the sneer his grin brought to my lip. He poured a shot of whiskey, slid it to me, and clicked one of his own against it.

I slammed it back and with two fingers, ordered more. Puck slapped a handful of twenties on the bar and nodded at the man, who seemed impressed.

"Thank you kindly," I said to the old man behind the bar.

Carrying both shots, we moved to lean against the wall by the jukebox. "And thank you," I said, handing my friend his drink.

Puck shook his head, his sly-grin dimple popped out. "Thank you, but I won't drink."

"You don't drink?" I scoffed. "What are you some kind of teetotaler?"

"Not *don't*, *won't*." He closed his eyes and leaned his head back against the wall.

"Well, now you gotta tell me why." I poked him in the ribs, feeling friskier than I'd been since my birthday.

He rolled his head to the side, dark eyes scanning my face. "Because if I'm drinking, you won't be safe."

"Safe? What're you gonna do, kill me?" I threw my head back. "I'm pretty certain I can take care of myself."

His lips pushed out and he clicked his tongue. "No.

Actually, I'm going to kiss you and I probably won't stop."

My heart snagged on a memory, dropping my grin. I loved Rusty. That I could be sure would never stop. Just like Nana never stopped loving Percy. But she married. He was a good man, my granddaddy, and loved her proper. I could love Rusty, but I couldn't have him. Stuck on earth for generations, trapped in a love I'd never know, a ghost of Lynnie's past. That certainly wasn't fair.

"I don't see the problem." I shoved a shot into his hand and clinked.

A charming, bright grin cut lines down his cheeks. "You really are something else, Carolynn Russell."

"Lynnie." Hot, spicy liquid slid easily down my throat. "You better believe it."

Lights flickered, washing the room from pink to green. Lime, olive, shamrock, crinkly, crackly shades touched everything, everyone. As if on cue, the front door swung open. Bathed in lilac, a long-legged man in heavy boots strolled in. Fiery soul ignited in my shared space.

"Hold on, girl, not here," I whispered, steadying my breath.

I looked back at Puck, a shimmering glitter of colors—turquoise among the brightest. His eyes shot to the man and back to me. "You know what to do," he assured me. "I'll be right here."

Daddy-long-legs slid onto a stool at the bar, tugged a leather wallet from his pocket. He reminded me of my daddy. Aging poorly, weathered, lonely. One of those trucks out front would be his. What atrocious things did he do in that truck? Out on the road alone.

Fae magic crackled over my skin. I shook it free from my fingertips, fearful someone would notice, and shoved my hands into the back pockets of my jeans. Black Sentry warmed against my chest. *Don't glow. Please, don't glow.*

Puck's energy swirled between us, gently nudging my back, a constant reminder I wasn't alone.

I slid onto the stool beside Legs, the target, and leaned on an elbow. "What's your drink?" He stunk like cheap cigarettes—Checkers or USA Gold, lights. I tucked my head close to him, looking up under lashes.

Tar-stained lips curled into a sneering grin. "Well, I'll be. Aren't you just a little thing."

I laughed, deep, throaty. Deadly. "You ain't seen nothin' yet, old man."

"I'll bet." He looked over, focusing on my lips too long. Zaps poked the barrier between the beast and me. "You on the job, darlin'?" He wasn't from around those parts. Georgia maybe.

I sat up, feigning offence. "You know any hookers buying drinks? 'Cause I sure don't." Weeks with Puck I'd learned a lot. More about how to get by, use my wiles, trick to survive. Not those kind of tricks.

"Guess not." He watched my face, still, quiet, figuring me out.

I held two fingers to Captain Longbeard at the other end of the bar. "Remind me of my daddy is all." I nudged him with my shoulder. "You like whiskey?"

Two shots sat waiting, he squinted at me. "What's your game, girl?"

Slow down. You've got him. Let him come to you. I snatched my shot from the bar. "I like to call it livin'. What's yours?"

A low groaning chuckle rumbled in his chest. "You're trouble." He tilted his shot toward me.

Puck pushed out the front door, shimmering waves of color surrounding him. I slammed my shot and clapped it back to the bar. "You gotta smoke?" I grinned, forcing innocence to my expression.

He looked around the bar at all the people not paying any attention to us. "I do."

"Let's get outta here." I pointed my chin at the door. "Unless you're not up for a little moonlight?"

"Oh, sweetie, *you ain't seen nothin' yet.*" His sneer was back and he draped his arm around my neck.

I shrugged his arm off my shoulder and wiggled ahead of him. His stench was too much. Not the smoke so much, the death. He reeked of it.

Darkness spread, thick and heavy over the trees and brush that surrounded Ray's Tavern. A slivered moon peeked through billowing clouds. Wet air clung to my hair.

The man followed as I made my way to the dark space— his death bed. "Where you headed?" He stopped at the back of a truck with Georgia plates. "I gotta nice warm place right here."

There was nothing on earth, or anywhere else for that

matter, that could have gotten me willingly into that cab. "That's no fun." I turned to face him, walking backward, coaxing his demons to come out and play.

He looked at the truck and back to me, the blackness at my back. "Gimme a minute, girlie. Hold on right there." He slipped his top half into the truck cab, gathered a few things, and shoved them into jacket pockets.

"Come on now, old man," I teased, "I don't got all night," leaving him at the truck.

"Slow down, girl," he demanded.

"Better catch up." I pulled my long-sleeve shirt off over my head, dropped it to the ground, and sauntered into the woods until darkness took me over.

"You're a long way from home," he called, trotting into the depths behind me.

"A bit."

I'd need to slip out of my boots and jeans before letting my girl free. I didn't have time to break in another pair of boots. Or jeans.

Glowing, a fiery amethyst in a sea of emerald, the man— the sinner—a beacon for the beast. I watched him stalk through the trees, vainly attempting to hunt for me.

I kicked a boot off with a toe at each heel. Jeans unbuttoned, I caught sight of glowing yellow eyes. Puck watched, waited. A wily grin curved my mouth. I wiggled my pants over round hips, piling them on top of my boots.

Ancient fire raged inside me. Vengeful flames licked bits of my soul, catching even the purest places ablaze. She'd come. In such fiery glory, my beast would break free and claim what was hers.

"Where'd you get on to, baby girl?" Puck stalked yards behind the blissfully ignorant target. "Best be careful, animals hunt these woods."

I slinked around behind him. "Aren't we animals too?" I said, ignoring the misty cold air stinging my skin.

He spun, hands wide, ready. "Oh, yes we are." Heartbeats thudded, a clanging obnoxious sound. Lips curled, his eyes touched every inch he could see in the shadows, worming over my skin, a serpent in man's clothing. Excitement, thrill dragged heavy, smoky breaths through grinning teeth. "You made this moment so very easy. I should be upset." Vengeful rage bubbled, threatening to boil over. "I typically live in that chase." He pulled a long blade from his pocket. "But I will certainly never forget you."

Fingers splayed wide, ready. My girl clawed just under the surface. *Now.* The man lunged, knocking me to the ground. She was there, right there, waiting. I needed her, but she wouldn't come. Not strong enough to fight him off myself, I'd surely die—or come close—in those dark woods.

His weight held me down, straddled over my hips. "You go on and fight, little thing. I like it when they wriggle."

He pressed the dull edge of his knife against the soft mound of breast not contained in my bra. "You certainly are a pretty one." Dragging the blade under the center, he cut it open, spilling boobs out.

Where the fuck are you? I punched and scratched and

kicked, bucking with every ounce of my hundred and twenty pounds. After all that restless anticipation…

Filthy, tar-stained fingers tightened around my neck. "Pretty girls have no place out in the woods with old men." His grip tightened.

Not. Like. This. Teeth clenched, my eyes blazed, amber reflected in his dead black pupils. He let go, falling back against my legs. "What in the fuck is that?" he screeched.

"That's better." I sat up, snatched him by the collar. "I am vengeance. Your sins are mine," I growled, low and menacing.

Back arched, eyes flamed on, a surge of energy rushed through me. Magic sizzled, dancing across even the tiniest hairs on my skin. *Come on, old girl. You remember how to do this.*

Erupting in a slop of skin and pieces of my human, she arrived, fashionably late, but oh so striking. I shook dense, shaggy fur, sending plops of goo to the ground, spattering his face.

My lilac sinner scurried away like a crab—if that crab were a scared little bitch. Hands clutching the dirt, desperate for escape. He threw a handful at me.

Snort. Huff. Snarling growl. Tail whipped, *twapping* him across the face with its girth.

She remembered. Our first go round had been clunky, rushed, a virgin in the back seat on prom night. We'd grown familiar in our time together. No more groping aimlessly in the dark. We knew what we wanted and every clever move to get it.

Magenta dripped from his nose. Dense, heavy braids had surely broken it. A rough tongue swiped across sharp fangs— memories of sweet, decadent vengeance hot on our tongue.

Three sharp barks whined high, ringing death's call. He cried out once, screamed, eyes full lavender moons on his face. A single swipe, four long gashes sliced down his shirt. Blood dumped from the wounds.

I clomped forward, following his body as it fell. On his back, he looked up at me. Heart slowly chugging, losing steam.

"God help me," he gurgled, color fading as his heart slowed.

God ain't got nothing to do with the likes of us.

Swarming, stinging shiny black hornets squeezed from his eyes, slick with a layer of oily sin. Drool fell from my curled lips, plopping in rivets across his cheeks. Black ooze strung from his teeth, water dripping backward. Upward. Toward me.

I stepped back, standing at his feet. From his ears, out his nose, buzzing, winged things fought to break free from their greasy prison. They schooled, drawing strays into their dripping pool, floating over top of him.

His breaths slowed, shallow, rattling. Blood oozed, a darkening eggplant puddle. Heart hammered one last rally. *Pop.* The universe sucked that black cloud of sin right out of existence.

Death had come for him, retribution for his murdering ways. I'd come. Eventually.

A rainbow on an oil slick, Puck shimmered in the dark, through the trees. His black wolf warbled, a shift in reality. Pale minty skin glowed in shadow. His wolf, the bear, my steed didn't live in a shared space inside him. The change was simple, just a suggestion, a shift.

I'd practiced, found my beast where she lived. Coaxed her free and home again. Letting her loose was like unbuttoning your pants on Thanksgiving, necessary and almost satisfying. Reeling her back in was like trying to zip them back up again.

She'd missed the hunt, the kill. Her one true reason for existing. If I'd let her, we'd have run off the excitement out in those woods. As it stood, someone would come looking. And finding. And that certainly was not on my agenda for the evening.

Puck shoved through bushes, barefoot, pants on but left to hang open, arms full of fallen clothing. "We don't have time for beastly games. Let's get going." He pulled a fitted gray shirt on and shoved his feet into boots.

Come on, girl. We're gonna get caught. I focused, searching my clouded memory for Mama Lee's humming, or Nana's smile. The pilot just would not light. We had to change, had to hide. Someone would come. I'd never fit in the back of Puck's car in my beast skin.

My turn now. Let me on out. The beast licked blood from her paw. *We don't have time for this.* A motorcycle roared to life. Ears perked. She lifted her head to scope the lighted lot in the distance. Through the trees, two men stumbled toward the woods. Toward us.

"Man, I wouldn't piss in that shitter with your dick," one laughed.

Unless they were really lucky and stepped right on top of him, they'd never see the body out in the dark. They'd certainly spot a giant green monster with fire in her eyes.

See?

Quakes trembled under thick skin. Jolts shocked just under the surface. A slopping sneeze of a thing and out plopped a girl. Me. The quicker the change got, the more remnants were left behind. Tickling magic and changling goo clung to my toes.

Puck held my jeans open, I slid fresh legs into the holes, whipping the shirt over my head. Boots in hand, we moved quickly toward the light. No beastly eyes to light the way, I tripped over roots and stepped on sharp sticks. I stopped, shaking hands pulled on boots.

The men pushed through the brush, just far enough out to piss in the shadows. A yard from where we stood. Panicked, Puck swung me by the hand, wrapping an arm around my waist, and pressed his lips to mine. Shocks of fairy magic still coursed through my veins, tingling places I'd been ignoring.

"Oh, well, don't let us stop you." The other laughed and clapped Mr. Funny on the back.

Puck pulled back and looked at them as if they'd caught us in the throes. "Shit. Sorry. We'll uh…" He pulled me by the hand. Face flushed red, I followed. "Just be going," he breathed.

My heart galloped long after we merged onto the main

highway. I'd found her. Not my beast, me. The girl I'd left behind in Havana was dead; I'd mourn her until my true and righteous demise. But the woman who'd slapped the devil in the face was alive and just getting started.

OGHAM & WHISKEY

Fresh from the shower, bare feet slapped kitchen tile. Puck lounged on the couch, feet kicked up on the arm.

Two empty bottles of top-shelf Irish whiskey stuck out of the top of the garbage can, I opened a fresh one. Quick in. Quick out.

"Feeling human again?" Puck asked, soft, slurred words clung together.

An old record player in the corner by the fireplace crackled another song. Blue button-down nightshirt tickled my knees while I danced through the kitchen. For the first time in what seemed like a century, I was happy, right down to my almost drunk toes.

I picked at the wrapper around the cap with my teeth, ripping it free. "I feel clean, if that's what you're asking." Even in the euphoria of the kill, I'd still felt those filthy hands on my skin. What alcohol hadn't washed away I scrubbed raw.

"Close enough." Puck watched me dance through the kitchen to him in the living room, that stupid permanent grin curled on his face. "You're happy."

I knew who I was and more importantly, what I was. My family hadn't shunned me like I thought they had. I had a purpose in the universe, and while it wasn't entirely obvious sometimes, I knew where I stood in the world— for the most part—and that was more than most people could say.

I sat on the floor in front of the couch and took a draw from the bottle. "I'm drunk," I snorted. "Sort of. But yes, I am happy. Or whatever that looks like now."

Puck rolled over onto his stomach, breath hot on my ear. "Whatever it is, it looks good on you." He took the bottle from my hands and slung it back.

"Why am I with you?"

He slid our bottle into the crook of my bent leg. "Because I can't find a reason for you to be elsewhere."

Cheeks flushed, I looked down at my hands. "You know what I mean. You've been around for… a long time. So many opportunities for so many things. Why'd you seek *me* out?"

Slow, even breaths flittered tiny hairs around my face.

"I want you, Lynn, like any man wants a woman. I need you like fire needs oxygen. You fuel my need to live. After centuries of a lone existence, I finally have you."

Nervous chuckles bubbled up my throat. "Jesus, Puck, you act like you've been waiting on me."

"What's to say I haven't?"

I turned to meet deep brown eyes, searched them for lies. "Puck, I have to be honest with you. I gave my heart to Rusty Kemp long before I knew you existed. I can't—*won't* take that back."

Black fanned lashes framed dark eyes. "The funny thing about love… there's more than enough to go around." One of his signature all-teeth smiles carved a line down a cheek and he kissed the tip of my nose. "We have decades to work out the kinks. You're not bound to human laws and emotions anymore. You're higher on the food chain, babe." He laid his head on the couch, twisting a bit of my hair with sure fingers. "Years will flow into each other. Time—hours and minutes—will fade, becoming something measured by events and moments. Your life will become more than a day-to-day grind. You will become more. I want to be here for that."

The spicy tang of whiskey caressed my throat in warmth on its way down. "What's in it for you?" I'd thought it for weeks. Why me? Why this life? Not just Puck's allegiance, but all of it. Rusty. Nana. The vengeful beast squatting inside me.

Puck slinked off the couch, soft cotton pants loose

around his hips. If I'd been more comfortable with it, he'd have worn nothing at all most days. He snatched the bottle from me, guzzling half in one gulp. Swiping the back of his hand across his mouth, he grinned. "You, stupid."

He smelled like soap and summertime, and whiskey. Scads of little brown freckles dotted toned shoulders. Floppy hair, badly in need of a trim, curled over his forehead. So many human imperfections for a mythological creature. No twinkling fairy skin, or wings, or pointy ears. Just a man, with many tricks.

I slung a leg over his lap, stealing the whiskey back. "Promise me something." Eyes wide, I'd surprised him. Something I wasn't sure possible.

Steady, his fairy heart thumped even and strong. "Anything." Warm hands hovered, tickling the tiniest hairs on my thighs, waiting for the green light.

"Don't break my heart."

Dark eyes looked up at me, brows pulled high, wrinkling his forehead. "Never," he breathed.

"Good enough." Static zapped my lips when I pressed them to his. Rusty Kemp had my heart, but I'll be damned if Padraic O'Kain didn't have everything else.

Confident, careful hands gripped my thighs, pulling me closer. Working up my hips, under my shirt, fingers pressed into my back. "Is this okay?" he mumbled, still connected to my face. I rolled my eyes under closed lids and moved his hands to my boobs. *The light's green.*

Puck dragged a shaky breath through his nose, eager,

ravenous, begging me to gobble him up whole. My girl, a wild thing meant for unearthly doings, licked hidden chops, eager in her own right for the familiar taste of fae skin. I ran my tongue up his neck, living for a moment in the heavenly scent of fresh rain, wet earth, felt in every sense at once. That beastly thing craved more, a cannibal fully prepared to eat her own kind. I couldn't give her what she wanted—wouldn't—but I'd take myself right to the edge of that feral madness. Stealing every blissful moment of him and that rainy bed he'd made for me.

"Did it hurt? The ogham?" Puck asked, tracing over the black lines up my spine.

I laid on my stomach, my head resting on my arms. "It did." Sunrise teased, turning the sky white. Tired eyes blinked lazily at him. "Like a glowing hot branding iron. Are they like Percy's?"

A few quiet breaths. "And all those who came before. Gort, ciert, fearn, dair, ruis," he recited the witches chant perfectly, tapping each group of black stripes from bottom to top.

"Does that mean something?"

"Tree magic. Older than me. Simple letters, swipes of

paint, lines carved into wood and stone. The power of the universe lies in every stroke." Puck drew the first in the curve of my back. "*Gort*," he whispered, brushing two lines on my skin. "Ivy. Like it, a parasite, the Cu needs you to survive in this world, but even in your death it will live on." Heat spread where he touched. "*Ciert*, the apple—her rebirth." Three quick swipes. "The bridge that binds you to this world and the other. Alder, *fearn*, the symbol of Brân Fendigaidd." I listened to every syllable, hearing in each the fantastical notion of what I was. "The mighty oak. *Dair*. Power. Strength. Enduring." My girl waited, anticipating the last, knowing it's weight. "*Ruis*." Five steady stripes, sealed with a kiss. "Death."

A hot tear plopped on my arm. Lines of black on human skin, the rock around my neck, the blood spilt from my veins—the whole of the *fucking* universe and it was all on me. Lynnie Russell. "That's all that's holding me together?" *And sheer will.*

He pressed his head against my lower back. "Isn't it something? One minute you're just an unassuming girl dying to get out of Havana, Arkansas, and the next you're branded in ancient script smiting the wicked."

My heart skipped a beat before righting itself. What I'd lost with Rusty, what I knew in my heart Garret would've never truly understood, I had in Puck. He knew who and what I was. No lies, no secrets, no fear I'd hurt him or lose him. He'd be there, forever. Beyond forever. I'd be dead and gone and he'd be young and perfect for centuries. Him and my beast.

DAYS GONE BY

A perfect little redheaded girl squatted in the dirt in front of Garret's doublewide. The butt of her jeans caked with mud, fiery red hair shimmered clean in the wind and sun. My new truck didn't rattle and clank like the old one had, and at some point, Garret had pea-graveled the rundown dirt driveway. Only the little blond boy sitting on the stoop noticed. His clear blue eyes, almost see-through in the sunshine, just like his handsome daddy.

I'd been gone a year when I sent Mama Lee the first postcard, Massachusetts scrawled across the front in blocked letters. I'd accepted my life, chosen to live it, but I couldn't let my life go on not knowing. Maybe it was the natural protector in me. I got that from my granddaddy, didn't have much to do with the beastly thing I'd become.

Seven years it took before I was settled somewhere long enough to get a letter back. A few days later and she'd have missed me.

I watched the two play in the yard for a minute. I hadn't been there when they were born. Hadn't smoked a cigar with my brother. Hadn't held Hattie's hand while she hollered and pushed those two angels into the world. I'd missed it all.

Just when I was starting to feel sorry for myself, my daddy walked out the front door and stood on the porch, white mug of steaming coffee clutched in one hand. He stretched and scratched at his chin for a second before he saw me parked a few yards from the house.

His eyes met mine and I realized it wasn't Daddy. It was Garret. Aged, weathered from years of being a man and raising up a family. He didn't do anything, just stared at me from the porch. I stared back.

What was I supposed to do? What was I supposed to say? The last time he laid eyes on me, we were pissing and fussing in Nana's living room. A lifetime had passed since Havana. He'd changed, grown up and settled down. I was exactly the same. I'd always be exactly the same.

I raised a hand from the steering wheel and waved. He sucked in a breath and took off running, coffee cup crashed against the wooden step on his way down. Barefoot and jean-clad, he ran through the dirt and pebble stone toward me.

Before I could get the door open, he met me, ripping the handle from my hand. He had a habit of yanking me from my vehicle, but this time I didn't fight him. I slid out and let my brother scoop me up in his arms, squeeze the breath from my lungs.

The screen door slammed shut, and a breath later, I was tackled from behind. Hattie wrapped thick arms around the two of us. Garret's back shook, sobs breathed hot air against my shoulder.

"Where in the holy hell, Lynn?" he said, muffled against my shirt.

Arms wrapped tight around his neck, I whispered, "You wouldn't believe me if I told you."

"Mommy?" asked the tiniest voice, melting my hardened heart.

"Someone is calling you 'mommy.'"

Everything I'd hoped for Garret had come true. Hattie was happy. Our family had grown. With or without the likes of Lynnie Russell, it happened, life went on. It hurt that I'd missed it all, but I thanked the heavens they hadn't waited around for me.

"Poop, Daddy," a rough, scratchy little man's voice called from the porch.

I laughed and Garret let me go. Sniffing back tears, he went to tend to his son. *His son. My brother is a daddy.* He scooped up the boy from the porch and took him inside. I smiled at Hattie so big, I thought my cheeks would explode. I didn't have to ask. She knew what I was thinking.

"We're happy." She smiled too and nodded. "He's a good daddy." She looked off at the house like she could see him through the walls.

I'd lived a thousand lives in nearly a decade. Felt raw,

untamed earth underfoot. Took from this earth the most vile, became a woman, a warrior, and hadn't felt tears on my cheeks in years. "My heart is so full I think it's gonna burst."

"Wouldn't that kill you?" Olive eyes stared up at me from above freckled cheeks.

I looked down at her. "Nothing can kill me." Hattie stared at me as if she suddenly remembered why they hadn't seen my face in seven years. I let out a breath and squatted down to meet the girl. My niece. "What's your name? It must be something exceptional." I lifted a thick lock of red hair. "With a head like that, you've gotta be special."

"Maureen Eleonore Russell."

I grinned. "Well, that's quite a name."

She clapped muddy hands together, admiring the splash. "Daddy says it's a strong name from strong women." Her round cheeks squeezed green eyes half-closed with a wide grin.

"I'd say so. You have my great granny's name. She was a strong woman. With a head of red hair just like yours. Your daddy made a good choice. It suits you right fine." I wanted to reach out and squeeze the life out of her. Scoop her into my arms and tell her I loved her, and I'd never, ever leave her, but I couldn't. I'd love her to the ends of the earth, but I couldn't say I'd never leave. Havana wasn't my home anymore. It couldn't hold the power I brought with me.

A scratchy giggle came from behind me. Garret hauled his son out the door by his feet, the boy laughing the whole way.

"That's my brother." She rolled her eyes and pointed at

the boy. "Rusty."

Air caught in my chest. A name I'd thought of every day for seven years but hadn't heard spoken once. It made sense my brother would name his only son after his dead best friend.

"Rusty... Russell..." I raised my eyebrows at Garret and he nodded. "Honor your friend, brother, don't torture your kin." I was proud of the name choice, but it did leave the poor child with a silly name.

"He'll be fine." Garret patted his son on the butt and set him down. "Missed the service," he said, choking back solace.

I blinked at him. "Garret, that was seven years ago. I'm sorry I haven't called. I just—"

"Daddy died, Lynn."

Breath shuttered. "What?" I swallowed hard. Tears clung to my lashes. His blue eyes met mine, looking so much like the man in question. "When?"

"Couple weeks now."

"I got a letter...." I let the rest go. Didn't want Garret to know Mama Lee had known all along where I was. Didn't need him over there badgering her for my whereabouts when I left again. He'd just come and find me. Leave his family behind to hunt a ghost long gone.

"He'd been sick just a month before the cancer took him."

"How's Mama?" I asked, voice hardly a whisper.

"Don't know. Ain't seen her since the funeral."

"Oh, Mama. Damn it." It was just like her to flit off, looking for a new man to keep her. "Garret, I'm so sorry I wasn't here." It was strange, daunting to feel so human. The beast turned and flopped in my soul, reminding me why it was necessary to shut that emotional, human place inside me off.

"You got things to do. I get it."

I looked at Hattie, unsure what Garret knew and what he didn't. She closed her eyes and nodded. He knew it all. Everything I was. Everything I'd done. "Garret, I'm so sorry for everything." My girl roiled, feeling every ounce of my human pain. "I…" *I'm sorry I killed Rusty.*

He looked away. "I know. I know." He ran a hand over his hair. "You staying for dinner?" Garret asked, without looking at me.

Head tilted at the morning spring sun, I pulled in the fresh spring scent I'd missed over the years, contemplating a full day in Havana. "The law still waiting around for the long-awaited return of Lynnie Russell?" I grinned, but it didn't reach my eyes.

Garret waved off the idea. "Been out here quite a few times asking for you. Some years now since anyone came looking. Wouldn't want you bringing attention to yourself. That *creature*." He flicked his hand angrily in my direction and I caught sight of four long scars across his forearm.

I cringed at the damage I'd caused, gulping back guilty bile. "I have control now. I know what I am and how to be. There's no choice in it, Garret. Like a heartbeat, I don't have to think about it anymore. I just do what I do. What happened with you and… Rusty was an accident. I was young and didn't know what I was. Puck helped me to come to terms with it, tame my beast."

"Puck?" Garret asked. Hattie smiled knowingly and looked at me from the corner of her eye while she watched the kids playing.

I nodded. "He's a good... *man*. Puck's like me. I can't hurt him." The end of my nose tingled, threatening a new stream of tears.

"What about Rusty?" Garret's tone teetered on hostile. "I thought you loved him."

"Garret... Rusty's gone." He scoffed. "He's been gone for a long time. Rusty Kemp will always have my heart, but I couldn't live the rest of my already lonely existence truly alone. I have someone I don't have to lie to. Someone I can't kill."

Garret sniffed back tears. "Well, looks like you've got it all figured out then." He looked back at the kids. "Looks like you're just fine."

"Fine? Not really. But surviving, existing, yes. I worked hard to be where I am now. To live without you all. It takes work to pretend like I'm not dying inside every single day." I turned away from him, swallowing the thick lump trapped in my throat. "I didn't even know y'all had kids. I'd... I'd have come back for that. I wouldn't have missed that," I said around the stubborn bulge.

I'd lie to myself, tell myself I'd have come running, but I knew better. Mama Lee's letter, *Come on home, one last time*, had arrived when it needed to. When I was ready. "I didn't have a choice, Garret. I was given this by birth and there's not a damn thing I can do about it but try my damnedest to keep those I love safe."

His eyes sparkling with tears. "Maureen…?" He'd spent my time away pretending too, hoping with all his heart it wasn't true.

"Oh." I looked at the little redhaired girl. "I don't know, Garret. I really don't. If I did, I'd make sure she was ready. I wouldn't let her be like Mama let me. It's just not safe." I wrapped my hand around his; it trembled, slick with sweat. "Nana, Granny Gwen, me…. Don't lie to her. To any of them." Tension squeezed his jaw tight. "Brother, listen, if I even think for a second that baby is next in line, I'll be back. I'll be here for her." I'd eventually die for her.

Glistening, red-rimmed eyes met mine. "I trust you."

"Thank you." Those three words were stronger than any others in history.

"Come on now, you two." Hattie hooked her arm with mine. "Let's make a plan for supper." I held Garret's hand up the steps and into the last home I'd had.

The three of us sat around their dinner table and visited until the night fell and darkness filled the sky. Maureen, a storybook held tight in her hands, asked if Auntie Lynn could read her to sleep.

I tucked that perfect baby into bed and kissed her forehead. We snuggled together, in my old room, little Rusty softly snoring in the crib he'd nearly outgrown. I read, twirling her fiery hair around my finger, and she listened.

At the end of the story, the knight had rescued the princess, riding off into the sunset to live happily ever after.

"Auntie," she yawned, "will you live here, happy forever after?"

I breathed, forcing steadying breaths into unwilling lungs. "Sweet girl, I'm always with you, but I can't stay." She whimpered. "There's a big, giant world out there to be seen and I'm not done seeing it. You'll be big one day and you'll leave this town in your dust." I kissed her head. It smelled like sunshine, reminded me of Puck.

She rolled, curled into my side. "Daddy says you have a very important job that needs to be done."

"That's true."

"He says you're something special," she said, and stole my heart right out of my chest.

A wide grin about knocked my ears off. "I guess that's true too. In my story, I am the knight." I took a breath "I'm a warrior." Her dainty lips fell open. "And so are you."

"*Me?*"

"Yup. And your daughter, and hers, and so on. My nana, and hers. It's in our family."

"What about Daddy?" she asked.

"He's special in his own way. He keeps my heart planted on the earth when my head needs to be elsewhere. And he gave me, and the world, you. Someday, I'll be back. You might be old and gray, but I'll be there. I promise." That promise I knew I'd keep. I'd be back eventually, if only to complete the cycle. *Ciert.*

"I wish you could be here always." My soul recognized hers. The same sizzling magic that vined deep in me, pumped through her veins. The Cu Sidhe would find her kin one day. Our fate would continue.

"I do, too. But the world waits for me. And it waits for you. Be strong, little one. Grow big and smart. Learn everything you can. See the beauty and balance in the world. Deep down in that heart of yours there is nothing on this earth that can break you. Raise your babies to be the same. Promise me?"

"Yup." She nodded and yawned.

"Good. Now, sleep, my angel. I'll be gone in the morning, but I'll love you always." I wanted to say more. I wanted to tell her everything she'd ever need to know about the world and how to survive in it. Instead, I kissed her one last time and sang her Nanny's favorite hymn until her breathing slowed and I knew she was asleep.

I pushed through the screen door where Hattie sat in the dark on the top step, a half-empty beer in her hand. Garret snored in the recliner. I'd kissed his head on my way out the door, waking him up to say goodbye seemed cruel. So did walking out for a second time. Remember those shit options? Life handed them out in abundance.

"Gonna just leave again?" she muttered, dragging a cigarette.

I sat beside her, plucking the smoldering thing from her fingers. "Still lighting up when you drink? Or'd you start up full-time?" Smoke circled my hand.

She scoffed, killing her beer in one swig. "He's never stopped looking out the window for you."

I pulled a long drag on the cigarette. "I didn't have a choice, Hattie. I could've killed him. You. Mama. Your babies," I croaked.

"What about now?" She took her smoke back, dragged until the end blazed bright. "You gotta choice?" Smoked billowed from her lips.

Moon high in the sky, half-full, lighting only what wasn't shadowed by trees. "Yeah." I sniffed. "I do."

She laid her head on my shoulder, sitting in the comfortable silence of our chosen sisterhood. "You better say goodbye this time."

I nodded, kissing the top of her head. "I'm glad I chose you."

Garret snored—exhausted from a week of hard labor. His beat-up old lunch pail, the same he'd snuck beers home in, sat on top of the fridge. Ready for a new day.

I knelt beside him, watching his eyes flutter under closed lids. A breath below a whisper, I cupped my hand around his ear, "I love you to the ends of the earth, brother. You are my heart. My tender soul. I am human because of you." Magic crackled the tips of my fingers, tickling his ear.

He groaned, not quite awake, not fully asleep. "Live in magic for me, Lynn," he breathed.

A final kiss on the forehead—deep lines cut across it, matching the whiskers starting to form around his eyes. "I love you, old man."

I was at the door when he said, "I love you too."

DAYDREAM BELIEVER

Puck—and the life I'd carved out for myself—waited on me in a cushy room just outside of Little Rock. I wouldn't make him wait too long. I had a few ends to tie before I left Havana for what I'd decided then would be forever—until my time came near its end. My soul just couldn't take the blows being home brought along with it. The cover of darkness would serve me well to not get caught.

Tires crunched along the gravel road that wound through grassy spaces around plots. There was only one major cemetery near Havana, not counting family gravesites on homesteads scattered about the county. Everyone I'd come to see would be right there in one place.

I figured my daddy would be to the west with the Russells and I knew just where Nana would be. Right next to my granddaddy. I parked the truck and tromped along the grass toward the Russell section. There were a lot of us, and most were laid to rest in one clump near the big tree in the back corner.

No true stone yet, a metal marker with a paper sign marked his place. Someone had left a toy truck—double trailers with a blue cab, just like his. He'd lived most of my life in that rig.

Ass over teakettle in love with Mama back in high school. It wasn't often a love burned so hot it lasted forever. By the time I came along, there was no turning back and Daddy knew it. He started driving truck that same year. Eventually, the hauls kept him gone longer and longer. Until the day came I knew my dad only by the trinkets he brought me.

I dropped to my knees in the dewy grass. "Oh, Daddy. I feel like I let you go long before you left." Sitting back on my heels, I took a big deep breath, pulling in the smell of the gardenias. "You did what you had to do. I get that now. I don't hate you for it. Thank you for bringing Garret and me into this world. Thanks for making up the human part of me. I don't know what I'd do without it. I love you, Dad. I guess…" I stopped to consider my words. "I guess I'll be seeing you."

I stood and brushed the grass from my knees. I had more goodbyes to say, and on a night so fleeting time wouldn't wait.

Standing tall, in near the center of a shallow hill, *Higgins* carved into a stone. I swallowed hard and shuffled to the place I'd visited more times than I could count.

Delma Devlin Higgins. Mother and Nana. Gone to the Heavens, etched just below the Higgins name. The silhouette of a cat carved beneath the date. A day I'd remember even in death. The sight of it dumped tears on my lashes. My bottom lip shook, and I thought twice about biting it off just to keep it from wriggling away and taking my resolve with it.

"Nanny," I said, and a full sob poured from my depths. Falling to my knees, every ounce of emotions I'd hidden away in my years gone from Havana bubbled up and out, soaking my cheeks with salty tears.

"I'm sorry. I'm more than sorry. I'm…" *Dying*, I wanted to say. But I didn't. It was a lie. I wasn't dying, because I couldn't. I sure wanted to. "I want you to be with God. I pray to whatever will listen that you've found your way home. With Granddaddy." I stopped myself. My grandpa was the only man I knew, but he hadn't stolen her heart, not fully. "I want your soul to be happy wherever you find yourself."

I left my knees to lay in the grass at the foot of the headstone. The tall, etched stone stood over me, my guard. I closed my eyes and pictured Nanny's face. Her curly silver hair and fingers filled to the tip with rings of all types. The way her eyes crinkled around the edges when she laughed.

There was nothing I wanted more in that moment than to crawl up her lap and listen to her humming a song deep in her chest. I thought maybe I could, one day, when I was allowed to leave the confines of earth and my soul flittered off to play with those who left before me. The thought became a hope and I tucked it away for safekeeping.

"My heart is filled with your wisdom and love. You taught me how to be a woman in this world. Your blood brought with it my gift to the universe. My gift of justice, my sacrifice of life for the greater good. Your strength, the strength of your family before you, courses through my veins and reminds me I have more to do than sit and blubber over my can't-haves."

Blue light cast eerie shadows. "I healed my cracks, but I never stopped to look them over. To accept them for what they were. It's about more than mending and ignoring," I reminded myself. "I needed a moment to step back and admire the work. Even the worst of the world needs attention. Even the hurt need love. Sometimes, saying goodbye is all it takes."

I'd say it, and I'd mean it. "Goodbye, Nana. I love you," I said after a long few minutes of breathing and reassuring myself that I knew what I was doing.

Too many years had passed and I thought in that time I'd moved beyond Havana and the losses my soul had seen there. I hadn't gotten over anything. I'd just put enough time behind it and my humanity forgot its hurt. It takes things like that, pain and sorrow, to remind us what it means to be a human in the first place.

Puck smiled about everything. Not because life was a happy place to be, but his lack of empathy for things that stung deep. I'd come to learn it was just part of his makeup and in reality, part of mine. My fae had begun to take over and steal away my human, leaving me content, indifferent with life and losses I'd felt. Immortality seemed to do that to people. Returning to the place I'd thought I'd forgotten ripped the human right to the surface and lay it out raw for the stings of the world to scratch over the breadth of it.

I clawed, digging at the earth. Nosed my muzzle into the deep hole I'd dug. My heavy paw scooped dirt away from a gray stone buried deep in the ground. Shoving dirt away, two round holes. I nosed against it and freed it from the earth. Swiping a paw, I tipped it on its side. Along the right side, a silver tooth shined in the moonlight. No stone, a skull. Our heart twisted and churned until it escaped from my throat in a howl that shook the forest. In the dead of night, in some woods somewhere, I'd dragged up the skull of my nanny.

I sat up screaming. Yellow sun blared into my eyes. Rode hard and laid out wet, I smacked away the tang from my mouth and shook the nightmare from my head.

A stiff breeze whipped through my hair. I closed my eyes

against the dust that stung my cheeks. Using the stone to brace me, I stood and turned my back to the wind. Off, beyond the blooming hawthorn to the north, a man stood, leaning against a tall marker. It was the form of a man I never thought I'd lay my eyes on again. Without thinking, I tore off in a full run. The heels of my boots dug into the grass and kicked up the dirt around them.

My eyes stayed trained on the figure. *I'm coming. Don't go. Don't leave me.* He flickered, his signal growing weaker the closer I got. A weak smile spread over his face, and in an instant, he was gone. I reached the marker where he'd been leaning. I scoured the landscape for any sign he'd been there. Searched the soil for boot prints.

"Rusty," I panted, clinging to the stone for balance. "Come back," I pleaded with the ghost.

I waited for a few panting breaths before giving up. Taking one last look at the dirt that surrounded the tall, slender headstone, I realized where I was standing. *Ruston Kemp - taken long before his time.* A wailing sob escaped my lungs before I could stop it. I wrapped my arms around the stone as if it were Rusty himself. It was warm under the southern sun, the edges sharp and digging into my skin. I let it. A pain I more than deserved.

"Are you here?" I whispered through my crying. "Or are you trapped in this place?" I asked and held a hand to my breaking heart.

In all those years, I'd never let Rusty go. His death was a mar on my human soul and his love was a thread by which

I was stitched to this earth. He was as much a part of me as my ancient fairy beast. Accepting my guilt, his death, I tucked away the hope that one day I'd see him again.

Bottom lip quivered as resolve bled from my core through the tips of my fingers and toes.

"My darling boy. Your life ended because of me. By my hand, you're not here with me. I will live with that until the day I'm finally free of this earth. Until then, I promise to keep you tucked away, safe with my raw human bits." I sucked up all my courage and let go of my selfish, human feelings. "I'm off to do special things, just like you told me to." More tears threatened to come. I wiped them away with the tenacity and resolve that came along with being an ancient creature. "You are my humanity. I love you with every last ounce of that. Until we meet again, my love." I closed my eyes. Letting out a breath, I sent with it the pain of Rusty's death that had festered in my depths.

With the cemetery in my rearview mirror, a longing settled in my soul I knew then would never leave. I would spend my life longing.

Sam's pump station—the place I thought I'd grown up—sat vacant. Boards nailed on the windows, a no trespassing sign plastered on more than one. I wondered what'd happened to Sam, the man who taught me the meaning of a dollar, what hard work and respect looked like. He'd called after me on those first days of my rebirth. Worried about me. Left a couple messages on the machine, the last sounded tearful. Another player in the game of my life, lost to memory.

Mama Lee's cluttered yard hadn't changed much in the years I'd been gone. Person-tall sunflowers jutted from the edges, framing the backside of the property. I grinned at the beaded curtain on her back porch. I knew, in my gut, she was just on the other side of those beads. Killing the engine, I hopped out, my boots puffing up dust around them.

"Well, I'll be. Lynnie Russell in the lovely flesh," Mama Lee called to me from behind her beads. "Get on up here, girl." Time, it seemed, had stood still for both of us.

"I got your letter."

"Well, never would've if you hadn't kept me up-to-date with your travels." Her smile spread from ear to ear and she opened her arms wide for a hug.

Stronger than she looked, Mama Lee's slender arms wrapped around my shoulders and damn near squeezed the breath from me. The beast tumbled inside, happy to see our old friend.

"You been out to see your nanny," she said like she already knew it to be true and wasn't bothering with a question.

"Yeah." I nodded and she let me go, making her way

into the house.

"Got to visit with Rusty?" She seemed to already know that, too.

I followed her inside. The room was still filled to the brim with trinkets and magical things. "I did." Drying herbs and flowers, wrapped tight in twine, hung from hooks in the doorway.

"Feel better?" she asked and poked her head from around the jamb of the door that led into the kitchen.

She knew exactly what she was up to even if I didn't. "I do."

"Well, then, how's about some breakfast? You must be starved half to death." She disappeared into the kitchen. "Getting skinny, too. That curly headed boy not feeding you?" She asked about Puck as though she didn't know his name. "Come on in here. I've got a pig frying."

I raised a brow at her. "I feed myself."

"Good to hear." She turned to look me in the eye. "Did you get out all that darkness that's been weighing you down all these years?"

Spicy smoke swirled from the end of a burning bundle of herbs, I breathed it in, remembering the day she'd calmed the beast and called me free. "I did," I said under my breath. "Didn't even know it was there."

"Can't let go of something unless you know where to find it." Drying her hands, she continued, "You won't be back, Lynn," she said, a matter of fact that I had yet to speak out loud. "This was your last visit to Havana… until your time comes, so I'm assuming. If you hadn't come back now, that hidden sorrow wouldn't've ever had the chance to come out in the open and blow away with the wind."

"I see. I didn't, but now I do." She slid an icy glass of tea in front of me. "You've been a friend to me when the world seemed to turn its back." I took a gulp, living in the memory of my youth for a moment. I couldn't stay there forever, in that place. It was a place of dreams meant only for memory.

"Your face hasn't changed an inch." She ran a rough finger over my jaw, taking in the magic of it.

"I was just thinking the same about you."

She swallowed hard and sniffed back something I couldn't quite peg. "You, my dear, have a long, interesting life to live. You leave us be here. We'll get on fine. You've done what you came here to do." She kissed my forehead and stood up from the table. "Cleaned house."

"I wish I could stay." I looked out the open door at all of her trinkets. "I'd like to get to know my niece and nephew. I miss my brother and Hattie." Sadness trickled its way over my heart and my feet hesitated to leave. "There are things here I want," I said without thinking.

"You've got a job to do. Go do it. We'll get on fine here."

"You trying to kick me out?" I joked.

She plucked a dried sprig of rosemary from a bundle and stuck it behind my ear. "For remembrance."

Havana needed me to say goodbye. I needed it too. Vengeance waited for no man. Or woman. As it were.

I hugged Mama Lee, tight and long. She held her breath in, perhaps fighting off tears. I didn't have room to cry anymore. It was a much-needed moment, a stitch in my existence that'd waited just long enough for me to grow unbreakable.

"Goodbye, old friend."

She sniffed and patted me on the shoulder. "All right now, be on with you."

I stepped off the porch steps and turned back over my shoulder. "I'll be seeing you."

"Long off." She shooed at me with a withered hand.

Before I drove off, she shouted one final bit of advice. "Be careful of your instincts, girl. They may not have your best interests at heart," she warned, and disappeared behind her curtains.

TAKING FLIGHT

Bright, white and charming, Puck's grin greeted me when I shoved through the door of our suite. "Miss me?" he asked, closing a book and setting it on the table.

"More than I expected, actually." I dropped my bag on the floor beside the bed.

Long legs cleared the distance between us. Strong arms wrapped around my middle. Small, intimate kisses covered my cheeks.

"You smell different," he whispered against my neck. "Like a spring breeze."

Ghosts of Havana dust peppered my cheeks. "And children."

I cleared the lump in my throat. I wouldn't go back. Couldn't. It wasn't my home anymore. They'd be my people until I was gone from the earth, but my home was with the beast. With Puck. Cu Sidhe didn't belong in Havana. She was a worldly creature with an Otherworld home of her own. A place that held the secrets of what we were. What'd been kept from me.

"I'm ready," I said quietly in his ear.

He walked me backward, plopping me down to the couch. "That wasn't my goal, but who am I to turn down a beautiful woman." A sly grin curled his lips. He kissed my neck.

"I'm ready to go home." I closed my eyes, sitting in the idea of leaving all I'd known. If it meant security for the future of my bloodline, I'd give it all up. Every day of earthly life. For that little redheaded girl I'd have done just about anything. "It's time I see Knockma for myself."

His eyes held mine for a long few breaths. "Are you sure?"

One good breath, a hard swallow, then "Yes." A simple word changed everything, as that word tended to do.

Eyes black as coffee and just as tempting scanned my face. "I knew this day would come. Never imagined this soon, but you're certainly ready." Eager hands groped the back of my head beneath thick hair.

My girl roiled inside, desperate to break free. Trapped inside her human too many hours while we traversed Havana. "Just one thing," I breathed, enjoying the weight of him on top of me.

"Anything."

Soft curls sprung free, falling over my face. "Can I trust you?"

"To the ends of the earth." His grin lit my soul on fire, stomach flipping somersaults. It could have been the beast, though. Maybe she knew where we were headed and was leaping for joy at the thought. She was finally going home. If *I* couldn't go home again, at least I could make sure one of us could.

"Now what?"

He touched the tip of his tongue to the corner of his mouth. "We fly."

My brows dropped. "Like with wings?"

He kissed my nose. "Like with Delta."

We'd packed so many times over the years neither one of us kept anything around that couldn't fit in a suitcase. This time though, we packed only what we couldn't absolutely leave behind. I'd shoved the photos of Garret and my family I'd been lugging around for years and the small cotton pouch that held the only piece of magic I owned into a small backpack already stuffed with tightly rolled clothes and my coffee mug.

My hand trembled, fingering the edge of the black leather folder that held my passport. Puck's friend, a *clúrachán* he knew out west, had made me a stack of false identification some years back. The drunk little thing said times had changed and *Tuath Dé*—which I'd come to learn was my ancestral heritage—better change with it. They'd lived among humans for centuries undetected; cleverness and adaptability had surely been a strong suit.

"You'll be fine. Promise."

Puck's voice cut through my own thoughts. He kissed my knuckles. It was more than the flight; it was the hours trapped in a tube of people. One of whom could cut to purple midflight and we'd be in a world of mess. I'd talked with my girl, warned her, begged her to let me be. But she'd been restless since we left Havana. Sensing home so close. I'd felt the same when we crossed the Arkansas state line for the first time in years.

Puck wrapped a warm hand around mine. A woman with a foreign accent announced over the loudspeaker, "Flight 136 for Dublin, Ireland now boarding."

LORD AND LADY MISHAP

Milky gray sky loomed overhead casting cinematic tones across the landscape. Puck's pale skin glowed, nearly iridescent in the light.

Thickets of trees hid away things I was sure ruled the earth at one time. Like the beast hiding inside me. For the first time I—the me I'd become—truly felt home. As out of place as I was, I knew within me was a creature born of that land and those people.

Puck mentioned more than once how it had all changed so much since he'd last been there. I could only imagine what it looked like. As it was, the cobblestone roads and aging brick buildings looked like something out of a storybook.

"It's like nothing I've seen."

He squeezed my hand. "From a place of knowledge you speak." He'd grown quiet since we'd landed in Ireland. Anxious.

"You okay?" I asked, watching the side of his face for any sign of worry.

He turned to me, charming grin spread wide. "Always."

Turning off the main road and onto a narrow hole-filled single lane, Puck pointed out a stone tower damn near taken over by greenery of all types. Castle Hackett, he called it.

"Fairy seers," he said with a wink.

With his nondescript accent and all-around boy-next-door charm, it was hard to picture him as an ancient fae creature roaming the rolling green hills of Ireland. Time had a way of stripping the true nature of folks.

The narrow lane ended at a pile of branches covering a path that disappeared behind a rounded mound covered in mossy overgrowth.

"There's not a road that leads to where we're headed. We'll need to walk the rest of the way. The entrance to *Cnoc Meadha*, the Otherworld, is through the trees and over the hill. It can't be found on a map and cannot be entered by a human." Puck hefted my bag on his shoulder. "Or an unwanted," he added, pushing the door shut with his foot.

Soft blades of moist grass tickled the tips of my fingers. A few yards up the trail, a waterless dam of old limbs and a fallen tree. Happy I'd laced my boots tight, I balanced on top, hardly clearing it with short legs and Puck's help.

A stone path, thick moss curling from between many cracks, led to steps that disappeared around the mound and out of sight.

Puck shrugged my bag from his shoulder. A bright grin eased fear that brewed, a slow boil in my gut. "Are you ready for this?"

I pinched my lips in my teeth, surveying the hill ahead of us. "You're sure it's safe?" It was the fifth time I'd asked something similar and just like the first time, he kissed my forehead, smiled, and nodded.

"This is your home. You belong here."

A smile lifted my cheeks and sent tears to my eyes. My girl grumbled, stretching, ready for home.

"I'll take you the rest of the way." He slid the straps of my bag over my shoulders. "When we arrive, you'll know. You will feel it deep within you. Just like I taught you, call to King Finvarra and ask for passage."

I swallowed hard. "What if—" He put a finger to my lips.

"You are Cu Sidhe. Warrior. Reaper of vengeance. Do not forget that." Eyes a shade above black held my stare, speaking to not just me but the beast. "You belong here. Always have."

Destined from birth, my beast, the fae in my soul, had always made me something different. Something more. I'd never truly belonged in Havana. Maybe my home was just beyond those steps.

Puck pressed his lips to my forehead, quivering breaths shook from his nose. Silver light shook around him. A breath and he was gone. In his place, my shiny black steed.

His hooves clomped over the stone steps. Footfalls hit without hesitation. My stomach jolted with each the higher along the hill we moved. I couldn't die, but I sure as hell didn't want to go tumbling down the side of a wet, grassy hill through a thicket of clawlike shrubbery either.

We rounded a bend into an endless arch of trees. Gnarled, leafless branches reached from either side of the trail. Boney fingers, threatening to snag hair and skin as we passed. Breaching the arch, a searing punch hit my gut. Puck shook his mane, flicked his tail.

Crackling magic rolled over my skin, vining lilac volts at the tips of my fingers. Only slight beams of muted light poked through thick treetops, casting crooked shadows over the trail.

The beast roared, baying, forcing room where there was none. Ahead, those jagged branches had grown together, overtaken by flowering vines.

Puck's hooves slowed to a stop. He puffed encouragement from his snout.

Cnoc Meadha. I let out a long shaking breath. "King Finvarra," I shouted, my own booming voice startled me. I swallowed back fear, squared my shoulders. "I am Sharlene Carolynn Diamond Russell from Havana, Arkansas. I am Cu Sidhe." Puck snorted. "I request entry."

Silence met me. A breath. Two. "Did I do it right?" I whispered.

Small yellow flowers, in full bloom, shrunk, pinching closed. Vines slithered over one another, leaving their home to twirl midair. The smallest reached first, skinny little things that flicked a snakelike tongue. Thicker, more menacing tendrils unfurled, reaching for me.

The first wrapped around Puck's strong legs, tugging

him forward. Heart wild, untamed, galloped in my chest. The beast roared, rumbling up my throat. Vines fell from overhead, curling into my hair, sliding down my shirt.

Spiny tipped branches poked into my back, claws capturing prey. Never penetrating my skin, those slithering vines wiggled deep into my soul, tickling my beast.

"Puck," I strangled, leafless branches growing up my throat and out my mouth.

Flowers bloomed at the ends, growing, spreading, engulfing me and the horse I rode in on. When the earth swallowed me from the inside out, I thanked the heavens it hadn't come with thorns.

Air sucked into my lungs, dragging in the taste of wet earth. Music played in the distance. Slender green vines slid up my back, uncurling themselves from my body.

I blinked. And blinked again. A constant motion, flowers and leaves and vines trailed over every nonmoving thing. Opening, closing, slithering.

Overhead, thick treetops filtered golden light, spilling in long strips on cottage roofs and ever-blooming petals.

Otherworld.

Green and purple waves of energy zipped up and down my arms. My girl wanted free. If I didn't let her loose soon, she'd chew her way out. A sensation I'd have rather not live again. I clung tight to my steed, silently begging Puck to come back to me.

Glittering specks, no bigger than a pill bug, flittered over and under and around everything. A horned being, tall as the nearest eave, eyed us over a furry shoulder. Wings surprisingly scant in the land of the Sidhe, it was overflowing with a bustling community of creatures. Most of which were starting to notice we'd arrived.

"Time to come back now," I whispered, keeping my eye on those things closest, with the biggest claws.

My beast, the Cu finally home after so long, fought to break free. Claws and teeth stinging my insides. Puck had been right, I'd've never made it past the vining gates without the control I'd gained in my years playing death.

Heavy footfalls quaked the tight village. "Padraic O'Kain!" a man's voice bellowed through the trees and over the rooftops, shaking loose petals and leaves.

All movement ceased. Critters scurried for shelter. Some, the bravest of them, stopped to watch, huddled together, whispering—pointing at the girl and her black horse.

Full breaths puffed from Puck's nose, heaving, panting. Without so much as a shimmer, he popped back into existence. Sending me crashing to the ground, knocking the air from my chest.

A giant of a man clomped toward us, shoving aside any creature not clever enough to move away. Long, braided red beard billowed in a breeze of his own creation. A crown of twigs and leaves sat on his head. Puck didn't take his eyes off him, kneeling to help me up.

"Remember who you are," he whispered to me, lifting me from the ground.

Feathers from shoulder to foot swooshed behind the heap of a man, a cape fit for a king. Puck's natural calm had been left behind in the human world. Now his heart fluttered, flipping over itself. My beast growled, rumbling deep in my chest.

Puck's hands clamped tight on my shoulders, silently begging, pleading for help. Whatever he'd expected from me I didn't think I could give it. Even held tight under my imaginary lid, the beast was wild, feral, home and happy to be there, ready to kill to be free.

Gigantor stopped a foot from us, towering over even Puck's six feet. "You have defied banishment, Puca. Exiled to earth for eternity. How did you penetrate my gates?

Puck stood tall, as though he wasn't completely naked, held his shoulders tight. Jaw clenched, he looked up at the man's murky olive eyes.

"King Finvarra, you will be pleased of my return. Of that I can promise you." Puck's naturally warm hand heated my lower back. "I've returned something you've been missing." He squeezed my arm, shoving me toward the man. "Your Cu Sidhe has come home."

CRIME AND PUNISHMENT

"*What?*" I growled, looking back at him.

Puck shoved me to the ground at Finvarra's feet and tore off into a sprint. The king groped for him, but Puck was too wily and quick. He snaked around the oaf of a man, white cheek clenched, an inch from being snatched up by the king's mitt of a hand.

The brutish king stomped after the naked Puca, reaching and just missing. Puck's feet hardly touched the ground. He leapt to a nearby rooftop, inches from Finvarra's reach.

I scurried back, frantically searching for a handhold to get to my feet. King Finvarra whipped his cape back, drawing a long sword from a sheath at his hip. Puck looked at the sword, then to me. The corner of his mouth twisted, curling into a grin. He winked. White wings flapped once, pulling his human form into the shape of a dove. A feather floated to the ground at the king's feet.

He'd left me. He'd tricked me. All that time. All those years. *To the end of the earth.* "Fucker."

"Cu Sidhe," King Finvarra bellowed. Those who'd stayed to watch the show turned to me, mouths and eyes full circles.

I gulped noisily and pushed myself to standing. On earth, I was stronger, faster, older than anything alive. In the land of the fae people, I was a human with a big, mean dog stuck inside me. A beast desperate to break free.

King Finvarra stood over me a good two feet. Ruddy, freckled skin more like an old farmer than an ancient fairy king. He bent at the hip, nose touching the tip of mine. A sinister grin curled wormlike lips over his teeth.

"Good dog." He patted my head and the beast growled, rumbling up through my chest, snarling my lip. The thin membrane that kept her inside rattled, stretched, almost broke under her pressure. "Hush now, *madra*. None of that."

The beast hadn't been happy to return home. She hadn't been tumbling around with joy. My girl wanted to be free to wreak vengeance on the things that lived there. "Why do I feel like you're not a good guy?"

"Good guy?" He looked confused. His thick accent muddling most of his words.

"Up to no good." Wooly brows pinched together. "Rotten… ornery…" He shook his head. "An asshole?"

He laughed again. "When *Croí na Tlachtga* planted my Cu into your kind, I thought it a curse on the house of fae and its king. Now, oh, now, it's a blessing. A feisty human woman come traveling right down to me. Aye, that's a sight." He looked me up and down.

"Now, you look here—" I started and pointed my finger in his face. King Finvarra chuckled and playfully bit at my finger. "I want to see Puck and then I want to go home. My *real* home."

"Puck? Your Puca betrayed you. Why would you want to see him?"

"I want to deliver him my thanks." Fire ignited in my eyes, glinting copper on his shiny nose.

"Oh, can't be having that now." The king snapped his fingers. A cloak fell around my shoulders, weighing heavy. Burdensome.

My stomach clenched, a fist tightening in pain. The beast reared, and bucked, and roared, and clawed, breaking the membrane, but trapped inside her worthless human.

Without another word, the king hoisted me up over his shoulder like a sack of potatoes. I kicked and screamed and cussed, but the thick cloak and Finvarra held tight. With a leather boot, he kicked open a wood slatted door, tossing me to the floor on a pile of animal pelts.

Eyes flaming, Black Sentry aglow, I growled, low and menacing, daring him to come closer.

Trunk-like legs straddled over top of me as he looked down over his thick beard. "Quite a shame I can't keep you, girl." Heavy, sneering breaths snorted from his nose. He climbed down to stand over me on all fours.

I refused to sit back, refused to make it easy. "You'd better pray my beasty stays put, asshole. She's dying for a piece of you." I longed for that sweet violet vision to call my girl out to play. The cloak kept us weak, jamming our signals.

"As I for a piece of you." Hot, steaming breaths heated my face. His slick, slimy tongue slid up my cheek. Crackles on my skin zapped his tongue. He moaned. "*Tlachtga* magic. Thought she could best King Finvarra." One loud bark of a laugh. "And here you are, delivered right to my lap." He thrust his wide hips against me.

"Careful, old man. I've killed things scarier than you." Which was mostly a lie. "My beast and I."

A sausage finger ran across my lip. "No, dearie, *my* beast. Come home."

He grunted and shoved his mouth against mine, probing my lips with his slippery tongue. No fresh rain, Finvarra tasted of human flesh—not salty, sinful. Predatory. My girl ripped me apart from the inside, anxious to tear the king to pieces.

Horse hooves clip-clopped outside, growing closer. A whinny caught the king's attention. He sneered and sat up to look out the window. My stallion clomped back and forth, taunting Finvarra.

"Godshite, Puca," he bellowed, hoisting himself from the ground. Finvarra, in two wide steps, flung the door open. "Padraic." His roar shook anything not nailed down.

Puck dashed in front of the king, tearing off through the crowd and out of sight. The door slammed shut.

I pawed at the cloak wrapped snug around my shoulders. No tie or clasp, it clung there, plastic on a square of cheese.

"Fuck," I hissed. "That son of a bitch." I'd followed Puck

to the ends of the earth for a chance at knowledge. The thought of home. If he'd just told me he wanted to go home, we could have made a plan. Formulated an attack. "How the hell am I gonna get out of this?"

"By your wit, I would assume," said a voice I hadn't heard in years.

"Avery?" I searched the room for her.

"Are ya kicking yourself in the arse yet?" She appeared at the window. White eyes glowed brighter than they ever had.

"How'd you get here?" I asked, more thankful to see her face than I'd admit.

She shook her head. "You missed the lesson and now you must learn the hard way." She cocked an eyebrow at me. "The hidden gates of *Cnoc Meadha* open to all Sidhe. I'm here now, but I cannot stay." Checking over her shoulder, she whispered, "You must escape at any cost."

And how the hell will I manage that? "I need the beast." My voice squeaked. "Come in through the door. I need help getting this thing off." I tugged at the cumbersome cape. "I don't have the strength."

"And you won't with it on. Woven with iron. It was the only thing could stop Cu Sidhe when it went feral."

"Help me," I begged, panic filled my lungs.

She shook her head, hair billowing in an unseen breeze. "You don't get it, girl. Noncorporeal." She ran her hand through the bars that made up the medieval window. "I have no touch in the Otherworld. A cruel joke courtesy of our king. Unlike your Cu, *Cnoc Meadha* is not my home."

"You've got to be kidding me," I shouted, slamming fists

to my head.

"Use your gut, girl. Trust it."

"I have and look where it got me."

Avery shook her head. "Cu Sidhe has the knowledge you seek. Always has. Trapped in a human body long ago, before I came to be. More fae than you and me combined. You can feel her, aye? Gnawing to break out." I nodded. "Her vengeance began in this place. With that king."

"*He* did this?"

White eyes darted side to side. Hushed, she said, "Finvarra's fairy wiles brought on the curse of the *Croí na Tlachtga*. Dragging human women to *Cnoc Meadha*. Leaving them broken, and with child. Generation after generation of men born to the same lust as the king himself."

My girl roiled inside, feeding on my newfound knowledge. "I've been ridding the world of a bloodline of… *rapists*? Why didn't Puck tell me?" I asked, mostly myself.

"Puck has his reasons, many are selfish. But these are lessons taught by your charge. Me. It's what you would've learned if you'd chosen me over the Puca. You're dafter than I thought."

I groaned, hands clenched in fists. "Why are you telling me this *now*?"

"Because…" Avery eyed a group of golden orbs zipping by. "…your time is almost up. You came here for answers, yes? Hunting long-lost stories for your future bloodline? This is the price you pay for the choices you make, dearie. Not knowing. You don't belong here, not anymore. Padraic may want you here by his side, but he cannot keep you. Not forever. Cu Sidhe *must* transition. The line must carry on. For the sake of the world, Lynnie."

She hadn't said my name once in almost a decade. In a flittering of dust, she was gone, my name carried off with her breeze.

I shouted after her, "Find Puck."

I chewed the inside of my cheek. Finvarra had been waiting on me, Cu Sidhe, not to come home but to loose the beast free from its curse. To end the killing of his kin.

I sniffed back fear and the tears that threatened to take over. *We got this, girl. I'll get you out of this place.*

A squeaking, scurrying caught my attention. From a large crack in the wall in the back corner of the room, a small gray mouse popped through. It scuttled around my feet and back to the hole. Silver shimmers glittered its fur.

"Puck," I snarled. "You get your naked rear end over here right now or so help me, I will bust outta here and when I do, you'll wish you *could* die." I waited, tapping my foot, hands planted firmly on my hips.

I trudged over to the helpless little thing, legs weak. One good stomp and the bones would crack around his teeny, tiny lungs. With a smile as wide as Texas, I lifted my foot dramatically in the air above the pathetic little vermin. A moment before I made contact with the dirt floor, its shimmering grew and Puck popped into existence. Hands up in surrender, crouched just enough to prove submission.

"Wait. Wait. Wait," he begged. Looking around, he realized he'd already changed into his human. "Lynn, I'm sorry. I'm so sorry."

"You lying," I said, swinging a fist at him. "No good." I kicked at his shins. "Piece of—" I reared back to lay a hard punch across his face. He kissed me instead. Our lips touched and the magic of the place filled my soul. Like nothing I'd felt on earth. Puck's lips to mine—rain so fresh I felt it on my cheeks— set fire to my human body.

He huffed, pulling in panting breaths, and ripped the cloak from my shoulders. Hand smoldering, he tossed it to the floor. My girl flared to life, a bubbling roar pushing from my lungs.

"Wait, just, wait." Bright smile wide, fake. "I didn't lie." I swung. He ducked. "Okay, I didn't tell you *everything*. I let you live your life until you were ready to come home."

"This isn't my home, Puck."

"I know. I know. Avery... I understand now." He shrugged. "*I* wanted to come home. This was the only way. The Cu Sidhe belongs in *Cnoc Meadha*. And you belong with me."

I kissed him. Long, deep. Living in the magic for one perfect moment. Letting out a slow breath, I whispered, "Not on your immortal life," sending one hard knee into his man parts. Immortal did not mean impervious. He wailed and fell to his side.

"King Finvarra," I hollered, dragging Puck out the door on a blanket of pelts, inhuman strength I could get used to. "He's here. I got him," I called to the king.

Footsteps shook the ground. Finvarra barreled around the corner. "Aye, a fast worker you are, my little Cu."

Puck groaned. "I will have your throne, Finvarra." He

coughed, and with an accent so perfect, I almost didn't believe it was him, he added, "Beidh mé go bhfuil tú marbh."

Finvarra fumed. Lip snarled, teeth bared. "You will die in your quest, boy."

A sinister grin twisted my lips. "You'll have to survive your feral dog first, King."

Eyes flamed golden embers. Hands trembled, waves of magic rolled down my arms. A pop and out burst my girl. A clean, flawless transition. Teeth gnashing, claws splayed. Finvarra's eyes rounded. A beast he hadn't laid eyes on in centuries, his loyal pup, rife with power and vengeance.

Puck may have been too quick for the hulking king, but I had the power. Finvarra ran, long, gaping strides carrying him through narrow dirt streets lined with stone houses. I gave chase. Hurling legs, bounding, dodging. His breadth did him no favors.

Swiftly I was on him, clinging to his massive back. Claws sunk deep into muscle. He refused to fall. Scaling his back, I met his throat with piercing sharp teeth and ripped a chunk from his flesh. Decadence filled my mouth.

The earth trembled beneath him when he fell. Blood glugged from his neck. Real, red blood. I'd torn holes in men half his size for years and not once was I faced with the sight of their blood. My girl didn't blink twice at it.

Finvarra gurgled, laughed. "Sidhe can't kill me. Nothing can." He coughed. "I am King Finvarra."

Puck caught up, skidding to a stop beside me. He patted me on the head. "That's my girl." The sound of a blade freed from its sheath churned my stomach. "What about silver?"

He raised Finvarra's sword high above his head. "Ainm daoine maithe." And plunged it deep into the king's belly.

Green tinged smoke billowed from the wound. It sizzled, spurted. The beast slinked backward, ready to flee.

Swirling winds rattled shutters. "Shit." Puck knelt in front of me. "Listen, you have to change back. Right now." Wide, black eyes pleaded. "Please. She can't see you and you'll never make it out on four legs." His Adam's apple bobbed. "Please."

Who? I snorted, shook my hulking coat, knocking my human free. Laying in a heap, Puck scooped me up across his arms. Whistling through branches and over rooftops, gusts nearly pushed him over. He ran as quickly as he could carrying me, back to the bed of pelts where I'd dropped my bag.

Even the bravest of the creatures took shelter in open doorways. Blonde hair flipped over my face with the wind. Those golden pill bugs zipped into hiding holes in nearby trees.

Puck set me down on two legs and shoved the backpack into my hands. "Head toward the hawthorn ring, to the west. Climb, dig. Think of home."

"Puca," a woman shrieked, opening Puck's eyes wide.

He looked back over his shoulder, curls whipping around his face. "I'm sorry I brought you here." His lips pressed to mine, I closed my eyes, clinging to the memory of what we'd been. "You were everything I hoped you'd be."

He'd lied to me. Tricked me. Loved me. Taught me how to survive. "Come with me." I grabbed his arm. "You don't belong here either, clearly."

He swallowed hard, solace hitting his face a second before a smile pulled wide. "Then how will you escape?"

"Padraic O'Kain," she wailed. "You'll burn for eternity for your crimes." Her commanding voice carried through twisting vines, curling them in on themselves.

One last glance over his shoulder, he said, "Listen to the old girl." He poked me in the stomach. "She knows what do." One last kiss on the tip of my nose and he was off. "Tell them about me," he shouted over his shoulder, bright grin wide on his face.

Sidhe moved from hiding places and gathered to watch the spectacle. I wrapped myself in the pelts, slinking into the shadows. Through an open door on the far side of a window, a woman approached Puck. With his arms open wide, he grinned.

"Queen Oona, I didn't realize you were back." Round butt cheeks clenched when she snatched him up by the neck without a word. "What a coincidence, so am I," he croaked.

Puck kicked and squirmed in the queen's clutch. Her wavy strawberry hair trailed the ground behind her, inches shy of the embroidered hem on her rust colored dress. Puck might've been quick, but the queen—just a little thing herself—was strong as an ox and had her own vengeance to reap.

I ripped a pair of pants and shirt from my bag and slid them on, hidden huddled in the fur.

She dragged him, dirt clinging to his bare skin, stopping at a series of posts jutting from the ground. Oona tossed Puck to the dirt. Squatty, furry goblins—swamp green with tall, pointed ears—scurried along to help her, quickly shackling Puck's wrists to the posts.

"Padraic O'Kain," she bellowed. "You are hereby charged with treason. Malice acts against the laws of *Tuath Dé*. What say ye?"

"Puca are wild, indulgent, and full of mischief. Can you fault me?" His accent rolled free as he grinned up at the queen.

"It is of the decree of Queen Oona of *Cnoc Meadha*, on this turn of Saturn, Padraic O'Kain is guilty and shall be sentenced to the bearing of iron. One for each act of treachery. Until the day I do deem him reformed. Do the people agree?"

"Aye!" many of the crowd shouted, fists in the air.

Slinking back, further from the action, I kept my eyes on the men in the center of it all. A large creature, all limbs and a pimpled pot belly, carried a handful of chain in a great gloved hand. Puck's dark eyes found mine through it all. I stopped. Frozen. Too scared to move and too prideful to look away. His jaw clenched and his chin jutted out while he stared at me, curling smile carving dimples in his cheeks.

The gangly creature laid one long iron chain across Puck's shoulders. Another chain and he closed his eyes. Pale skin around the chain smoldered and festered. Three. Four. By the fifth, he couldn't hold back his pain anymore and he let out a scream of agony that stung me square in the center.

The beast roared back through my lips and I knew it was the only chance I'd get. I took off in a full run toward the west—I hoped. My feet cut into the dirt, kicking up dust at my heels. I'd wanted to stop and look, marvel at the beauty of it all. Soak in the world that'd birthed my lineage. The crowd's echoed cheers promised I wouldn't survive if I stayed behind.

Tiny white flowers dotted a group of trees ahead. I pushed forward, toward the pungent stench of a hawthorn in full bloom. Without stopping to think, I slammed against a twisted trunk. I climbed. Gripping tightly, afraid to slip, scaling the prickly tree for my life, I dug in my toes and pushed up. Thorn-barbed branches poked holes into my palms, leaving spots of blood behind as evidence.

Puck cried out again when I reached the top. The sound brought bile up my throat. He'd been my friend. An ally. Leaving him felt wrong. Lynnie wanted to go back, rescue my friend, save the day. The beast clawed down my center. A warning. Time's up.

Impenetrable overgrowth held me tight in the Otherworld. Limbs curled, slipping up a pant leg, around a wrist. Clinging to the branches, I shook loose leaves with the force of my whole body.

Another scream caught in the breeze trembled my insides. My girl hung on the fringes, dying to burst from my seams. I nearly let her.

Teeth clenched, I rumbled, "I just wanna go home."

White petals swirled in tornados, falling through from the tip top of the trees. Tingling zapped my center, tugging an invisible line. I growled, shoving through thick branches. They slid free from each other, cradling me in their spiny grasp. Lost in a sea of white, the hawthorn trees, to the west of *Cnoc Meadha*, swallowed me whole.

THE MEEK SHALL INHERIT THE EARTH

Tiny round petals floated to the ground around me, falling to my cheeks. A familiar ring of Hawthorn trees surrounded me—not a bloom in sight. Spiny branches jutted overhead, creaking in an autumn wind. Leftover magic fizzled on the tip of my nose.

Panting, the Otherworld still tight in my chest, I crooned, "Let's see the Ozark Howler do that." Leaves rustled in the grass.

A gun cocked half a second before something shadowed the sun. "Lynn?"

I sat up, nose to the barrel of a rifle. Circled in a ring of whitecap mushrooms. "*Hattie*?" I asked, squinting at the figure of an old woman with familiar brown eyes. Her hips had widened and the set of her jaw had changed with age, but the grandma I stared at was my best friend.

"How in the holy hell did you end up out here?"

Puck's cries echoed. I closed my eyes against the ghost. "I escaped," I croaked.

"I thought I'd never see the likes of you again."

I blinked over and over again, taking in the map of lines carved into her face. "I just saw you. A week ago if it was a day." *Where's Garret?* "You had two little ones toddling around the yard." I whimpered, "What happened?"

She blinked right back. "Lynn, I ain't seen your face in fifty years."

Head swam. Fifty years gone in a day—in a matter of hours. An immortal existence spent.

No. No. No. The price you pay... "Hattie..." My eyes filled with tears. "Where's my brother?"

She looked down at the ground, sorrow set on her face. "We lost him last year."

I'd missed it all. I'd left them behind to follow a fantasy, a trick. A blink in the Otherworld had stolen decades from me. Any options I had for my life gone. I wanted it all back. The heavens could take my last breath for one more moment in Havana. *My* Havana.

"Mama?" Hattie shook her head. "The kids?" I asked with hope.

"Rusty joined up with the war." *What war?* "He's out in California now. Haven't heard from him since his daddy passed. My girl, bless her heart, met a good man, Carrington Mallock, from Danville, and moved away after college. She lives in Shreveport now with my grandbaby." She'd done just what I told her to. She'd left Havana in her dust. A look passed over my face that scared Hattie to a fit. "Don't you even think about it, Carolyn. Not for one second. You stay away from those two."

"Maureen is in her fifties now, right?" About the same age as my mama was when—

A gut-ripping tug yanked in my center. Ancient magics come calling. Avery'd said my time was up. Another day, two—a matter of minutes in the Otherworld—the beast would've missed her appointment with *Croí na Tlachtga.* Trapped in Knockma, she'd have been freed from this human prison. I could've ended it, this curse on both our houses. Freed the Cu Sidhe, my kin. Hattie's grandbaby would've been free to live and grow. Generations of women would never know the power of Cu Sidhe. Finvarra seed would spread, tainting the world with its lustful greed. Choices, shit stink of the universe.

Hattie held her face and shook her head. "No. Lynn, it ain't gonna happen."

I stood, kicking a mushroom from the ring. "Hattie, you didn't tell them?"

She leaned her rifle across broad shoulders. "Not a word. You was gone for good and there was no sense in it continuing."

I didn't know the person who stood in front of me. Behind

those familiar eyes was a grown woman with demons of her own. I was one of them. "It must, Hattie. I'm sorry." I didn't have anything else to say. There was nothing else I could say. I'd royally screwed the pooch and there was no taking it back. Nothing left to do but try to make things better. To not let my life happen again.

"Where've you been?" Tears filled her eyes.

"You wouldn't believe me if I told you." Snatching my mostly empty bag from the dirt, I swallowed hard, not sure how to ask what needed asking. "Hat, can I borrow Garret's truck?"

She looked at me like I'd shot her cat. "You pop up here out of the blue and have the nerve to borrow your dead brother's truck?" She set her jaw and glared at me. "You're going to them, aren't you?" she asked but knew the answer.

There was no way I couldn't. Either I went on my own, or I'd be summoned to die when the time came. The least I could do was to make sure my successor didn't meet the same fate I had. She'd know more. She should have known from the day she was born. It was my fault she didn't and I was going to fix that.

"Hattie, please. If you love your grandbaby, you'll let me go to her. She needs to know. Our bloodline depends on it." I wrapped my arms around her, breathing in apple shampoo. "She's a warrior, Hattie. Destined to smite the wicked."

"Do you know? For sure?"

I stepped back, hands wrapped tight around her arms. "Sure enough to claw my way from the Otherworld to be here. There are things she'll need from me, people out there who will prey on her. Without me, her life will be just like mine. Gone before she knows it."

I'd always thought Hattie and I would get old together. Die gossiping about the town on our front porch. It tore my heart into a million fiery pieces knowing I'd missed Garret's passing, Daddy and Mama's too, and sure as the sun rose, I'd miss Hattie's. To make things fair, they'd all miss mine.

Her nostrils flared. A woman hardened by time and heartbreak. I knew in my heart Garret never did stop looking out the window for me. I read it in the lines on her face. "You take care of her, Lynn."

"For the rest of my life." Pulling her close, I squeezed, soaking in one last drop of who I'd been so many years ago. Wiry gray hairs popped from her bun, tickling my nose. "She'll need you too. Know her. Love her. Remind her she has the knowledge right inside her. All she has to do is listen." The beast rumbled, anxious, tense. "I love you, Henrietta, with all my heart," I said into her shoulder.

"I love you, too." She sniffed and wiped away tears. Stoic in her old age, her tough skin had only gotten thicker. "Now, get on with it. Oh, Lynn, the keys—"

"I know," I yelled over my shoulder while I ran to a fancy truck parked out front of an aging blue house. The old brown doublewide had been replaced years before with a sturdy two-story. I grinned. "Good on you, brother."

Throwing my bag to the passenger seat, I slid behind the wheel. I reached to open the glove box for Garret's keys. Time reached out and cold cocked me square in the jaw. Like nothing I'd seen in my lifetime, screens and buttons and things I had no clue what to do with. "Fuck. It'd be really cool if I had time for this kinda shit but…" I opened my eyes wide to the heavens, waving hands over my churning stomach.

The door flung open, and I nearly fell out. "Listen, I'm older than you and I deserve your respect. When I'm talking, you do not walk away from me." Hattie stepped up on the side, leaned over the top of me, and pushed a button under the steering wheel. Lights popped on inside, the engine so quiet I wondered if I imagined it. "I want to slap you across your face right now. I want you to know that." Maybe she was still my Hattie.

"I'd let you." A punch to the gut ticked my running timer, doing her job for her. "I'm losing time, Hat."

She watched my face, surely seeing in the anguish festering in my soul. "Tell her to come see me."

I pressed my forehead to hers. "I'm so glad I chose you."

"Get the hell on outta here before I knock you into next century."

"Love you too."

Desperate for help, frantic to put what pieces I had together for my successor before my time was up, I drove down a pocked dirt road I hadn't seen since I left running.

Nana's old white house, hardly standing, sat half caved in at the end of the drive. I'd hoped Garret had fixed it up. Even if he sold it. It needed life. I gulped back aching sorrow at the sight of my childhood in shambles.

Recent rain caked my tires with mud. I didn't bother closing the door. And to be honest, I worried I'd lock myself out somehow.

Granddaddy's old hawthorn still stood guard. Colorful fabric had been tied around barren branches. They hung in strips that whipped in the wind.

The closer I got, hot tears welled. I gulped, pressing a hand to the faded carving. "Divine providence." Cheeks wet, lilac crackles sparked at the tips of my fingers. "Where are you now?"

"All around you, sweet pea."

I jumped and swirled around to a pair of eyes I knew had to be a ghost. "You gotta be dead."

Mama Lee tied an orange ribbon on a low branch. "You outta be old." She winked.

"Touché." I blinked at her. "Am I dreamin'?"

She reached out and pinched me with strong, leathery fingers. I flinched. "Doesn't look like it."

"How is this possible?" I asked while a furry green beasty rumbled inside my own self.

She plucked a piece of fabric from the tree and tied it in a knot around a chunk of my hair. "That, my angel, is a knowing you don't need on your soul."

"You don't know what I got on my soul. I promise whatever you're carrying is no burden on me."

Mama Lee patted my shoulder. "Don't you argue with me, dear. I've got work to do and so do you. Now, what in the world are you doing all the way out here? There're no ghosts here for you."

I shook my head, eyeing the decaying house. "I ain't here for her. I'm here for her." Hand pressed to the tree, magic sizzled on my fingers. "I need a fairy. Granddaddy said fairies lived in this tree and seeing as though everything in the universe seems to be up for grabs, I thought, why not?" Panic set in and it was unbecoming, speeding my voice and tangling words. "You seen a crazy Irish woman floating around in a white dress?"

"Should I have?"

I closed my eyes. It was worth a shot. "No." I breathed, refusing defeat. It'd happened to me without Avery; it'd happen without her now. I went on faith that she'd find her in time, my successor. Or come at all. "If she stops by, tell her I survived. And she was right. Mostly."

"Did you enjoy your adventure?" Her eyes glittered, mouth curled into a grin, she reminded me of Puck.

The consequences sucked. But getting there... "It wasn't the life I longed for. I'll mourn that life for the time I've got left, knowing I was one of a kind. Dying in the name of justified vengeance, I can live with that."

She pressed a hand to my heart. "I'm glad to have known

you, Lynnie Russell."

"I don't know what you are, or why the beast brought me to you, but I'm grateful she did." Fire burned inside, my timer ticking away. No matter how badly I wanted to lay under that tree or slip on up to the porch for a visit, my time was up. Nearly.

Mama Lee's strong arms wrapped around my middle. Her ear against my chest. "Welp, better get to it." She sucked her teeth and let me go.

Over my shoulder, a few yards away, I asked, "What's with the fabric?"

"Wishes. For the fairies. Before they tear it down."

"Tear it down? That tree is more than a hundred years old." A new panic rattled my soul. Everything that was Lynnie Russell would be dead and gone. No sign of who I'd been. That naïve girl falling in love under a full silver moon. The boy who'd given his life. Nana and Garret and Hattie.

Refusing to let myself and my people die out, I dug around in the truck, finding a pad of paper and drafter's pencil. They had to know. Someone. She. The next in the line. She had to know this was here. We were here.

Scrubbing the pencil over a piece of paper pressed to the tree, I rubbed the impression of Granddaddy's carving into life. It wasn't pretty, but it'd do. Proof I was there. They'd been there. That magic did live in Havana. In the hearts of my people.

Mama Lee ran a hand over my arm when I shuffled by, hurrying back to the truck. Our fingertips grasped at the last second, tangling crackling tendrils of magic. A final farewell.

The little red-haired girl I remembered seeing not a week before answered the door a grown woman. Crow's feet, and the skin around her jaw sagged, but her daddy looked back at me in her eyes, and I knew I had the right house.

"Maureen Russell?" I asked.

She blinked a few times before settling on my eyes. Shock took over her expression and the thought of slamming the door in my face passed over her before she quelled it. I was her long-lost auntie come for a visit looking not a day older.

"It can't be." She shook her head. "Are you a ghost?" I pinched my lips between teeth, shook my head. "I thought you were a dream." She stepped back, hand on her chest. "Daddy always said you were special, doing God's work. When Nana died she said.... She was all doped up on morphine, I didn't believe her."

It hurt to hear about Mama on painkillers before she died. She'd been in pain. She'd probably been scared too. I shook off the hurt and focused on my last duties on earth.

"Your blood, mine, chosen by women, powerful and ancient, carry a burden. It's hard, and it's lonely, but it's necessary for the world. I wish I could stand here and tell you every secret I know, but I can't." The beast roiled.

"There's just no time. Where is she?" Maureen shook her head. "Whether you want it or not it's coming. I can't stop it. Neither can she."

"She's not." She shook her head. "She can't be. This… this is hogwash. I can't be a part of this abomination." She pushed the door to close but I caught it.

Eyes flamed, Black Sentry sprung to life, lighting my face green. "Maureen Eleonore Russell, you listen to me." She gasped. "I promised your daddy I'd come and I did. I'm here. I should've been here sooner, but I can't change that now. It's coming, you hear me. It's coming fast. You can choose to pretend I'm a ghost and this is all bullshit, but the long and short of it is your daughter, my great-niece, is very close to becoming something that will change her life forever. Her pain, her existence, everything she will become has the potential to destroy her. It can turn her into something inhuman. A beast that without a rein can and will hurt people she loves. Your actions from here on out are the only thing that will prevent that. Your knowledge, her knowledge, my being here is the only thing that will make her life better than mine was. I don't know everything. Hell, I don't think I even know half of it, but I sure as hell know I screwed up and lost more than I thought I had." I looked her in the eyes and saw my brother. "I need to see her."

"She's not here," she said after a long pause. "She's at a church retreat in Flag Lake." The look on her face sent chills to my toes.

They needed the quiet. I wondered if they laid in wait for

the moment to find them. Cool soil underfoot. Moon high, trees and nature to draw from. *Croí na Tlachtga* will find her, change her. I let out a shaking breath, closed my eyes, and forced that ancient power back home until it was time.

Glowing dimmed at my throat, eyes fizzled to blue. "I'm sorry I scared you. Know that your daughter will fight that same fight and she's going to need her mama to keep her tethered to the earth. Like I needed my brother." She nodded. "You're so beautiful." I reached out and squeezed her hand. "Have your daddy's eyes."

She searched my face, looking over every smooth inch. "You told me once you were a warrior. Is that what my baby is? A warrior."

I sucked in a gulp of air. "She is."

"Will you bring her back to me?"

No. "That's not how it works."

"Then I'm coming with you." She turned to snatch keys from the peg. I stopped her with a hand on her shoulder.

"I can't let you do that." Her brows pulled together in the middle. "She'll need you alive when she comes home, and she will. Trust me, it doesn't work out well for those not meant for magic." I touched her cheek. "Here," I said, pulling a stack of photos from my bag. "These belong with family."

Maureen flipped through the photos of her parents, me, Rusty. "I've never seen these." She looked at me with tears in her eyes. "You never came back." Hurt hit her face.

"I know. Sometimes the choices we make cause more

problems than they fix."

She sniffed, looking back down at a photo of Garret. "That's life, I guess."

I nodded. "A series of shit options."

"He loved you. Until the day he died."

I swiped away a loose tear. "Yeah." Without warning, I pulled her into a hug. "Call your brother, huh?" She nodded, warm tears soaking my shirt. "Your mama got a shock this morning, too. Check on her for me."

Her hand wrapped around the back of my head. "I never forgot you."

"Me too, baby." Lavender veins zipped along my arms and I let her go. "Time waits for no man—or woman." I held up a hand that crackled with magic. Her eyes went wide. "Tell her I tried."

Maureen stepped off the porch after me. I didn't turn back. Couldn't. Time would soon run out, nightfall would come. Her time would come. So many things she needed to know and no way to tell her. I should've been there. Before. Long before.

Knockma should've been my refuge, a place of knowledge, understanding. A way to help my successor reign mighty in her quest. I'd learned enough to know the Cu Sidhe must continue. The pain and fear would not. I'd stop it. Somehow.

Fiery pain seared my gut. I leaned, panting against the side of Garret's truck. Sun blazed its final rally against the night. Lime, magenta, violet, and jade, waves of crackling light zipped over my skin. Hands shaking, I pulled the cotton pouch from my bag. I squinted against the brightness of the Black Sentry, lifting it over my head. It dimmed, blinking out when it left my skin, sliding into the bag.

Would she miss me? My beastly sister. I closed my eyes, living one final moment in the world of the Sidhe. Listened to animals scurry home for the night, drawing in the scent of fall. Wet rain. Chin quivering, I swallowed any idea I would get out of this alive.

"Accept what you are or it'll eat you alive," I repeated Puck, desperate for something I couldn't put a finger on. Life? Or was it salvation?

Whizzing power that stitched us together snapped, one string at a time. I bent in half, doubled over. Black vomit poured from my lips. Remnants of a decade of souls reaped. She roiled, fighting to be free, knowing what was to come.

I folded pages of yellow paper into a square and pushed them into the pouch. The last words of a dying warrior. My final grasp of a world I hardly knew.

Sky turning a deep blue, a single star twinkled overhead. Night had officially arrived. A shift in the universe— something I'd come to know as Puck's magic—gripped hold of me. Searing pain etched lines down my back. If I'd had a mirror, I was sure I'd see the ogham carved from my skin. Not Puck's magic, fae magic.

"Hold on, old girl, we'll get there."

Pouch clenched in my trembling fist, I stumbled off into the darkening woods. Skin glowed, vibrant, wild. Feral. Lighting my way. Ancient magics calling me home.

SUCCESSOR

I had no real reason to be in the deep woods. Nothing that I could pin down to a set of steps, down one specific path that led me there. But there I was. Alone, scared, cold, and something I couldn't explain. The blood of four women dried around sharp claws.

A fire that once blazed a vibrant green was a pile of glowing embers. Rust splattered drips crusted on stones surrounding the pit. I'd never intended on venturing off on my own, leaving the campsite behind, making myself vulnerable. The night beckoned me. An invisible crooked finger, whispered promises in words I didn't understand.

I died tonight, beside that roaring fire. Sliced open and bled, lamb at the slaughter. Resurrected in the body of a creature. A monster.

"I've been hunting for you all night, sweet pea." A blonde woman stepped out from a line of trees. She looked down on the pile of dead things I'd left in my wake. "Well, looks like you've already gotten started."

She let out a long whistle and walked toward me, fearless. "I know what you're feeling right now, and I want to tell you, it'll be all right." A small baggy dangled from her fist. "First, these women aren't what you think they are. You did your job just as you should've. Leave them where they lay. They'll pull a disappearing act soon enough and no one will be the wiser. Second, I know you're scared, *alone*. Be grateful. It was better that way, trust me. Third, and this is the most important, so pay attention. Keep your soul about you, baby, in the end, it's all you've got. It's all that matters."

The monster I'd become growled, low and deep, at the woman, but she didn't flinch. Without a word, she set the pouch on a large rock, patting it once. "This is yours now." She shrugged a bag from her shoulders and set it on the ground. "You'll likely be needing this too."

The woman closed her eyes and nodded once, falling to her knees in the dirt. Her eyes, wet, glistening, half closed with a sad grin. Scratching along my chin, she said, "Don't worry about me, baby. I'm not what you think either. I'll pull a disappearing act soon enough too."

She looked off into the still darkness, listening to the sounds, feeling the cool breeze on her cheeks. "You've got lots to learn, little one. Trust your gut, she knows what to do. Don't be afraid to love and be loved." She patted the small cotton bag. "I did my best to say what needed said."

The monster licked her face, a face I realized I'd seen before. Only in photos. Old pictures my granny had. She bowed her head, exposing the back of her neck. "I'm tired, baby. I've had my fill of this place. I got a sweetheart waiting on me, and you've got a long life ahead of you. Be swift. Be just." She swallowed, and whispered, "Listen to that *fucking* Bean Sidhe like your life depends on it. It does. Stay safe. Stay alive. And whatever you do, stay the hell away from the *Otherworld*."

A banshee? I asked, but she couldn't hear me trapped in the monster.

Curved, deadly claws stretched. One heavy paw slashed at her neck. Blood splashed in long lines across my face, plopping in blobs to the dirt. *No!*

Shouting did no good. Amethyst blood glugged from her neck, pooling in blackberry under her body.

Breaths uneven, shaky, I could hear her faint heartbeat slow. Eyes glistened, glazing over with coming death. "Oh, there you are," she breathed, sucking in her final, ragged breath.

The monster sniffed the air—piney aftershave—knowing that scent well. It snuffled at the woman on the ground, nudged her shoulder with a snotty snout, and let out a quiet whimper.

Golden dust glittered in pitch black, swirling down from thick treetops. The twisting wind picked up leaves, spreading them around her.

A shimmering gold angel in blue jeans stood over the women. "Come on, girl. I've been waitin' on you all night."

He grinned at the monster—me—then looked at the girl again and ran his hand through sandy hair.

Golden specks flowed from her, spinning through the air, mingling with his before whisking away in the twisting wind.

The monster flopped in the dirt beside her body and stayed there. I couldn't say for sure I'd had any control over that, but I prayed all night we stayed right there. Right near that pouch she'd left just for me. I wanted whatever was in it. Something told me it was my deliverance.

Dawn chittered in the air, the sky turning white through the trees. Chirping and singing, day-loving animals woke with the sun, as I did. A tingle hit deep in my stomach and bled into my limbs. The monster stood on all fours and panted—a rolling discomfort, like squeezing into shoes that were a size and a half too small.

Fur and teeth sank into my skin and gums the same way they'd grown out—a squelching crackle that turned my stomach. A slurping pop and out I slid, spilling bits of the creature onto the forest floor. A lavender current zipped up my arms.

The blonde girl's body remained where she'd fallen, the sun beginning to glisten against her tan skin and golden hair.

Dark blood dried in stripes on her chest. With a shaking hand, I cleared her face of wild hair. I *had* seen her before. My papa called her a warrior.

Morning breeze chilled my skin, drawing out shivers and goose bumps. On all fours, I scurried to the black bag she'd dropped beside the rock. Light, I almost wondered if it was empty. Unsteady hands—coursing with adrenaline—fumbled with the zipper. Inside, a pair of pants and a tank top.

"Thank you," I whimpered, cold setting in.

Grateful, I pulled the clothes on. The pouch lay exactly where she'd left it. I snatched it from the rock. Fragile cotton felt like it might fall apart in my hand. I pulled the aging drawstring gently and tipped it over to spill the contents into my hand. A small rolled up piece of parchment, a black stone that hung on a strap, and a thick, tightly folded square of papers spilled out.

I opened the roll. Scrawled in lines of rust colored ink, centuries old script spelled out what seemed to be a poem. I clutched the trinket and square of papers in my hand while I read the words under my breath.

"By the Moon, power in thee, this stone charged in protection be. Who wishes harm render still, not spoil a soul nor bid thy will. Hear my plea on this night; impart protection on this bearer of fight. By these words power shone, grant your guard upon this stone. Wholly in power and divinity, by these words so mote it be."

Hot poker jammed against raw skin, I cried out. Light glowed a horror-movie green from my fist. Searing pain cut in lines across my thigh. Heavy black hash marks swiped across my skin, engrained bone deep.

A weight, heavy and suspiciously unending, fell on my shoulders. My gut rumbled as something inside me stirred. The monster? Trapped inside me? The idea bubbled nausea in my stomach.

I plucked the black stone and folded papers from the ground and pulled open the square. The first few lines confirmed a lifetime of hushed secrets. My heart sank as I read them aloud.

"I can't tell you what I *really* am without telling you how it came to be. Most stories start just before the action begins, when the juicy bits are ripe. I think mine is better told from the beginning. Or close enough to it."

My name is Georgia Lynn Mallock, but most people call me Lynnie. Papa named me after a warrior.

Like my auntie before me, I am death. Vengeance. Justice. I am Cu Sidhe.

Today was my becoming and this is where the action begins.

Right, impart protection to this. By these words, powers show, grant your guard upon this stone. Wholly in power and divinity, by these words, so mote it be. By the Moon, power in thee, this stone charged in protection be. Who wishes harm render still, not spoil a bit nor bid thy will. Here my plea on this

A bloodline that will reign until the last man walks the earth

Gwendolyn McNab

Fergus Whelan

Maureen Whelan

John Devlin

Delma Devlin

Morticae Higgins

Sue Ellen Higgins

George Russell

Georgia Lynn Mallock

Carrington Mallock
Maureen Eleonore Russell

Henrietta Willits
Garret Llewellyn Russell

Sharlene Carolynn
Diamond Russell

CPSIA information can be obtained
at www.ICGtesting.com
Printed in the USA
LVHW010329130521
687287LV00007B/48/J